Praise

FIELD BLENDS

"Such a rich and immersive trip. From a winery in Virginia to a bar in Madrid to a hotel in Prague, I couldn't help but think I want to go there! And I want to taste that! Meanwhile enjoying the world through the eyes of these characters. Welch is a storyteller with the pen of an experienced travel writer, pulling sensual and evocative details from each scene. Readers that have dreamed of seeing the world need this book for their carry-on or nightstand. *Field Blends* is the modern reader's guide on how to experience the world, with the reminder that we are all human, sharing a diverse planet."

—Jill Barth
Wine and Travel Writer, Contributor to *Forbes* and *USA Today*

"New author Andrew Welch has a passion for life, wine and nuanced ideas. Building on his extensive European travels, he spins a tale that explores the amorphous boundaries of identity, relationships, where we call home and political ideology. It is a story well-suited to our shifting contemporary world."

—Michael K. Powell
President and CEO of the Internet & Television Association

"I've always said that we are all a product of our environment. This book truly shows the strength and resilience of being raised in a God-fearing, loving, compassionate environment that never leaves you. Congratulations on a book well done."

—Senator Joe Manchin
United States Senator from West Virginia

"Andrew takes readers with flying colours into a beautiful journey through the world, vineyards, wine bars, big cities and friendships. *Field Blends* is a book for every wine aficionado and world citizen. It gives matter to think about wines, society, our roots, friendship and more generally what is life. Like its author, this book is deeply human."

—Carole Bryon
Lady of the Grapes, Covent Garden, London

"Luminous, compelling and lyrical, *Field Blends* plumbs the angst of a generation's search for meaning and purpose within a society that seems to be shifting from under their feet. Andrew Welch's characters—complex, diverse and universally uncertain—come together and apart in a common quest to get beneath the surface of things, to find who they are meant to be and where they fit in an increasingly unrecognizable world. With its elegant style, vivid imagery and remarkable insights, *Field Blends* is as intoxicating and delicious as the wines that provide the narrative's backdrop."

—Greg Fields
Author, *Arc of the Comet*, 2018 Kindle Book of the Year Nominee in Literary Fiction

"Andrew Welch's extraordinary imagination and energy were apparent during his undergraduate days at William & Mary. Now he has written a first novel, informed by his roots in a tiny town in a mountainous state, then by his delight in the liberal arts and sciences in college, and global travel thereafter. *Field Blends* is a richly drawn account of complex friendships evolving amid great wine and great cities, with a strong undercurrent of millennials seeking meaning in the troubled world in which they must make their way. This is a challenging, engaging story."

—W. Taylor Reveley III
Former President of the College of William & Mary

"With a sparkling wit and a keen eye for details, Andrew is a born storyteller. He's an observant world traveler with a wry affection for home. The debut of his first novel, *Field Blends*, is an exciting event."

—Katie Cristol
Member of the Arlington County Board, Virginia

"Neither the romantic passions of youth, nor the intoxicating glow of wine, can keep darkness from the door."

—Jim Greenwood
US Congressman from Pennsylvania from 1993 to 2005

"With his first book, Andrew Welch has invited us to a delightful and entertaining journey of characters traveling near and far. Sharing their discovery of interesting people and events is a delight. I found myself smiling with fond remembrances of my own similar journeys. Based on *Field Blends* we will be hearing much more from Andrew in the future."

—Dr. William Stubblefield
Rear Admiral (Retired)

"*Field Blends* is a tale of modern professionals in a contemporary and contentious environment. The crisp, wine-enhanced dialogue adds a distinctive flavor to Welch's thought-provoking story. A really good read."

—Richard Knott
Author, *A Heritage of Wings*

Field Blends

by Andrew D. Welch

© Copyright 2020 Andrew D. Welch

ISBN 978-1-64663-068-4

Published by

köehlerbooks™

3705 Shore Drive
Virginia Beach, VA 23455
800–435–4811
www.koehlerbooks.com

FIELD BLENDS

ANDREW D. WELCH

VIRGINIA BEACH
CAPE CHARLES

To the many, and the few
For those who lift us up
For those who bring us together

For those who honor the roots whilst they climb the highest tree

For those who—free of prejudice—remind us how grand
the world can be

Chapter One

Early August's summer sun rained down from a pale-blue sky, hazy yet bright, mottled by streaks of white clouds leisurely meandering from atop one mountain valley to the next. Gravel crunched beneath my feet as hot air whisked outward from a truck bellowing too quickly down the narrow highway just outside of town. The scent of motor oil and an honest day's work—that trademark permeating the air of every car shop—filled my nose. Sweat formed at my collar. It was hot.

An older man appeared in the open door beneath a freshly painted sign engraved with the words *Warm Springs Garage*. Weathered and hard, skin long ago turned to leather, colored and disheveled as only a fellow for whom every dollar had turned on the skill of his wrench could be.

He grinned. Another truck barreled past.

"We got her fixed up for you," he called out.

"Thank you!" Barely audible above the din of trucks. "Anything wrong?"

"None that you need concern yourself with. She's working pretty well. You shouldn't have any problem getting to where you need to go."

Some days before, a self-styled reverend and a doctor of philosophy in testament to a series of online degrees had shared how badly he felt for me that I had not seen the wisdom of attending college more locally. He had, apparently, always seen me as more of a West Virginia University man.

Studying locally was not my intent.

"What do I owe you?" I opened my wallet.

"Nothing."

"What?"

"You don't owe me anything. See, isn't too often we see a kid go away. Think of us here in town when you're gone. This is what I can do to help you get there."

"That's incredible, thank you. . . " I trailed off.

"Good luck," finished the older fellow. "Go to it."

I packed that car the next day, and drove south and east to Virginia, where that afternoon I moved in at school. You might say that it was there in that gravelly parking lot beside a highway in West Virginia that one life ended so that the story of another life could begin, carried on a free oil change and a Ford that just worked.

Erik Weber was one of those profoundly thoughtful people whose moments of exuberance were so well timed to correspond with something actually meaningful that the world around him seemed to slow as he accelerated. We shared that country town of our upbringing but fell out of frequent contact to some degree for several years after leaving it. He somehow managed to find his way onto the cover of a national weekly after ensconcing himself at Harvard, the poster boy for all those who had ostensibly come from not much of anything before—allegedly through nothing but his own intellect—finding his way into the most rarified of academic and professional circles.

The truth was a bit more complicated. In high school he and I benefited immeasurably from a bizarre investment made by the public school in training a small cadre of teenagers to build computers, run networks, and otherwise cause mischief amongst traditional folks who preferred for kids to mind their place. Erik had been born in suburban Maryland during a time in America's history when it still seemed every year would be better than the last. His father had lost his job in a scheme, and for a moment around the age of six, Erik had lived with his aunt and uncle in Fairfax, Virginia, whilst his parents deliberated between divorce and moving to West Virginia to embrace a *Green Acres* lifestyle far from the city.

He arrived in the country about a year later after having spent first grade cast as brilliant whilst living in the grasp of modern education, whose method of teaching a kid to read was far more concerned that the kid learn to think than that the kid memorize words. The peculiar upshot of this was that Erik's second-grade teacher in West Virginia immediately identified him as being slow, thus putting him in the odd position of being simultaneously enrolled in both remedial reading and a program for the gifted and talented.

Erik found his intellectual footing and chewed through the entire Microsoft Windows NT administrator manual sometime in junior high school. There was a glorious moment around the age of fifteen on our first day of paid employment at a local computer shop during which we managed to knock out power to the entire building whilst setting fire to the server on our workbench. We lived out the rest of high school zipped up in suits meant to protect us from the itchy agony of too much building insulation, pulling wires through attics and walls whose confines were better suited to quasi-children like us instead of full-blown adults.

In any case, Erik's moment in the national spotlight on the cover of that magazine came a touch too late, for he had already taken scholarship money from the Navy by the time a San Francisco venture capitalist came across his story and decided to treat the kid like his personal starfish, as if the man were living out the old fable of the fellow who snatched the creatures from the beach and tossed them back into the sea. *I can't save them all, but perhaps I can save this one*, he must have reasoned.

Erik returned to visit our hometown a while later driving a beautiful black-on-black German automobile. Everyone whispered that his relationship with the Left Coaster might have amounted to more than mentorship.

Off he went to his first Navy ship, and then to school where he became a nuclear power officer—a *Nuke SWO*. He internalized every moment and detail surrounding the experience. After several years, the call of the unicorn beckoned, and he hung up the uniform at the end of his contract so that he could return to his software roots and chase his billions in an understated, self-reflective way.

At some point he had settled in with Emma Cuevas, a remarkably fun and free-spirited human being whose only offense was to be employed as the press secretary for a Republican senator in 2018, a situation made bizarre—or at least ironic—by her blend of Cuban and Finnish ancestry. Her father's antipathy for the Castros from whom he had once fled bent Emma's politics to the right. Her cantankerous maternal grandfather on Cape Cod—self-described as having grown up speaking Swedish in the school and Finnish on the street—imbued a fondness for the thoughtful Lutheran-cum-atheist type. So, Erik Weber.

I stood under the majestic vaulted ceiling in the great hall of Washington's Union Station. The clicking of a thousand shoes on the marble floors beneath my feet echoed from the gold-flecked dome that wrapped up, like a classic painting, every statue, goodbye kiss, and mid-evening scurry off to New York. Just as the infamous 9/11 attack showed us that the surest way to humble an empire is to destroy its cathedrals, so too did this place suggest that if you want to proclaim an empire, build a cathedral. Indeed, some of the most beautiful works of architecture on earth are those that greet the visitor—Union Station in Washington and Kansas City, Grand Central and the old Penn in New York. All are the rolling-stock forebears to those grand airports which followed: Madrid-Barajas in Spain, Seoul-Incheon in Korea, even the beautiful National Hall at the airport just across the river from where I then stood.

Erik approached, fresh off the latest train. "Chris Jacobson. Hello, sir. Good of you to wait."

"A gentlemen's evening is well worth it."

"I might disappoint you. I'm beat."

"It's never too late for Joselito."

"Never. Until it's closed, that is."

We caught a ride and inched along the stately Columbus Circle in front of the station before breaking out onto North Capitol Street, connecting with Massachusetts Avenue via D Street, and ultimately down Seventh to its corner with Pennsylvania.

"Where the hell is Emma?" I asked. "I haven't seen her in weeks."

"Down to San Juan with her boss. Trying to convince everyone that someone cares."

"None of them care."

"Emma cares."

"What a strange place that must be. Caring, passionately caring, in a sea of human beings who care nothing."

"Hilarious, since as an intern she once developed this odd expertise in flood insurance."

We got out of the car.

"This the spot?" the driver asked.

"Yes, thank you, sir. Enjoy your night. Be safe."

The driver sped off in search of his next customer. I turned and faced Erik.

"She's a good girl. I just don't get it."

"She barely gets it herself, anymore."

We went in.

The great European cities, and many of the American variety they inspired, are marked by their great restaurants, splendid places that wrap you up inside and treat you to an irresistible menu of food and drink. Like Bluestem in Kansas City, the best ones tend to be understated with nondescript front doors and remarkable attention to detail: a heavy slab of quartz laid as a placemat; a parade of wineglasses coming and going to ensure you're always drinking from the glass most appropriate to your wine; each element in every dish impeccable and artistic; hustling staff that stays cool at every turn. And since the town had crossed my mind twice in this late-evening meetup with Erik, I'll just say how much I love Kansas City. It's my favorite city in that part of the country. Kansas City is filled with good people. It is a place I'd live if I were keen to give up the Atlantic Ocean.

We stepped through the door of the all-too-familiar Joselito: Casa de Comidas, and as ever found ourselves transported to a bygone world both elegant and intimate, where you'd expect to see Hemingway at a nearby table. It was the picture of charming city dinner café. As if we were looking through the window on Madrid, Paris, or New York. Javier, the proprietor, managed to bottle the essence of the classic city in this delightful restaurant serving exclusively Spanish food and wine.

The place was obviously the product of immense and deliberate care. At its heart was a tribute to Javier's roots. He had built the place around its good people. He seemed truly invested in them. In return, they had helped him create the sense that when we walked through the door, we were walking into the closest thing to Spain in America.

Indeed, Joselito's enchanting details reflected a very intentional effort to take us back in time. Black-and-white photos adorned the walls rising to the high ceilings. The marble tabletops sat next to wine buckets on silver pedestals. Tiles fit the decor. I feared that it would take me days to shake from my mind the music of decades past. Better to think of a new song and recite it mercilessly to myself until this classic music faded away.

Then there was Billy Grant, Javier's English bartender.

"Hey, gents."

"See you haven't Brexited from our fair city."

"Fuck off, Chris."

"That was one of the worst jokes you've ever told." Erik feigned disgust as he looked at me.

We sat at the bar.

"I wouldn't let Javier hear you say that to a customer." I grinned at Billy. "You'll go the way of Sarah Sanders at the Red Hen if you're not careful."

"Please, who do you think I am? Erik's lady friend?"

"Hey. Fuck off," Erik groused.

"Aurelio's got this great new bottle on the glass menu."

Aurelio was rather a legend in Spanish wine circles. Years earlier he was said to have had a vision for the future of American wine drinking and had set about discovering emerging producers in the heart of Spain's north-central red-producing regions—Ribera del Duero, Toro, Rioja. Then he began importing them into the States. He had once arranged for Ava Murray and me to visit the San Román winery in Toro, country that would have been wasted on anything less than the vineyards. About equidistant from the small towns of Morales de Toro and San Román de Hornija, the winery sat just a couple of kilometers inside the Province of Valladolid, east of the border with Zamora about two hours northwest of Madrid. A remarkable characteristic example of what makes wine from Toro so unique, we found the San Román wine and its cousin, Prima, to be spectacular fusions of Old-World grapes and technique with the big and bold qualities so loved by many modern wine drinkers. We had fun with our host, Juan Ignacio, moving about the cellar tasting and comparing wine from barrel to barrel.

In any case, after leading us to the precipice of early-afternoon inebriation, Juan had sent us to lunch at El Chivo in Morales de Toro with a bottle of his finest in hand. There the chef sat at our table and asked us if we had brought the wine. We had just walked through the door into what appeared to be a small local place fronting a charming yet luxurious dining room in the back. Yes, we had the wine; a blessing, for the meal that followed had been paired specially not just for any bottle, but for that particular bottle. Our host grinned. So, at El Chivo, in the tiny Spanish village of Morales de Toro, began one of the most spectacular three days of lunches that Ava or I had ever experienced. "Phenomenal and amazing" were all we could choke out when we first tried the contents of the mythical bottle. There was raspberry in front, followed by black currant. Truly exquisite, a great pair with root vegetables, brilliant with the chickpeas and calamari of the first course, and particularly so with the traditionally prepared lamb in the main course.

But that was years ago.

I share all of this here in a feeble effort to articulate how truly legendary Aurelio was in the Spanish wine community. Friends of his were friends of everyone to be found there.

Billy set two glasses for us on the bar.

I read the label: *Bodegas Arrocal Ángel,* from Ribera del Duero. The 2011 vintage seemed to be a higher-end selection from Bodegas Arrocal, a winery I had heard of in the village of Gumiel del Mercado in Ribera del Duero. A mix of blueberry jam and bright-red stone fruit with a little rough-and-tumble rusticity made for a highly dynamic nose. There was also a dusting of dark chocolate that turned into cacao on the palate. It was cool and like biting into a juicy piece of fruit, curiously mellowing out whilst taking on additional structure once we'd swirled it in the glass for a few minutes. The beautiful balance made it a classic Ribera del Duero that I swear I would have recognized as such in a blind tasting.

"England destroyed Panama today. Barely a match." Erik woke me from my reverie.

The Englishman fired back. "You can have a team filled with lots of stars, but the team is better than the sum of those stars. Or you can have a team like Real Madrid that is filled with stars but really is just shit."

"Don't let them hear you saying that in here."

"They can fuck themselves."

"Chris is a bit full of rage about Sweden's loss to Germany."

I came from a Swedish family.

"Who the hell tackles a man next to the box in the last minute of stoppage time? Who the hell? What the hell was that son of a bitch thinking?" I was enraged by the whole affair.

Billy grinned. "I'm just happy for a sporting event without that incessant singing before the game. Your American national anthem is really quite absurd. I mean, no one can hit some of those notes, and the World Series is always filled with tension waiting to see if the woman is gonna do it. My national anthem, 'God Save the Queen'—I mean, how about 'Let's save some tax-exempt hereditary billionaire!' Now that's a national ideal we can get behind!"

"Eff *Tyskland*," I grumbled, not ready to let go my ire.

"Sorry, the whole World Cup thing upsets me. It's hard to be European and see vast groups of Germans waving flags. It makes us nervous."

"Make Germany Great Again," Erik quipped.

"Cheers."

We paid our check and shoved off.

Several days later, in one of the most extraordinary turn of events I have ever seen in sport, Sweden defeated Mexico to win the group stage whilst South Korea sent Germany home from the tournament, last place in its group.

Chapter Two

Earlier I mentioned Ava Murray, who possesses the dual distinction of being perhaps my best friend and the wife of Peter Dean, my nearly equal friend and college roommate. Ava and I had dated for several years whilst serving together in the Coast Guard. I will forever remember the moment I fell in love with her, days after she reported aboard. I was in charge of the ship at that moment and sent her to the chart table to instruct several of the cadets in the finer points of paper-based chart navigation. She called course changes with pencil and eraser in hand as we weaved between channel markers whilst the chief and I monitored the situation from a computer screen. Chief looked at me after about three hours and said, "Well, you're never going to believe this, but we're about twenty feet from where she thinks we should be. I think the kids have gotten their lesson's worth tonight."

Anyone who has spent time on the water understands why a twenty-three-year-old junior officer would be inescapably attracted to a twenty-two-year-old just-slightly-more-junior officer—a pretty brunette with nerves of steel. I had loved the Coast Guard, and I had loved her more.

Ava was with me from nearly the first moment I grew serious about wine, and over time we grew serious about wine together. I have the most wonderful memories of picking a different wine and cheese pair each night and excitedly bringing them home for the two of us to sample. She had a predilection for Chardonnay, never my favorite, but rather a varietal whose best editions I grew to appreciate. There were other adventures, careers, a new city, and bottles of wine that followed, but I will forever count amongst my most treasured moments those spent with Ava near the beginning of the journey through wine and through life.

Eventually we said goodbye to the Coast Guard. There was much hand-wringing about the difference between friendship and romance. So, we also relinquished our previously romantic relationship. We loved one another intensely yet never touched again. We were soulmates, indivisible by time, but incompatible under the same roof.

Ava at some point spent the night with my cousin Geoff, a seemingly insignificant event that would take on outsized relevance. She took up with our friend Peter after she moved to New York for law school at Yeshiva University. I was happy that the newly relocated Ava and the notoriously selective Peter had connected.

Their first date was at Wine:30, a bar near the corner of Thirtieth and Park. They had planned to split a bottle, of which Peter ultimately drank three-quarters and Ava had a glass, around which time arrived some girlfriends whom Ava had asked to come to save her from a potentially bad date.

Peter ordered two more bottles.

Eventually the conversation turned to one concerning anatomy, whereupon Peter looked Ava in the eye from across the table and slurred together the following prophetic statement: "Well, you know what they say, 'It's not what's in your pants, but what's in your wallet that counts.'"

He winked.

She laughed uncomfortably.

They were married eighteen months later in a wedding that was stupendously extravagant yet brilliant, the most appropriately ostentatious yet strangely tasteful bookend to the singularly inappropriate comment through which the relationship began. Emma Cuevas—Erik's new girlfriend at that time, the one who worked for the US senator—shared a drink with me at the open bar and commented how presidential inaugural balls seemed pedestrian in the shadow of Ava and Peter's extravaganza.

Construe none of this as an indication that the two were not in love. Rather, they were two of the most visibly in love people any of us knew.

Peter had this notion around the time he married that he ought to acquire a bottle of rare whisky for his bourbon-loving fiancée, a wedding gift for the ages. *The Wall Street Journal* had recently published a column suggesting that Pappy Van Winkle was the one bottle to rule them all, so I made inquiries with Pascual, a friend who ran a small shop in Manhattan.

He called me one morning about six months later and left a message. "Chris, I have what you're looking for, but you need to come soon."

I took a train from Union Station that afternoon.

Peter met me at Pascual's shop where Pascual pulled out three bottles and set them on the bar—Old Rip Van Winkle aged ten years, the twenty-year-old Pappy Van Winkle's Family Reserve, and the twenty-three-year-old wrapped in black velvet.

Peter began counting out a stack of hundred-dollar bills on the counter.

A woman came into the shop and asked Pascual for a wine recommendation. He held up his hand. "So sorry, but not now."

Peter and I galivanted home to the apartment he and Ava shared in Murray Hill, like two Stone-Age men who had just slain a mastodon, and laid our winnings at her feet. That wedding gift came a bit early. I walked away one twenty-year bottle richer and $400 poorer. It was well worth it, and even today, I still have about half that bottle on my shelf.

Ava and I had once visited Barboursville Vineyards near Charlottesville, Virginia, home of the University of Virginia.

Incredibly, as it turned out, Thomas Jefferson had been correct in his quixotic dream that Virginia could make great wine. We had been to most of what I'd call the great wineries of Virginia, but on this occasion we chanced to stop near Jefferson's famous home at Monticello. I was initially skeptical, but I was blown away in the end.

Like many of its cousins, Barboursville Vineyards was in beautiful countryside with a run-up of winding roads through towns you've never heard of. We were personally greeted and shown the ropes as soon as we entered, which was welcome if for no other reason than its immense number of different bottles on offer made it all quite overwhelming. The higher-end tasting room in the back—Library 1821, it was called—was a true temple to great Virginia wine. It managed to be simultaneously elegant and cozy. They had maintained an extensive library of past vintages of their signature red called Octagon. Those bottles had been made in the style of a French Bordeaux. A girl named Chelsea patiently hosted the perfect tasting. She was herself an aspiring winemaker at another nearby winery. Virginia was developing a culture.

Peter had never been one to keep bottles on the shelf, but he started his own collection at mine and Ava's prodding around the time they moved in with one another. Of course, he could not allow it to be a thing collected and treasured over time. Rather it had to be acquired through a whirlwind of activity that involved a trip to Napa, membership in the *Journal*'s wine club, and far too much money spent on *futures*. That would be wine purchased on faith before being bottled.

I tended to dislike wine clubs such as the *Journal*'s or any of the online services that had recently become popular.

Wine could be complicated, and complication begets intimidation for the uninitiated. Wine clubs were great to the extent that such misadventures helped novice wine drinkers feel comfortable with a foray into wine. Fine to the extent they helped their customers learn about new wines from new places they hadn't previously considered. Peter was not a novice wine drinker. He was just impatient.

The dark side of this phenomenon was much the same as with other forms of self-gratification in the cult of personalization that technology made possible. We had lived our lives in quite an era. Lower costs for newcomers had led to the proliferation of online news sources to fit every niche view and persuasion. Social media allowed us to surround ourselves with friends who thought as we did and news that reinforced our own ideas. Dating websites allowed us to refine and locate the ideal romantic partner with an astounding degree of precision. Similarly, online wine services allowed us to target what we already knew we liked, and then get more of it. So that meant less of what we didn't like and, sadly, what we didn't know.

Thus, whilst I was supportive of anything that introduced people to wine, I also felt that online services risked pacifying one with the good-enough whilst withholding the opportunity to fully experience what really made the stuff interesting. Wine is made great by its ability to expose the curious drinker to different things that he or she didn't know existed, to take us to other lands and climates, to teach us history, and to enrich our knowledge of the world. Like so many other things in our modern technological society—news, entertainment, friends, lovers—these wine clubs allowed us to indulge our narrow bias, whilst simultaneously isolating us from the outside world of the new and different.

Curiously, this stood in stark contrast to a countervailing trend in the habits and preferences of younger folk. I had recently read an article suggesting that many millennial wine drinkers were eschewing points and ratings-based wine recommendations. Instead they sought out wines that told a story or otherwise carried some interesting cachet. The article cited a craze for Slovenian sparkling wine, suggesting that the wine tastes of the largest generation were driven at least in part by a search for something between the cool and the uniquely undiscovered. That instinct rang true for those of any generation who knew that the best bottles were not necessarily the most popular. Finding great things in unexpected places really delighted me.

I suppose the real question was which modern instinct would win in the end. Would technology-enabled selection and consumption relegate stories and artistry to history? Would data-driven personalization send us delights ever more perfectly suited to our known tastes at the expense of ever fewer opportunities to learn something new? Or would we actively seek out the next adventure, the next story, the next piece of masterful craftsmanship hewn from an unknown source in a little-known part of the world? Ava and I were unapologetic advocates for the adventure.

I've found that wealthy men share much in common with peacocks. Dressed-up weddings and extravagant wine collections are of a piece with the brood of children, attendant nannies, and large houses in well-to-do neighborhoods that follow. They are plumage, a visual indication of their master's success.

Children terrify me. Not so much that I might have some, but rather that others might have some and I should find myself alone each night in my apartment. But it happened that by the time we were in our mid-thirties, Peter and Ava had three.

Catherine, Meghan, Patrick. I was godfather to the first—Erik was godfather to the second—and no one as yet to the third. I had become more comfortable with the role as Catherine got to be three and now four years old. She was her mother, complete with those high cheekbones and thick dark hair, the latter of which pulled an ancestral string that the ever-meticulous Ava had recently tracked to a rather surprising conclusion.

In the lore that surrounded her family's history there was seemingly no genetic reason that Ava should have ever required the services of, shall we say, an ethnic hairdresser. Born and raised in Boston, she was ostensibly the product of an Irish father, a Danish mother, and somewhere a line of Ukrainian Jews. But Catherine's arrival as yet another generation to wear that unexplainable hair coincided with the advent of mail-away genetic tests, so Ava was taken by surprise six weeks after spitting into a tube to learn that

her top-ten most-likely countries of origin included the expected
Denmark and Ukraine alongside Spain and a smattering of its former
empire. There was no trace of anything resembling Ireland.

It turned out that our grandparents had played together as
children in Boston. Mine had no recollection of the particulars of the
family, only that Ava must have been named after her grandmother,
and that surely they had been Irish. The family friendship had been
lost to history at rather a young age, not be rekindled until the Coast
Guard brought us together by chance.

Pete's family background, on the other hand, could be described
only as "Ohioan." His father had been a good friend of a young local
congressman who, being unmarried and childless at the time, had
on several occasions taken young Peter to Capitol Hill as a stand-
in on Bring Your Child to Work Day. That congressman was now
the state's outspoken governor. He had run for president two years
earlier. When he traveled Peter packed a small waterproof radio
to listen to Rush Limbaugh in the shower each morning. It was a
predilection that reminded us that the world takes all kinds. Though
it made him by far the least popular of our friends with whom to
share a hotel room.

He called me the day after I fetched Erik at the train station
in late June. Erik had seen him in New York several days earlier. It
seemed that Peter had undertaken some scheme to acquire top-tier
airline status by flying a number of miles within a certain time period
that ended on the last day of the month. He was 510 miles short.
Inconvenient, given that a one-way from New York to Washington
would yield him only 500. He'd need to actually fly home in order to
pick up the last ten. I was surprised by all of this given the amount
of time he purportedly spent jetting around the world in first class,
visiting one business interest or the next, generally feeling important.

Chapter Three

I was downtown a few days later, after which I headed over to Joselito on Pennsylvania Avenue. Andrew Jefferson sat at a table out front reading a book. A glass of ice was decaying in front of him. There was a dilapidated leather bag at his feet.

"How goes the war, Jake?" He preferred shortening my last name—Jacobson—to calling me Chris.

"Pete's in town tonight. Didn't expect to see you here."

"Odd. I'm here whenever I've a spare dollar in my pocket."

Andrew looked terrible. Whether it was late June or the darkest moments of winter, the man wore a cardigan every day of the week. Sometimes, on weekends, you might catch him in a short-sleeve buttoner. Sweat beaded on his brow. Glasses rolled down his nose.

The waiter came to check on him.

"Another gin. Why the hell not? And why the hell is that son of a bitch coming to town?"

The waiter looked at me anxiously.

"Café con leche? No, wait. Whatever is Aurelio's latest white, I'll have that. Ask Billy." The waiter scurried off.

"How long have you been here?"

Andrew stared at me. "Not long. Where the hell have you been?"

"I wasn't supposed to be here at all."

"Damn right."

"How is it?"

"Well, the drink is fine."

The Spanish loved gin. Andrew wasn't the least bit Spanish, though he shared their fondness for gin.

"You going to be here later?"

"Not likely if you're coming back with Peter. I've had a hell of a bad time, and I've no interest in his opinions."

"How long have you really been here?" I asked again.

"Hours. I've been here hours."

"Have you eaten?"

"To hell with eating."

We had been friends since college. There he had often worn three-piece suits, and a straw hat if he was feeling festive. He had feuded endlessly with his roommate, an even stranger fellow who became as famously obnoxious a lawyer about town as he was a student about campus. Andrew spent a few years shamelessly manipulating our fraternity elections in a bid to "keep the lunatics out." He became fluent in Arabic, Turkish, Farsi, and Hebrew before getting bored of it all, developing an acute case of uncontrollable insomnia, and dropping out.

From there he made a futile attempt to save a local bookstore—whose owner eventually chose cannabis over literature—and later managed to get himself deported from the United Kingdom for overstaying his visa after falling in love with a man from Kentucky who was then studying at the London School of Economics.

"What have you been up to?" I asked.

"Better you not know. Better for everyone."

He had once told me that he made most of the little money he never seemed to have introducing people who should not have ever met in the first place. I was damned curious, but I preferred not to know. In any case, he seemed to have garnered a reputation as an enigmatic genius of foreign affairs, perpetually down on his luck, yet a haughty liberal from San Francisco who hated humans but loved humanity. He was too brilliant to pass up if one was in the market for someone with his unique skills. A drunk, to be sure, but an uncommonly gifted fellow with a knack for matters of international politics and law backed up by a talent for languages that few could replicate. To hell with degrees.

Our waiter returned with a gin and a glass of white, a Rueda from Marques de Tomares that I swirled in the glass. It was a characteristic verdejo from Rueda, dominated by immensely floral notes. Lemon zest followed juicy grapefruit, though the thing nonetheless felt like drinking a flower. It turned pleasantly sweet at the end, and paired well with Manchego cheese that had somehow appeared upon the table.

Ava and I once made our way to this winery's tasting room in Rioja where our host, Sara, had paired various meats and cheeses with what was, perhaps, a bottle of an earlier vintage of this very wine. Its verdejo grapes had been grown in Rueda, around a three-hour drive southwest towards Portugal. We had gone down into the town of Fuenmayor for lunch at Restaurante Alameda, a charming yet unassuming façade behind which we had found a delightful, bright dining room in which we enjoyed one of the most spectacular gourmet lunches I could remember.

Tomares and Alameda together paired soup, Norwegian lobster and chickpeas, beautiful salad, and the best croquetas I have had in all of Spain with, of course, a delightful bottle of the Marqués de Tomares Reserva from a vintage year that will forever remain a mystery to me because the bottle bore no label.

"Where will you go from here?" I asked Andrew from across the table.

"I'd love a good cuddle, if you're offering, but I'd prefer my fellow from across town. Little twit is still married to that imbecile from the voting rights group, so I don't think that's in the cards for tonight either."

He took another swig of gin and slid a newspaper—he still enjoyed newsprint—across the table.

"I can't read it. Can't bear to read anything more these days."

"The Republic endures, Jake, at least for another day."

I smiled back at him, lost in some combination of frustration with the world and fondness for the odd company. He continued.

"I do love drinking too much with you, Jake."

"You seem to have done fine on your own before I sat down."

"True, but I do love you."

"I love you too, Drew."

"Fuck off. That's not my name."

It was oddly cool for late June. The sun hung in the sky like a boy on a ball field who just wasn't ready to go home for dinner. I turned and looked west down Pennsylvania Avenue. It was a broad boulevard lined with a mile of trees at whose end the Capitol's dome was lit from behind by the brilliant yellow light of the late-afternoon sun, illuminating the wineglass in my hand in the final hours before it sank further on the horizon and turned to blood orange, a fiery metaphor for the ghastly business upon which it gazed each day.

I finished my wine.

He downed his gin.

"I better go to fetch Peter."

"I'll miss you."

"You always do."

"Goodnight, Jake."

"Goodnight, Drew."

Lyrics to some Spanish song or another often filled my head whenever I walked away from Joselito. Lately, I'd been humming in my mind something specific for no discernible reason.

Sale de la niebla de un bostezo lunar
Descalzada y despeinada, corre
Corre hasta sus brazos como nadie lo hará
Jamás, jamás, jamás.

I walked alone, northwest towards the Capitol but without a particular destination other than that in the back of my mind I knew I had to get home to Arlington. Peter could get himself there from the airport. Pennsylvania was mostly quiet as I passed through Seward Square, named for Abraham Lincoln's secretary of state, who had arranged the purchase of Alaska from the Russians in a decision ridiculed by some at the time, but altogether prescient years later.

After about ten minutes I turned onto Independence Avenue at the Library of Congress. I thought it might pour rain, but the scene of pristine trees and hollow democracy bathed in sun-streaked mist was beautiful as ever. I turned down First Street at the Cannon Building, and a moment later disappeared underground into the metro station.

Chapter Four

The phone's chimes shook me from sleep.

"There's a Mister Dean here for you. Shall I send him up?"

I had told the concierge downstairs to send him up, but they seemed to have lost something in the shift change that transpired during my nap.

"Yes. Send him up."

A bang at the door a few moments later, and I knew it could be no one other than Peter Dean.

"Christopher!" A grin on his face.

He tossed his duffel to the floor and hugged me.

I poured him a whisky.

"How you doin'?"

"You're the one with a story to tell."

"I missed you." He grinned again.

"Nonsense."

"It's true. Also, as of twenty minutes ago I am now only ten miles short of top-tier airline status."

I was sincerely jealous.

"We need to take a trip," he continued.

"With the gentlemen? So you can show us all how great it is to be you?"

"Sure, with the gentlemen. What's Erik up to?"

"Being a gentleman, I imagine."

"How about Nashville?"

"Nashville sounds like hell this time of year."

"Montreal, then." It was a near fact of the universe that Peter Dean was always two degrees of separation away from thinking that a trip to Canada was a good idea, mostly on account of it being imminently possible for him to manipulate his employer into paying his airfare.

We sat in quiet contemplation of this idea, sipping whisky, staring out the big window to the Potomac River.

This is how it always began. Though we had become much more civilized since our youth.

In college we had hosted a gathering at which the local police felt obliged to visit. Noise complaint. They knocked on the door, and Peter beelined for the basement. I discussed the matter with the officers for about ten minutes, after which they seized a pair of coolers. Nobody thought much of Peter when the officers departed until after another twenty minutes and another knock at the door. Pete's heavy footsteps bounded up the stairs, and he threw open the front door, babbling in Spanish at the fellow delivering pizza, whom he had evidently called during his brief subterranean exile. The delivery driver left.

"Why were you speaking to him in Spanish?"

"Chris, he was delivering pizza."

"He was also Asian."

"Was he?"

"You're an ass."

He called the police department the next day, reporting that two men posing as police officers had robbed his house and stolen his coolers.

We each downed our hundred-dollar whisky. Etched tumblers upon the table, artisanal ice melting slowly into oblivion. We called a car and went to Joselito.

Nine o'clock and still packed on a Friday night. In Spain this would be early. Andrew Jefferson was long gone. Javier hugged me, and I introduced him to Peter. Billy came to the table as we sat.

"Gents."

"Billy, meet Peter Dean. I think you'll get along well."

"Why so?" Peter grinned again.

"You seem likely to agree on approximately zero things save fondness for wine," I explained.

"Seems like enough."

"He listens to Rush Limbaugh in the shower."

"America is rather like a bookstore. It's filled with people who don't realize that their time has passed. And that's quite a condemnation coming from an Englishman. You know that damned bookstore down the street? The one with the lousy coffee shop? It's the only place I've ever seen with all those right-wing books, the Clinton-bashing books here, the religious books there, and the biggest stack of pornography I have ever seen sitting a meter away."

"The wine, Chris, the wine," Peter implored me as he scanned the list.

Billy reminded me that he had one bottle left of the Cartago.

Cartago Paraje del Pozo, from San Román, the Toro winery that Ava and I had once visited. We had tasted this one straight from the barrel, and I would have killed to see how it ended up now in the bottle.

"Ava and I once visited that winery."

"Settled on the Cartago?" Billy was waiting.

"Absolutely not. Unless Peter's buying." It cost $190.

"I'll buy. What the hell." Peter shrugged. He was an extraordinarily generous human being.

Billy ran off.

"Bless you, old friend."

It really was delicious wine.

"How's my goddaughter?" I asked.

"She talks about you all the time. Always asking, 'When's Uncle Chris going to come visit me?'"

"Seems all the women in your house love me."

"Just two. The littler one wouldn't know you from Adam."

"Or Erik, or God . . . She's two? Can't imagine either makes much of a difference to her yet."

"You'd be surprised. But Catherine, she's a little Ava. She is her mother. Has a bizarre reverence for the rules that she certainly hasn't inherited from me. She's become utterly fascinated by clarinets, any wind instrument, really. Strange thing."

It was odd. Best friend of half my life, years into a family on account of a girl I'd once parted ways with but would forever love. I was grateful for the history. We were living in perilous times for friendships. I feared it might come to the point where I had nothing left to talk about with a man for whom I felt brotherly affection.

I changed the subject.

"About our trip. What if we went to Spain?"

Now was the time, if I was going to steer the plane in that direction. The country's incredible wine filled our glasses. The Hemingway effect—that notion that Americans would keep falling in love with the place based on any exposure whatsoever—was in full swing.

I made no secret of my love for cities, and less secret still of my affinity for the capital of Spain. Indeed, much of my idle scheming turned out to be an exercise in getting back to Madrid, as was the case a few years ago when I strung together a bizarre itinerary that sent me on a grueling Washington to New York to Madrid to Stockholm itinerary all so that I could have a stopover in Madrid a week later on my way home from Budapest. Wherever I went, I always seemed to return to the European city with which I fell in love on a childhood visit with my grandparents. I still sent my grandmother pictures whenever I walked past places we first visited together. As if I were building a visual monument to time lapsed in my mind, as best illustrated by the peculiar multi-decade string of photos depicting my grandfather and I sitting in the same spot along Calle Cava de San Miguel.

"What's wrong with Montreal?"

"I don't suppose there's anything wrong with Montreal."

"We could go to Cartagena."

I knew I had him now. I would just have to endure the banter about every other random place he could think of before agreeing on a trip to the place to which his glass was already leading him.

We ordered tapas. Erik Weber called me.

"Emma's back. And her cousin is in town from Stockholm. Where are you?"

"Joselito. With Peter Dean."

"We'll see you soon."

I hung up.

"Erik Weber is coming."

"Fantastic."

Javier arranged a larger table for us. Erik, Emma, and her cousin Simon arrived twenty minutes later. We ordered more tapas and wine. It gurgled from bottles into beautiful glass decanters that resembled swans. Laughter and happy conversation filled the room adorned with polished marbled tables and glasses, twinkling as the candlelight refracted through their sparkling contents. The party's blend of elegance and warmly familiar charm could only have been the work of Javier. He guided us through a lineup of wine from Bodegas Elias Mora, a lovely winery up the road from the tiny town of San Román de Hornija, the last winery in the Province of Valladolid before crossing into Zamora. There a winemaker named Victoria produced wines rich in character and purity. Each was made from Tinta de Toro grapes grown in vineyards no more than a ten-minute drive from the winery, a walkable path from vineyard to the many bottles produced each year.

The wine on our table, Descarte, came from a specific vineyard whose fifty-five-year-old vines produced something especially captivating. Freshly cut pepper on the nose, balsamic, and a touch of cinnamon evolved into nice mineral notes, cedar, and, I dare say, root beer when aired in the glass. Aurelio stopped at the table to tell us how we could age this wine in the bottle for fifteen years. It would be difficult to spend so long not drinking it. It finished with dark raspberry jam notes on the palate, the sense of biting into milk chocolate with gooey raspberry.

"Hello, boys."

"Ashley Maria Luciano." Peter grinned.

"Hello, Ash." She sat next to me.

I smiled and turned back to my conversation with Simon. Erik and Ash struck up a chat.

The growing party ordered more food. Most dishes could be had in three sizes—*tapa, media ración*, like an entrée, or *ración* as a family-style portion meant for passing. The menu changed often. At my end of the table we had been working on a year-aged Manchego with spicy tomato marmalade and rosemary together with *jamón iberico de bellota*. I was attracted to the *raya al pimentón*—skate wing, of all things—and a lamb dish called *costillar de cordero asado*.

Ash opened her own proceedings with a sangría prepared with striking flair. It was delivered in a small spherical glass bottle to be poured over large ice cubes into which pieces of chopped fruit had been frozen. This prevented ice from melting into the wine whilst sitting in a carafe. Rather that its slow melting should add fruit to the mixture as time went on.

Simon told me how he was working on something or other up in Boston. He had come down to Washington for the weekend to see Emma. We were excited that Sweden had advanced in the World

Cup. I longed for him to speak with me in Swedish, though I prayed silently that he'd not put my poor skills to the test.

I turned back to Ash, who had grown quiet when Erik and Peter disappeared into a moment of serious conversation.

"I've not seen you in weeks."

"Oh. You know me." She trailed off.

"I do indeed. How has it been?"

"It's been dreadful, Chris, dreadful. I've missed you."

"What have you been up to?"

"I don't even know."

"Feeling good about reengaging the world?"

"Why do you ask so many damned questions?"

"I was inquiring because I care."

"I know. It's not your fault. It's a terrible business. You shouldn't want anything to do with me. I've spent too long telling you that. It's not fair."

The skate wing arrived.

"Good news, Chris!" Peter jumped in. "Erik's going to Spain with us."

Apparently, we were going to Spain. It had only taken $400 worth of wine.

Ash perked up. "I want to go to Spain!"

Javier visited the table to pour more wine. He and Ash began babbling at one another in proper Spanish at a pace far beyond my ability to keep up.

"I said I'd think about it," Erik clarified.

"He said he'd think *seriously* about it." Peter grinned.

I asked if the ladies would be joining us.

"We'll see. I need to talk with Ava."

I hoped Ava would come.

"Forget Spain. What are we doing tomorrow?" Emma asked.

"Tomorrow?" Peter stared back at her.

"Yes, we should do something decent tomorrow," she said.

"We should do something decent tonight," Peter countered.

"We are doing something decent tonight!"

"Some more decent."

"You're drunk, Emma."

"Of course I'm drunk."

Simon chuckled at his cousin.

I suggested that we visit a winery.

Peter took out his phone and called Ava.

"We're going to a winery tomorrow. You should come down on the morning train."

Silence as we all stared at him.

"Leave them with the nanny. You'll only be gone a day."

Peter listened.

"We can fly back together on Sunday."

He grinned.

"I'll buy you a ticket now."

He hung up.

"Seeing Ava in the morning?"

"Yes. Around eleven?"

"That sounds civilized."

"Where we going?" Billy asked as he returned to the table.

"The *boys* are going to Spain." Emma smiled.

I asked Billy if he wanted to come along.

"Haven't got the funds. I need to go to London to visit my mother."

"We could go to London," I offered.

"I'm from London, and I work at a Spanish bar in Washington. How do *you* think I like London?"

"Valid."

Peter interrupted. "You really should come to Spain with us. I'll buy your ticket."

He really was very generous.

"That's very nice. Truthfully though," Billy clarified, "I was asking what was happening tomorrow."

"We're going to a winery." I asked Billy if he cared to join.

"You clearly haven't been to enough brunches if you think there's a chance in hell I can be somewhere other than this spot."

"So you were making a courtesy inquiry?"

"I was just making damned conversation."

Peter asked who would drive. This was a good question.

Billy told us a story.

"I'm a terrible driver. Seriously, I had eight driving instructors, and one of them had a stroke. So I didn't drive for ten years. Then I moved to California where the test is much easier. I cheated. Seriously, I got into the car and the instructor said, 'You probably have a license in Britain.' I said, 'Probably.' I didn't lie. The laws of probability were that yes, I probably did have a license in Britain. We drove around the block whilst he told me about his trip to Stonehenge, and then I passed the test. I drove around the next four years just running into shit. Ask Aurelio; I hit a brand-new car—my first $3,000 accident—with him in the passenger seat."

"That's a cheery thought before we go spend the whole afternoon drinking wine and driving home."

"You've spent the whole night drinking wine."

"Only after nine."

"Yes. We drank whisky before that."

"Thanks, Peter."

"Cheers." Billy ran off with our dessert order of *torrijas*—an Andalusian-style bread pudding—and *sopa de chocolate blanco y fresas al Jerez*, a warm white chocolate soup with strawberries marinated with sherry vinegar.

Javier had grown up in a town called Huelva, in Andalusia, in the south of Spain.

Ornate little cordial glasses appeared on the table. Javier poured something or other from his private stock. He was famous for making his own liqueurs.

"What are we doing tonight?" Emma asked.

"What the hell? It's almost midnight," Erik huffed.

"Alright. What are we doing this morning?"

"Nothing good happens after midnight anymore."

"Anymore! You're only thirty-four . . . That rhymes." Emma giggled.

Simon was in town, so we called cars and went back to my place for akvavit.

Ash decided against it. "I hate akvavit," she said. "See you crazy people in the morning."

◦◦◦◦◦◦◦

The ice had long ago melted in the whisky glasses by the time we returned home.

I cleared them away and took out the small fluted glasses that I used only for akvavit. They were strange glasses, three flutes connected at the base atop the stem such that drinking from one would cause all three to be drained. The trick was not throwing it back so quickly that you ended up with a face full.

I fetched a bottle of O.P. Anderson from the freezer. Simon was visiting, so I considered this a special enough occasion to go straight to the Swedish stuff. It was difficult to find Swedish akvavit in Washington, so I normally settled for the stuff from Norway or Denmark.

Simon pointed out that it was just past Midsummer, the high holiday in Sweden when akvavit was typically drank. I poured five glasses and passed them around. We raised them and I began singing. The Swedes knew the song, and I had been making Erik and Peter sing the thing for years. We sang.

Helan går
Sjung hopp faderallan lallan lej
Helan går
Sjung hopp faderallan lej
Och den som inte helan tar

Han heller inte halvan får
Helan går!

We downed the glasses. Peter tossed akvavit in his face. Emma giggled.

"*Sjung hopp faderallan lej!*"

"Disgusting stuff." Peter wiped his face.

"You either love it or hate it." Erik loved it.

"Again! Again!" I collected the glasses and began pouring.

Peter asked what the song meant.

"Eh." I poured and distributed the last glass. "Here's the first drink! Drink up, because if you don't drink the first you won't get the second, and what would be the point of that?"

Peter looked at Simon.

"More or less," he said.

Helan går
Sjung hopp faderallan lallan lej
Helan går
Sjung hopp faderallan lej
Och den som inte helan tar
Han heller inte halvan får
Helan går!

We downed the glasses. Peter did better with this one. He just needed practice.

Sjung hopp faderallan lej!

Chapter Five

We plucked Ava from the train a bit after ten. She had caught an earlier train. Peter and I hugged her. I lingered a moment, happy to see my friend before we shuffled back into the car we had rented just that morning. Erik drove the six of us. Emma had decided to not come.

"She's ill," Simon explained.

"Ill in a grocery bag in Chris's elevator last night," Erik snickered.

Constitution Avenue runs from the Capitol along the Mall until it crosses the Potomac River into Virginia. It's pleasant for a time, but later there is suburban wasteland lined with the next real estate developer's take on unoriginal dining and tawdry conveniences. A burrito joint. A hair salon. An office park. A Lexus dealership.

"I knew someone who died there." Ava pointed to a hospice facility.

We each labored to produce an unintelligible acknowledgement of loss for someone nobody else had known. It was the sensitive thing to do.

Suddenly it became very rural. We drove off into the Virginia countryside. There are few cities from which such thriving wine-making is as accessible as Virginia is from Washington. Urbanity melts so quickly into rolling hills, quiet roundabouts, villages cropped in by forests, and within an hour the pastoral beauty of horse country. Stone walls and split rail fences hemmed in the road as if they were keeping automobiles out as much they were keeping horses in. It's one of those stretches of highway with a vineyard around each bend, up each hill, down in each little valley and hollow.

At some point Ava and I began discussing which wineries to visit.

We came up a hill onto a flat stretch of road where a mass of cars and horses were gathered around a large complex of stables. I wished I had learned to ride. Green branches bent over the road like a tunnel as we disappeared back into the valley below. John S. Mosby Highway it was called. I wondered who John S. Mosby had been.

My phone knew that he had been a Confederate cavalry commander in the Civil War. The countryside through which we were now driving had been called Mosby's Confederacy. He had apparently managed to befriend Ulysses Grant prior to the latter's ascension to the presidency, played a part in an amnesty bill for former Confederates, and served as the American consul to Hong Kong, after which he lived another thirty-one years.

A Confederate who found common cause with his former enemy. Another road named for a former traitor. Could one be a *former* traitor? A segregation academy—one of the private schools set up in the mid-twentieth century so that white parents could avoid sending their children to school with black children—was named in his honor forty-three years after he died. It closed a decade later.

I was depressed and bored of the topic, so I stopped reading.

We drove through Middleburg. Charming, idyllic, like everything else here. We passed the Red Fox Inn and Tavern. At the corner, one would turn for the Foxcroft School where well-to-do families sent their teenaged girls. I found myself wondering how Ava and Peter felt about educating their children. Ava had grown up in a New England boarding school. I grew up in West Virginia, a place that so seldom saw any of its kids go away to college that the local mechanic had felt compelled to give me a free tune-up before leaving.

Hunters Head Tavern passed by on our right.

"I'd have loved to go there." Erik really loved Hunters Head Tavern. The sleepy village of Upperville, the brick path and stately stone arch covered with ivy, the whole scene here in the heart of wine country fit his penchant for old, interesting things. It was the type of place through whose door you might slip to a time long past in an authentic English pub, a true tavern house built around 1750, laced top to bottom with rustic sophistication. Old plank floors, fireplaces, exposed beams, farmhouse tables, and wooden chairs of which no two ever seemed to be alike conveyed a homey sense of somewhere far away. It was like stepping out of a fox hunt. Actually I had once heard some fellows there discussing fox hunts.

Hillsides rolled into one another through cow-filled valleys and over crests of open fields lined with roadside trees providing shade to passing cars. Stately Trinity Episcopal Church appeared as we slowed through town. Light-grey stones, dark-grey roof, a quiet courtyard surrounded by more trees.

There were exquisite restaurants in the countryside. As with wine, the best restaurants are those that take full advantage of the terrain. The string of towns and villages—Middleburg, Upperville, Paris—dotted the highway through Loudoun and Fauquier Counties, serving a compelling terroir.

We stopped at the Ashby Inn in Paris, an unincorporated village that seemed plucked directly from the English countryside. An old church rose up on the quiet little street next to the inn. Birds chirped. The setting was positively idyllic, the type of place you stop for lunch between wineries, and then realize hours later that you've sat in the garden until your next destination has closed.

A path led us to a covered terrace as we wandered up through the garden. Ours was a beautiful day, so we took brunch outside, sitting under vines meticulously maintained in the ceiling above the terrace. We angled for a table near the steps so that we could stare out into the garden and the unobstructed view of the hills beyond. Inside was a bright, light-soaked dining room, rustic tavern, and cozy library. I thought that we all should return to sit and drink in them when winter came.

The Bloody Mary bar tempted Peter away from the wine the rest of us had come seeking. The generous cheese plate and our crepes kept us happy. Stuart, the sommelier, had crafted an excellent wine list from the best of Virginia and a wide net cast to other regions around the world. He was spectacularly knowledgeable as he guided each of us to pairings we craved, clearly happy to banter with us.

I had been lost in my thoughts for some time and would have been lost for more time still, sitting out in the garden with my wineglass, had Ash not interrupted my silence.

"I think I'd like to move."

We all stared at her. I asked her if she thought she might like to move out here.

"No, I want to get out of here. Take a little money to a place where I don't need much."

It was a ridiculous statement. Ash never did anything with a *little* money.

"What is it you do for work, Ashley?" Simon didn't know better than to not ask.

"She wanders about town."

"Pardon?"

She told Peter to go to hell. He promised that he didn't mean it how it sounded.

"I have many friends."

That was mostly untrue.

"And I always find something useful to do with my time."

That was most certainly untrue.

I didn't much know what she did with her time, but I did know that she got her money from her father, who had been dead for twenty years.

Ashley Maria Luciano had not been born Ashley Maria Luciano. Her father had been Colombian, and had not exactly come to America on the up-and-up. He was evidently brilliant, working his way through school flying crop dusters and those airplanes that pull advertisements aloft above crowded beaches. Then he got involved with the crowd who built the early internet. After that he flew for love rather than money. He didn't need the money. He died in an aviation mishap in the late nineties when Ash was six.

Her mother, a second-generation Lithuanian from Chicago, remarried an American fellow named Luciano. She changed her daughter's name in desperate grief and longing for a happy family.

Ash sat at the table, visibly annoyed.

She asked Simon, "What do you think of Americans?"

Ava shifted uncomfortably in her chair. Marital harmony asked only that her pragmatic sensibilities not get too mixed up with Pete's stubborn brand of America-first conservatism when in polite company. Ash had only asked the question to get back at Peter for his petulant little dig earlier.

"You have beautiful wine country." Simon sipped awkwardly from his glass, unable to wipe the smirk from his face.

"No, but what do you think of the people?" Ash pressed.

"Have you really got many flat-earthers? You know, people who insist the earth is flat?"

"I've never met a flat-earther," Peter blathered from the lip of his Bloody Mary glass.

Ash laughed.

"It was funny to me, Chris, when Emma told me that you were Swedish. When I hear that someone is Swedish, then I talk to them in Swedish."

Now it was my turn to feel uncomfortable. I was terrifically embarrassed by how poor my Swedish was.

"Jag är trött på min dålig Svenska," I sheepishly choked out.

Ava exhaled in quiet relief that we were moving on from the flat earth discussion. Her husband didn't believe in the nonsense, but he was particularly sensitive to the notion that haughty liberals and Europeans might associate him with all manner of American fringe.

"Well, I think that's a fundamental question of this moment," Erik interjected.

"What is?"

"What Simon just said." Erik paused. "See, we are almost exclusively unique among countries in that to be American is not about blood and soil. Now that might be changing."

Simon asked Erik to tell him more.

"Well, most other countries are defined by the born qualities of those who find themselves there. 'I speak French, my ancestors have lived in France for a thousand years, my waiters are rude to everyone, therefore I am French.'"

"But not here?" Simon asked.

"Our waiters are friendlier." I tried to lighten the mood.

"And poorly paid," Simon added.

Erik was undeterred.

"No. Historically speaking, when someone chose to come to America, to become an American, they were swearing off that blood and soil stuff and instead dedicating themselves to an idea."

"And that idea was?" Ash looked at him skeptically, likely thinking of the Spanish, Colombian, and American passports that she carried in her bag like religious objects, a tribute to a man long dead who she barely remembered. She was all emotion, unable to recognize that her father was in fact the human embodiment of the point Erik was making.

"And speaking Swedish to Chris?"

"Chris isn't Swedish. He's American." Erik shot me a look as if to say *I'm sorry.*

I bristled.

"We don't think of it the same way here." Ava came to my defense. She knew how important this was to me.

I stared half drunk at my wineglass swirling mindlessly in my hand upon the table.

I had plans to visit Sweden soon. My family came from Grundsund where about 700 people live on the coast of the Skagerrak, the strait that connects the North Sea to the Baltic. There I had cousins descended from my great-grandfather whose son had once immigrated to the United States.

My head swam in the Swedish traditions and practices that had been passed through my family over many years. I served meatballs at Christmas. I grew up on *plättar*—Swedish pancakes—at breakfast. My mother had decorated her Christmas tree with Swedish flags. We drank akvavit and sang "Helan Går," despite the fact that only a couple of us actually knew the real words and what they meant. Most were just Americans swinging glasses and singing gibberish.

How odd to Simon the notion that I should think of myself as being Swedish. He was as Swedish as I was American. In the typical American telling, we often equated nationality with citizenship, not with ethnicity. Because most of us descend from people who came from somewhere else, and because many of our families have not, in the grand scheme, been here long, the distinctly American concept of ethnicity is one of a fellow like me—somewhat Swedish, a bit English and Native American, and the remaining fractions an indeterminate blend of God-only-knew-what. The more blended we get, the more American we become, whilst the ethnic heritage that characterizes the individual or the family is often the one spoken the loudest. The one whose stories get told. Whose songs get sung. Whose food gets cooked. Whose drinks get poured.

I contemplated my wine again. Like so many of its people, American wine came from somewhere else, too. France's pinot noir grew splendidly in Oregon, whilst Germany's riesling had made it big in Upstate New York. Vidal blanc, a French hybrid created in the 1930s, grew well in Massachusetts. Chambourcin was the child of unknown French and American parents. Several years ago, the

Spanish winemaker at Virginia's Potomac Point Vineyard and Winery created Vino Camino, a blend of Virginia's excellent cabernet franc and monastrell imported from Spain. I had once tried a lovely bottle of tempranillo—Spain's noble grape—produced in Texas.

Just as Americans tended to equate nationality with citizenship rather than ethnicity, so too did we know our wines by their grape, what they are—tempranillo or pinot noir—rather than the European way of naming wine by place, where they're from: Rioja or Burgundy.

The American people had been imported and blended from the good stuff of other places, tempered and given unique character by their new surroundings, the terrain and climate of human experience. Whatever greatness one ascribed to America, the thing that made America great didn't happen in spite of its fractional origins. It happened because of them. America had grown up and grown rich because those who came before lived in a nation where they could pass on the richness of their cultures, such that today I could raise a glass and sing Swedish drinking songs with my Swedish-Egyptian-Jamaican-English-German-Mexican-Irish-Portuguese-Jewish-Catholic-Protestant-and-whatever-else family.

America was supposed to be about content of character, not birthright.

I downed the glass of wine, and we departed.

It was a short drive to Delaplane Cellars on nearby Lost Mountain. The winery itself seemed almost cut into the hillside. Its big windows towering above the vineyard and the road below to boast spectacular mountain views from its patio and tasting room. In the distance I noticed three mountain peaks that inspired the elegant labels adorning each bottle.

There was a sign admonishing us that all who entered must be twenty-one years old. Groups larger than six were not permitted. Buses and limousines must keep away.

Sounds of a lone man playing his guitar wafted through the high vaulted ceilings and out the open door onto the patio. Friendly people poured glasses for a throng of revelers at the bar. Light shone in, reflecting angelic white from puffy clouds in the sapphire sky that stretched over rows of grapevines sloping down gentle hills and across lush green fields to the blue mountains beyond. A white manor house and impeccably kept white country fence hemmed in the yard below.

I bought a bottle of viognier and sat with my friends on the deck. Virginia produces excellent viognier. And I hoped that we'd not revisit the conversation from the inn. Andrew Jefferson saw us and came to say hello. I felt badly about not having invited him. He told me not to feel badly. He was here with friends from Fauquier County.

Later I bought a bottle of cabernet franc. Virginia produces excellent cabernet franc. Sometime after that Ava decided that she wanted sparkling wine, so we drove back the way we had come, towards Washington to a winery that we knew made sparkling wine. Virginia does not often produce good sparkling wine, but I knew this bottle to be quite good.

You'd be forgiven thinking Greenhill Winery larger than it is when driving up. The people there had done a splendid job creating something that was both expansive and personal: farmhouses spread across acres, stately and stone walled next to the pond yet intimate in their myriad little tasting rooms, open fields, open skies stretching out to the thick tree line along the opposite side of the vineyard.

Then there was the barrel room, a cathedral of wine where barrels were stacked five and six high to form a broad aisle under the tall, vaulted wood ceilings from which twinkling lamps were hung. Light shone in through the large round window in the apse, bathing the would-be altar in a yellow glow that fell like a spirit upon barrels encircling the center as an ambulatory, years-old witness to the quiet aging that was done here. Neither a cathedral nor church of any kind, but I might have married a girl in that cellar.

The porch of the main house was less majestic, but equally

captivating for its simple charm, a place you'd spend the day letting warm summer breeze pass over you, food from the kitchen fill you, wine delight you. Their sparkling was notable, a Chardonnay made in the classic style of a French blanc de blancs. I would not ever suggest growing Chardonnay grapes in Virginia, but this sparkling wine—rare in the Commonwealth—made excellent use of them and was reason enough for a visit.

Peter bought two bottles. We sat together on the back porch in the late afternoon. Ash and Peter carried on in some ridiculous discussion. She frustrated me when she was being difficult. My phone rang at some point. I was surprised to see that it was the most interesting man that I knew.

I took the call and walked out into the yard.

"Cousin!" I greeted my cousin.

"Mister Jakey!"

I had no idea why he always called me Mister Jakey.

"Where in the world are you?"

"Well. At the moment I'm sailing around Anegada and headed south to Saint Croix. But I'll be off to Bermuda in a week."

"Lucky man."

"Care to join?"

"Join what?"

"I need you to help me sail up to Bermuda and on to New York."

"When?"

"Like I said, in a week."

"Not possible."

"Why?"

"I'm up to Provincetown on Monday morning. Then off to Stockholm next week."

"I'm entertained that you can't help me sail to Bermuda because you'll be in Sweden."

"What lives we lead."

"Well."

His life was far more interesting than mine.

I asked him when I would next see him. He said that he planned to be in New England for a stretch during the summer hurricane season. We said goodbye and hung up. I had no idea when I'd next see my cousin.

I stood there in the field. Late afternoon's warmth floating over me, glass of sparkling wine in my hand. The world seemed to go on forever from here. I was happy that I had turned off notifications on my phone earlier in the afternoon. One couldn't trust it. Today's America was, if nothing else, good at producing a string of daily calamities. I had to get away.

Ava walked out and stood close beside me. We looked out in silence for a moment. That happy sense of having been drinking sparkling wine filling our senses. She asked me who had called.

"Geoff Gamal."

"Oh my." She giggled. "Love Gee Gee."

"Everybody loves him. I love him dearly."

"What did he have to say for himself?"

"Wanted me to help him sail to Bermuda."

"I'll help him sail to Bermuda."

"You should tell him so. I can't do it."

"Mothers of three don't sail to Bermuda."

We were quiet for a moment. It occurred to me that I neither knew if Peter was aware of Ava's and Geoff's long-ago dalliance, nor was I sure how he may have felt about it.

I asked her if she wanted to walk.

We walked out on the little road down towards the stone manor house by the pond. It was a longer walk that stretched the length of the main vineyard. Ava seemed happy to step away from the group on the porch. I was happy to be walking through a vineyard again with Ava. I missed our adventures in wine.

We walked for a few minutes in contented silence. Sometimes these things are best done sharing everything and nothing at all.

She asked me how I had been.

I told her that I had been fine.

"And?" she asked.

"And?" I had so much to say, but couldn't think of anything to say.

She laughed, and smiled at me as we paused for a moment.

There were some people playing by the little road, on the side where it met the head of the rows of grapevines. One of them was taking a picture of a beautiful young woman posing beneath a tree in front of the vineyard. She told the girl how happy she was that they could visit together now. I imagined she might be turning twenty-one—beautiful smile, full of life. I wondered what books she might write one day, or paintings she might paint, or software she might create. Tall, flowing hair, auburn made just a bit blond by the sun. Quirky round sunglasses, flowing white top. A woman who may have been just in her sixties joined them and called the young woman Emily. They all looked alike. I imagined they were three generations, playing by the side of the little road.

Ava and I walked on towards the pond. Everywhere we were surrounded by green. Grass. Vines. A leaf dropped like a feather on my shoulder from the tree overhead. One day it would turn to brown, but for now, it too was green. It was a beautiful day we were sharing together.

I asked her if she might go to Spain with us.

"Perhaps," she answered playfully.

"I hope you will."

"It's not a trip for the boys? What's it that you call those?"

"A philosophers' journey?"

"Yes. That."

"I don't know. It would be good to have you."

"I'll talk with Peter about it when we're back in New York."

"Good." It made me happy.

Eventually we returned to Peter, Ash, Erik, and Simon on the porch of the big house. A little wine had done well for Peter and Ash.

They were all laughing and pouring rosé. Ash and I locked eyes and shared some indiscernible thought.

Later we drove home. The setting sun shone between the trees like orange tears crying over the day's inevitable end. I drifted off to sleep in the back of the car.

That evening was lonely.

"To hell with Ash," I said to myself alone in my room.

I was angry because I knew how this was going to go, how it always went. *Damn you, Ashley Maria Luciano.* I was angry with myself.

I lay in my bed and drifted off to sleep for the second time that day.

Chapter Six

Spain met Russia in the World Cup at ten the next morning. It was Sunday, the first day of July, and oppressively hot—not a day to be outside. I wore linen and poured a glass of albariño from Rías Baixas. I would have preferred cava, but the Catalans didn't want to be Spanish anyway. *Why should I drink their wine whilst watching this?* I thought.

Simon came to watch the game with me. Emma came with him. She was still not ready for wine. Simon asked me about Peter Dean.

"Peter seems very nice," he said.

"He's a good man."

Spain played poorly and lost to Russia on penalty kicks. I hated to see the Russians win. This silly sport spoke volumes in that moment. The Russians had just embarrassed a superpower.

I hated drinking wine when the sun was up, but I had done so three days in a row—Friday with Andrew Jefferson, Saturday with the gang, Sunday in some superstitious notion that perhaps my choice of beverage would have any influence over the outcome of a sport played half a world away. We three sat and chatted until it was long past time to say goodbye. I had grown fond of Simon, and felt I might miss him.

Peter and Ava had gone to New York. I was sad to see them leave, so I took a nap and awoke during the golden hour when the brilliant light just before twilight guarantees that any fool with a phone can snap a stunning photo. It was about the same time at which the spaces between the trees had cried their tears for the end of the day before. The room was bathed in light, and I was very happy for a moment.

⌒⌒⌒⌒⌒⌒

Later I called a car to take me to Joselito. It was quiet, not many people on the Sunday before a holiday, but the music of decades past filled the space as usual. Javier had gone home. Ash sat alone at the bar, staring up into the enormous mirror that reflected the room behind her. I greeted her.

"I thought I might find you here."

She mindlessly swirled her sangría and stared forlornly into the glass.

"How did you know?"

"Spain lost."

"Am I that predictable?"

"Yes."

Billy poured me a red from Navarre. I swirled it mindlessly and stared forlornly into the glass. Then I grabbed it with two fingers by the base and spun it with vigor. It settled before I smelled it. A good, deep, hard smell. I said nothing as I lingered there before taking a sip, smiled, and exhaled.

"I can't believe you drink wine from Navarre," she said, looking judgmentally at my glass.

I stared back at her, and was not in the mood.

"I'm an ass. I'm sorry," she recanted.

Ash looked as though she was fighting back a tear.

"It's not the game, you know."

I knew very well that this had nothing to do with the game.

"I'm sorry I was such a bitch to Peter yesterday. And to you on Friday night."

"You were far worse to Peter."

"Yes. . ." She trailed off.

"You seemed to work it out with him by the end of the day?"

"That was the wine talking," she corrected. "I'm still no good to him or you or anyone. And you all take such good care of me."

"You noticed." I grinned.

"Go to hell." She fired an awful stare and then smiled a bit in the corner of her mouth. Her lip twitched. She pursed them together and looked away.

"Peter seemed to like you," I said, addressing Billy from the other side of the white marble bar.

"He's not my type, but he's not a bad fellow for a crazy person."

"He *is* crazy," Ash piped.

"Told Billy he'd buy him a ticket to Spain," I offered.

"I know. I was there."

"Ash, why do you have to be so rude to your friends?" Billy grinned at her. I snorted with laughter. She shot that awful stare.

"Go to hell, Billy," she said.

He laughed and walked away to carry on with his evening chores behind the bar.

Ash and I giggled, staring at one another.

"He's funny."

"At least you're self-aware enough to not be angry when he asks you things like that."

"Oh, I'm self-aware. But Billy can ask me anything he likes. He's funny."

"How many glasses have you had?"

"Not many."

"Good."

"Why?"

"Because I'm enjoying this too much." I paused. "As you said on Friday night, I've missed you."

We sat quietly for a moment, listening to the music and the sound of some other guests saying goodbye, sipping our drinks. Ash finished her sangría. Billy brought her a glass of wine from the same bottle I was drinking.

"Glass from Navarre?" He winked at her.

I looked around at the gold frames that encircled the towering mirrors, the old photographs of Javier's family and life growing up, his mother, his father, the framed posters from Sevilla and Huelva.

"Have you been to Huelva?"

"No. Why?"

"Idle question. Javier's hometown. Perhaps we should go."

"On your boys' trip?"

"Why does everyone think it's a boys' trip?"

"I'm not aware that anyone thinks that."

"You just asked me if it was a boys' trip."

"No, I asked you if you were suggesting Huelva for your boys' trip."

"Actually, I thought you were going to join us."

"Of course I'm going to join you. Don't be silly!" She smiled.

"I've not seen you like this in weeks."

"You've not seen me like anything in weeks. I've not been anywhere. And for good reason."

"In spite of those penalty kicks."

"In spite of those penalty kicks." She then asked, "Why are you so good to me?"

"I'm not anything to you."

"Shut up."

"Shut up?"

We resumed drinking and listening to the music. There was nobody left at the bar or restaurant. Even Billy had disappeared. A waiter was cleaning up in the side room.

There were silver candelabras on the bar, every four stools or so. Ornate, and caked with wax of many evenings past. The candle at our place had been burning low when I arrived. Now it was flickering inside its well, persisting, hanging on as if it had lived this latest episode with us and couldn't bear to be extinguished until it had seen us through. A dab of wax dripped into my hand. I kneaded it before returning my attention to the wine. I was content with this moment.

A few years earlier when younger and less patient, I'd have asked questions. I'd have wanted to know what I could not have ever possibly understood. I suppose that was how it always was with these things. I imagine that's how it had always been for her. Questions. Sympathy. Bewilderment. And eventually, as it always was, resentment.

Lost in my thoughts again.

"I see you playing with that wax."

I cast it aside and looked at her. I had indeed begun playing with the wax again.

"Always fidgeting," she added.

"Just waiting."

"Waiting for what? For me?"

I smiled.

"You've become more thoughtful as you've grown up, you know."

"Please, I'm seven years older than you."

"Good thing you found such a mature young lady, then."

"Ha!" I actually laughed.

"You're all so good to me. See, I can admit it when I'm in a good place."

"Joselito?"

"You know what I mean." She smiled that smile that melted worlds and erased time.

"I just realized who you look like," Billy said to her as he returned to the bar.

It irritated me that he had returned at this moment. I felt like we had really been getting somewhere without him.

"And who is that?" she asked.

I was suddenly curious myself.

"Do you know Leire Martínez?"

I had never considered this, but Ash struck a stunning resemblance to the singer whose lyrics I had been humming to myself days earlier when I walked into the sunset, away from Andrew Jefferson sitting out front with his gin. Striking eyes. Charming, lopsided grin that conveyed the countenance of a real person with real thoughts, real inquiry, real substance, always somewhere between skeptical and amused. Flowing auburn and dark-blond hair.

She seemed flattered.

"Of course," Billy added, "only when you're not in one of your surly and disagreeable states."

She scowled.

"You certainly know how to ruin a good moment," I told him, thinking that he had no idea how correct he was.

Billy laughed, refreshed our glasses, and scurried off again.

Ash and I swiveled on our stools to look at one another. She laughed and then looked down.

"You really up for another one?"

"I'm still here, aren't I?"

"Ha!" It was her turn to laugh. "Though I can't imagine why."

"Certainly against my better judgment."

"That's for damn sure." She shook her head. "You're a fool, Chris Jacobson, a damned fool."

We swiveled back to the bar and sipped our wine. It was getting late, but Billy wasn't one to let good company walk out the door in a straight line. The wick was sputtering its last gasps in the little molten wax that was left in the candelabra.

"Where you off to next?"

I told Ash that I was leaving the next day.

"I'll miss you."

I knew that she wanted me to tell her that I'd miss her, too.

"You barely saw me."

"I saw you three times. That's practically a record."

"Not untrue."

The candle flickered and died.

We sat in silence for a moment, finishing our wine.

"Shall we?" I asked.

"Yes."

I paid and said goodnight to Billy. He was nearly finished anyway.

We walked out the door, and, without words, turned up Pennsylvania. The Capitol was stately lit under the moon that had been full just nights ago. Warm breeze rustled the leaves on the trees that grew on either side and in the median of the wide avenue. It was still dreadfully hot, but we didn't yet care. Ash draped her arm on mine.

My mind picked up where it had left off walking this same sidewalk several days earlier.

Y María le dice que sí,
Dice sonrojada que sí,
Y se esconde en sus brazos.

Eventually we called for a car, and disappeared silently into the night.

Chapter Seven

I would have preferred to leave for Provincetown straightaway in the morning but went to my office instead. Working in software is strange. Being anywhere but the office is common. All the freedom in the world, yet sometimes one just feels the need to go in. In any case, I had this notion that I'd accomplish a great deal on a quiet morning wedged between a summer weekend and a midweek holiday.

The office was a ghost town. A bit after ten o'clock I stopped at the desk of one of our junior software engineers, weeks out of college. I had taken an interest in her and hoped selfishly to direct her obvious talent towards projects important to me. I also felt badly that there were so few people in the office. The ability to work anywhere is a blessing, but I imagined it had to be difficult for her just starting out. How exciting could it be to come to an office and find nobody there, or to have no need to come at all? Opportunity is so often the result of chance. When you interact with no one, your chances for serendipity are slim. Human beings had never been better connected, nor lonelier.

I returned to my office and passed the time replying to emails. This was apparently what it meant to accomplish a great deal. They never ceased. *This*, I thought, *is how well-to-do, educated children should be told their lives will shake out*. I thought about the fellow who had repaired my car as I headed off to college sixteen years earlier—

weathered and hard, skin long ago turned to leather, colored and disheveled as only a fellow for whom every dollar had turned on the skill of his wrench could be. I wondered if this was the life he had intended for me in that moment when he thought he was doing his bit to send me off to some brighter future. I wondered if I had let him down.

Shortly after eleven in the morning, the receptionist called. "Someone named Emma Cuevas is here for you."

I looked out my window down to the street. I sighed and walked out to the lobby. It wasn't that I didn't want to see her. I was quite fond of Emma Cuevas.

"You metroed thirteen stops to see me?" I asked her as we exchanged a hug in the lobby.

"Straight from the Hill. There's nothing happening in my office," she sighed, "and the boss has gone home."

"Are you here for coffee? Lunch? Good company?"

"All of the above?"

We walked up the street to SER, Javier's restaurant on the Arlington side of the river. It was his first restaurant, the place where we had first met him. There were eccentric yellow leather seats at the bar, a wooden farmhouse table the centerpiece of the room, saucers and table settings different enough from one another to impart the character of home. I was sad that we were hours too early for another warm summer's evening.

Simple. Easy. Real. Javier's original vision. He had created something special. In Spain, the staff at most restaurants were truly invested in their craft. Less so in the United States, where servers so often changed jobs. Sometimes, in the slow mornings, his kids and the kids of his staff would crowd together around the long counter learning from Chef David how to cook a dish.

To the surprise of some, I was sure, SER did not revolve around tapas and small-plate dining. The staples were there—*pan Catalana, croquetas de jamon y pollo,* Manchego cheese. A salad promised to bring us "the most beautiful things found at the market today." Various fish appeared on the special menu. I had recently tried a delicious preparation of blue fish. *Cochinillo* and paella were always offered. I was only mildly ashamed to admit a fondness for the cheeseburger, prepared with Spanish flair, topped with Mahon cheese and bravas sauce.

In the evenings, Javier would roam the tables in his trademark jeans, blazer, and Chucks, personally thanking every guest for coming. He stopped often to make real talk about the wines with anyone who was interested. One sensed that everyone who worked there was truly grateful that you chose to spend your time with them. Happy hour until seven each evening was a real deal, with homemade red, white, and sparkling sangría done properly—poured over ice in the glass rather than diluted with ice in the bottle. And for dessert, one of several liqueurs made in-house and aged in glass orbs high above the bar. There were delicious brandies aged with peach and cinnamon, and also with black tea. Just as at Joselito, the gin tonic was the best I'd encountered.

I didn't want to think about returning to the office, so I ordered a sangría instead. Good Lord. It was only lunchtime.

"An early start," Emma flatly judged.

"Don't judge. I'm just having one."

"I might have three." She smiled at the waiter. "For now, I'll just have one."

He ran off.

We talked about why she had made the trip across town. Absently at first, then more to the point. She was troubled by Simon's account of the conversation at the Inn on Saturday. I told her that Erik had been the voice of reason as usual, always something insightful to say, rarely alarmed, never off kilter.

What Erik may or may not have said was not what bothered her. We meandered through a few minutes of this when she finally admitted that the visit from her cousin Simon had been difficult for her.

"It's nothing about him. I love Simon." She stared off.

"It's—" I pressed and then lingered.

"He doesn't mean to pass judgement."

Emma wanted *me* to tell her about *her* feelings. She had come here looking for a narrator. I lingered another moment before giving in.

"You don't like going to work when he's here."

"I don't much like going to work when he isn't here."

"You used to, I think?"

"I used to believe . . . I used to believe something."

"You used to believe that you mattered." I let that idea hang in the air for another moment.

"I used to believe that it was a good thing," she replied, sheepishly, and looked away.

This was, of course, nonsense. She still believed it was a good thing. At least, she believed that what she believed was a good thing.

"Listen," she suddenly and confidently reasserted herself. "We're doing good work for Americans. We're doing good work for our country, despite it all. This wretchedness is a passing moment. We're still here."

This is what she told herself to make it all go away.

"You don't have to defend yourself to me."

"But I do; you know I do. I have to defend myself to everyone."

"Even Simon?"

"Especially Simon."

I was going to need another drink. I ordered a café con leche and asked Emma if Simon had ever said anything about this.

"Only ever out of curiosity. Only ever because he wants to understand. He's a good one."

"He cares about you."

"Yes. But I confuse him. Why would I be so invested in something that looks so terrible to him? His perfect little Nordic world."

"Multiethnic democracies are messy."

"Thanks, Professor. Now you sound like Erik. If I had wanted a lesson in sociopolitical theory, I'd have gone home."

"Come to see me for a little emotion? A little fire?" I didn't mean to sound mocking.

I was sitting staring at a beautiful woman on the verge of tears for the second time in less than twenty-four hours. Emma struggled to pull herself together whilst my thoughts drifted into contemplation of the night before with Ash. The waiter returned with our coffee.

"Why did you people have to do this?"

"Me people?"

"*You* people," she sneered apologetically, if such a thing were possible.

"I don't have people in this."

"You cried the day of Obergefell."

"I cried for Andrew Jefferson."

She consented whimsically. "One step closer to being the kind of country we always should have been."

"To Andrew Jefferson."

"To Andrew Jefferson."

We raised our cups.

She took a sip and finally spoke again. "But that wasn't enough. It was never enough."

I would have preferred to not go down this conversational road, so I waited for her to continue.

"It wasn't enough to simply make things right. They had to make believers out of everyone."

"They?"

"You liberals . . . you know what I mean."

"Ah, yes. *Those* people." I couldn't help it. I must have sounded like I was mocking her. I didn't mean it.

"They had to have their cake."

"This isn't about the cake."

"No, it isn't, and you know that. I mean, I get the business about how this nation wasn't built by those who waited and rested and wished to look behind them. But Jesus, couldn't they have given everyone a minute?"

She may have had a point, though I didn't want to admit it.

Perhaps we had come too far, too fast. Perhaps this moment in the world wasn't a question of righteousness, but of the speed at which most people could take the whole business. Perhaps we had tried to ice the cake too quickly. I wanted neither to believe this nor apologize for it, but only fools fail to consider that they may have been wrong.

Erik and I had grown up in that small town with a fellow who later became a pastor. Actually, we grew up with a lot of fellows who became pastors. Meanwhile, we had become sailors and geeks. Others had become builders, butchers, and social workers. My mother had called a few years earlier to tell me about a nice girl who had just checked her out at the grocery store. The girl had asked about me, hoped I was doing fine. "He was a nice boy," my mother told me she had said.

I grew up with another girl who married another fellow we had known. He had been a good, funny kid when we were young. I remember seeing their wedding pictures on Facebook. He in his uniform, she in her white dress, beautiful smile, ready for life together. Now they had a tribe of little boys whose every expression was painted with an adorably mischievous grin. But I heard that he was never the same after the war.

Now she was a social worker. Went to work every day to look after someone else's children, to give them their shot. She was doing more *real work* for America's future than anyone I knew. From time to time she would like some piece of progressive hopefulness I posted online. She understood what needed to be done.

Emma believed she was speaking up for good people who were just living their lives. People like the ones in the conservative little West Virginia town where Erik and I were raised. The two of us hoped that the place would produce a billionaire. Could have been either of us if we had our way. It at least succeeded in producing good people.

Then it voted.

Perhaps we had pushed them into it whilst we were busy trying to ice our cake.

I didn't know.

There was nothing hateful or backward about Emma Cuevas.

She spoke four languages. She wasn't in it to fight a crusade against social change. She was old school. Her Cuban father couldn't get over what the Castros had done to his beloved island. So, she hated them for what they had taken away from him years before she was born. It was as if generations of her father's family were cursed to wander the world hating anyone who showed any inkling of rapprochement with his old enemy. So she had gone to work for conservatives. And she had bought into the rest of it. But she didn't believe in half of it. This was just who she was. Now her loyalty to one tribe made her an outcast amongst her other tribes. City dwellers. Washingtonians. Finns and Swedes. Well-to-do thirty-somethings with college degrees.

She was in this way a throwback to a time past, when an American might have spent Sundays in church and weeknights in a union hall. Or when a devout fellow might have lived next door to a strident atheist, but none of it mattered when they were cheering for their kids from the bleachers at a little league game. She was trapped between identities: Cuban. Conservative. Finnish. Under forty. College degree. Urban. American. Those were her pages of the story.

And in her telling of that story, she was the one willing to speak up for good people. One day she woke up in a country where half of us, high on the successes of our world having become a bit more just, were demanding ideological fealty to all that we believed was true. Just like Emma said, it hadn't been enough for us to make things right; we wanted to make believers out of everyone.

Now she had to wake up every day and justify to everyone in her life why she still defended the indefensible. Why she still worked in those halls. Her own cousin likely thought her complicit.

We set our empty cups on the table.

She expressed her satisfaction in some barely intelligible Swedish. She was much better with it than me.

I smiled at her. We had resolved nothing, but I was happy to have passed the time with her.

Looking around, I thought of how table arrangements on the patio would evolve as the day and night went on and the happy hour crowd migrated outside. It was tough to not smile at the world as we sat there. Work seemed a million miles away.

We parted ways and returned to our offices.

I decided that sometime soon I ought to go visit that pastor with whom I had grown up. I hadn't seen him in sixteen years, but he said wise things on Facebook. It was hard work steering good people clear of the Devil.

Chapter Eight

Later I went up to Boston. The airplane took off facing northward, and I drank in the view of the city from my window. Late afternoon's summer sun shone from the west, bathing the white stone monuments in its glow. Cars raced around the Lincoln Memorial, between the golden horsemen and over the Memorial Bridge towards Arlington. The Reflecting Pool mirrored Apollo's daily journey as if it were a lake of fire. Fountains sprang forth around the memorial to the Second World War. The Washington Monument's long shadow cast momentary darkness on the Mall beyond.

We banked left as we flew up the river past Rosslyn. I looked down onto the ferries and small boats crisscrossing the Potomac River. Georgetown was filled with people at the waterfront. Soon it would be the Fourth of July.

Goodbye, beautiful, complicated, wretched city of dreams, I thought before dozing off.

We had become increasingly unmoored from sense of place. We could live anywhere, work anywhere, travel anywhere, go anywhere. The world is small yet filled with opportunity and possibilities made boundless by the sky. Yet we yearn for roots as we travel farther afield. Every airplane must eventually touch down.

Airlines take us where we are going and remind us of where we are from. They move people. They are with us when we set out into the world. They are with us on our honeymoons. They help us launch our businesses and win the big deals. They get us home just in time to see the ones we love one last time. They take us on all our journeys. Yet, though they are there every time life really matters, they are loathed, commoditized, barely more than a utility. The great American airline of times past had been more than a flying bus. It was the only commercial enterprise that resonated in peoples' lives the way that teachers, doctors, the military, police, and fire departments could. They were with us when it mattered.

Another failure of potential in a world of missed opportunity.

Nowhere on the planet did aspiration to a proud past, the importance of home, and the imperative of progress resonate more strongly than in transient Washington, DC. We might venture far from home, yet every pilot and flight attendant I had ever befriended could wax eloquent about love of home and family. They were, at their best, deeply rooted in sense of time and place.

The plane returning a congresswoman to her district was the same plane that returned a weary business traveler to the birth of his child. A flight attendant once told me that Hawaii was her favorite route. She told me about the people she served who had spent years saving for the trip of a lifetime. They made her smile. They reminded her that there was purpose in her work. Real human stories lay behind the transience of Washington.

At our best, we could say to everyone who came here from somewhere else, "We serve who you serve. Our story is everyone's story."

Jarred awake as the airplane thudded down on the runway in Boston, I scrambled across the harbor to catch the late ferry that was running special for the holiday.

A group of men frolicked about just in front of me as I walked down the World Trade Center pier. We were all happy being off to Provincetown. The boat was filled with the laughter of people rollicking on colorful drinks served in plastic cups from the onboard bar. Other groups of men and dogs and a few pairs of women lined up at every table, window, and railing as the whistle blew and we pulled away from the dock.

Flags were stretched out atop the wall of the World Trade Center that passed us by as we pulled into the shipping channel. Portugal. China. Australia. Saudi Arabia. Panama. South Africa. The world was here to see us off. The sun had begun to set over the harbor, and I felt for the first time in a long while entirely at ease.

I left my things and ventured out to the catamaran's bow. We passed the airport, and the planes passed us overhead. Azores Airlines was off to Ponta Delgada. Aer Lingus headed to Dublin. Icelandair off to Reykjavik. Iberia to Madrid. British Airways—who this time of day flew from Boston to London like they were running an hourly bus service in the sky—was, well, off to London. Japan Airlines would be aloft to Tokyo sometime after sundown.

We left a tanker at anchor in our wake as we passed Hull. Faster now. This was a fast ferry, a quick cat. I was filled all at once with airy euphoria of knowing that we would soon be in Provincetown, and the deep-breath, spindrift, one-with-the-waves quiet calm one feels when he goes down to the sea in ships. Spindrift is a spray blown from a rough sea or surf, the sweetest of natural drugs.

Green bell buoy to the right. We were headed out to sea. Houses clustered on an outcropping of land spit into the far reaches of Boston Harbor. At some length the boat passed a lighthouse built upon a rocky ledge such that it appeared to have been born on the crest of a wave and rocked in the cradle of the deep. Minots Ledge, it was called. Its light shone in a pattern of seconds. One second. Four seconds. Three seconds. *One. Four. Three. I. Love. You.* One letter. Four letters. Three letters. The locals in Scituate, for whose harbor it was the lonely sentinel, called it "lovers light." Every day, throughout the months and years and decades whose waters had battered its stone walls: *One. Four. Three.*

Out in the expanse now. Halfway between Boston and Provincetown, where there's no land to be seen. So close, yet not even in sight. I turned back to the ship's stern to see the sunset.

There are few places in the east where one can see the sun set over water. Cape Cod, bent and bowed and angled back on itself, is one of those places. The American flag flapped in the stiff breeze, strung from a pole on the flagstaff out back. The sun burst forth in its last moment of brilliance, bright enough to pierce the star-spangled fabric with light, a wash of translucent red, white, and blue flapping in the wind. Apollo sank beneath the horizon.

I went inside. What a party it was. There were more colorful drinks now. More cups strewn about. The dogs had made friends with one another and their adoring human fans. The men were happy. Women carried on being paired off, seemingly just happy to share with one another this little stretch of ocean on the way to Provincetown.

An outline of sand dunes and beach shrubs appeared in the twilight of the rising moon. We passed Wood End lighthouse, then around the bend of Long Point, turning hard around another green buoy as if it were the sun and our boat were a comet eager for its course. Engines quieted. The ferry slowed. We drifted past the breakwater and the yachts at the pier and the sailboats on their moorings in the moonlit harbor. We were wrapped in summer's heat, floating into town on this ferry after the sun had set. I'd only ever come in under the cover of darkness in the late fall, after the time had changed, when the weather was cold and the harbor empty.

***

I caught a cab from the pier. Wendy was driving. I gave her $20; I had owed her $10 since last year when her credit card reader was broken and I was out of cash, and $10 for the interest I thought was due after having floated my debt for a few seasons. She laughed. I told her that I'd not forgotten.

A man dressed as a pilgrim rang a hand bell. *Clang. Clang. Clang.*

"And all is well now that you are here!" he shouted in an accent that was both very New England and very gay. Surely the world had room for but one gay town crier dressed as a pilgrim. I was happy that he lived in Provincetown. There were many people in the streets. Wendy broke us free of the traffic in Portuguese Square, and we headed home.

Later I walked down to the beach.

Crickets sang in the tall grass as I felt the breeze, smelled the salt, heard the waves lapping against the shore. And I looked up to a bowl of stars, sparkling like diamonds as if God were offering tribute to the spirits in the clouds as they streaked across the sky.

The dippers led one another in their summer-long dance through the heavens. And I thought, *Seeing all this unfold, year after year— perhaps this is what life is for?*

Turning around to walk through the dark of night over mismatched planks in the dock, boardwalks that meandered vaguely straight through the thicket, but which over years had become predictable, with no contrived light to illuminate the path, I found no element of it frightening, no shadow disconcerting. Just the most familiar thing that I had ever known, as if it were the first thing I had ever seen. It was certainly the first thing that I remembered.

Then I turned the corner, in dark clothes fading into the shadow beneath the trees, realizing I was for a moment part of the scenery but for the contrast of white shells against my tired feet.

Moments later and I was exhausted, sinking into sleep unencumbered by the sounds of the city. Pure to a fault. Cool breeze stroked the curtains of my open windows. I smelled the salt. I heard the waves as they lapped against the shore.

Chapter Nine

Extreme tides are a curious phenomenon at Cape Cod. A boat floating in ten feet of water at high tide can be keeled over in the sand six hours later when the tide is low. It was Tuesday, the third day of July, and the tide was an hour short of its ebb when I awoke. I walked about on the sand bars where at their most extreme low point one might be able to meander a half mile from shore and be only knee-deep. Boats sat idly chained to their moorings. I had found these contraptions interesting as a child.

One summer around age ten I arrived in town and immediately hauled from my grandmother's basement a brick and buoy joined by a rope, emphatically telling a friend, "This is what we do every year," as if some outside force were compelling me to bury that silly brick in the ground for no reason whatsoever. Another summer I found a large mushroom anchor to bury in the ground. My mother was unhappy having to pull it out of the sand as the tide rolled in ahead of an oncoming storm the last day of the season. Our personal histories are curious things, fixed in time yet nearly blank pages upon which we write any particular interpretation depending on our mood when we tell the story. Who knows where the real memories ended, and the tale began?

I walked on and decided after a time that I ought to go up to my aunt's house so that I could watch Sweden play Switzerland in the next round of the World Cup. Anyway, I hadn't seen anyone since arriving the night before. And there sat Geoff Gamal at the table, grinning like a Cheshire cat.

"You're late," he said.

"What the hell are you doing here?"

"You, sir, were not here on Monday morning as we discussed."

"We discussed nothing of the sort."

"Nonsense. You said that you couldn't help me move my boat because you were coming here on Monday morning."

I looked dumbfounded.

He continued. "I was here Monday morning, and you were nowhere to be found."

"Where the hell is your boat?"

"Oh. I left it in Red Hook when I decided to come see you."

"What about Bermuda? And hurricane season?"

"Hell, hurricane season started a month ago. What's a few more weeks? Besides, there are other boats if this one doesn't work out."

"You're a strange guy, Gee."

"Indeed," he managed to choke out with wholly unconcealed glee, his eyes twinkling.

I gathered my thoughts. "I'd want to spend the Fourth with no one but you. Besides, who knows how many of them this country has left."

"One assumes the same number as all the other the countries?"

"Don't be a dick."

I was happy to be watching the game with Geoff. He was just as Swedish as me, though his Egyptian father made him a trifle darker and entirely less blond. He was a beautiful human being. Dark curly hair. Skin that never burned. A charmingly wide, white-toothed smile. Everyone loved him.

He was the type of ridiculous person whose story—both the long arc of his existence and the churn of his daily life—defied reason to the point of absurdity. My aunt was of course a white-bread American whose people happened to have come from Sweden. Her marriage to my Egyptian uncle may have begun as an act of youthful rebellion, but she had at any rate given birth whilst on an overnight layover in Canada. So, Geoff somehow managed to crawl away from the whole affair a citizen with three passports in hand. It was said by someone with alleged first-hand knowledge of the situation that in the height of the Arab Spring, Geoff had camped out on the roof of a Cairo apartment building that his father owned, ready to shoot would-be vandals.

Those who knew him were fond of his story about the rigmarole through which he sought to get on the right side of American traffic laws. His driver's license had somehow managed to be suspended in two states because a computer glitch caused considerable disagreement between the two jurisdictions as to which should properly have issued him a license to begin with. His novel solution was to return to Egypt and obtain a license there after which he might go about his business as an "international driver" back in the States. The fellow who checked him in at the licensing center in Cairo asked if he wanted to rent a luggage rack to use during the test. He refused the absurd suggestion, and summarily failed the test. He returned the next day, rented the luggage rack for a sum of cash that was no doubt shared under the table with the driving instructor, and passed.

I am more confident in the equally odd story that he spent several years receiving his mail at a beach bar on Jost Van Dyke, which was near where he anchored a sailboat. I once visited him in that bar. I had seen his mail there.

He was professionally respectable enough, having at various points applied his intellect towards lawyering, and his charm towards raising money for our alma mater. It was Geoff who introduced me to our shared fraternity, through which I came to know both Peter Dean and Andrew Jefferson. Lately he had been putting his skills to work lawyering, delivering supplies by boat, and raising investment to rebuild following the past year's hurricanes in America's island territories that he called home for six or so months out of a year.

Otherwise he and a girl shared a flat on the Upper West Side. She was a doctor whose people came from Nogales. None of us had yet gotten to know her well, though I was told that she had bootstrapped her way through undergraduate and medical school before winding up at New York Presbyterian Hospital in Manhattan. I don't think that Peter or Ava had ever met her. I did not imagine it would have pleased her to know that Geoff had just flown over New York in an ill-conceived dash to Massachusetts simply to prove a point to me.

He was a good fellow, though, the most interesting person any of us knew. He could be rather introspective, religious even, and deeply reverent in the moral thoughtfulness he devoted to people, causes, and beliefs. He was a man of contrasts. Privileged by intelligence, good looks, and wealth. Yet not above buying junked guitars at estate sales and fixing them up to sell for an extra buck.

We watched Sweden beat Switzerland whilst drinking akvavit at ten in the morning. Geoff was always up for anything. We were excited for the win. Though I am reasonably sure that had they lost I could have gotten by just telling everyone that our people had been Swiss all along, and that we were ecstatic to see the land of our forebears advance to the next round. Nobody in America knew the difference anyway. Spotify, Ikea, Volvo, and the Scandinavian social welfare state all hailed from *Swederland*, didn't they know?

Then we went to lunch.

Geoff kept a moped upon which I once had a mishap. He had for years insisted that I wrecked it. I maintained that it had been an accident and nothing irreparable at that. I had been on my way to a haircut and offered our friend Pancho a ride downtown. We spun out in some sand turning into the street, and I somehow ended up knees down in a gravel pit by the side of the road, the moped on top of me, and Pancho atop the moped laughing hysterically. Geoff's Canadian then-girlfriend came running out of the house and asked mockingly if I needed a bandage. Pancho picked the moped out of the gravel and drove us the rest of the way into town. Hence my argument that it had not been *wrecked*.

I must have looked terrible and bloodied when the delightfully crass, unusually tall lesbian woman who cut my hair took one look at me and asked, "What the hell happened to you?"

I explained the situation, and she said only, "Well, if that isn't the most fucking stupidest white-boy thing that's happened all day. Get into the bathroom before you bloody up my carpet."

Later she came to fix me up. She was nice about it, aside from the profanity.

A lifetime of memories in Provincetown.

So, on this afternoon, like every time since, Geoff drove the moped with me on the back. We rode off to Ross' Grill.

I always ate my first lunch of any visit to town at Ross' Grill. Were I to conjure in my mind one picture summing up the good life in summertime, I would be hard pressed to find something more compelling than the sight here of a sangría on my table and the harbor view from the balcony. The restaurant was on the waterfront side of Whalers Wharf. The original had been fashioned from the old Provincetown Theatre. It had burned to ashes in the nineties.

We ordered blackened scallop wraps, the best French fries either of us had ever eaten, and a pitcher of sangría. The sun shone high over the harbor, and there was nowhere to be.

"So, are you coming to my party tonight?" Geoff asked.

"Party? What the hell, you're having a party?"

"Oh. Yes." His voice tended higher and a touch squeaky when he was excited with a surprise. He couldn't contain himself.

"You've barely been here twenty-four hours. How have you gotten a party together?"

"There's not much to do. Nobody has *Third* of July parties, so there wasn't much competition."

"Who's here? You're the first person I've seen."

"Everyone is here."

"The Canadians, too?"

"The Canadians, too."

"Alright, good work. So we're having a party tonight." I exhaled and waited to see what he'd ask me to do.

Then he asked me to do nothing.

"What's wrong with you, Jakey?"

"Me?"

"You're in your favorite place. I flew over seventeen-hundred miles to see you. I'm throwing you a party on your favorite holiday. Your team just advanced to the group of eight."

"And?" I cut him off.

"And," he exhaled, "you seem miserable."

"Ha. That's a bit of an overstatement. You know good and well what's bothering me."

"That's a bunch of nonsense."

"Is it? The country is going to hell and we're launching fireworks."

"In the gayest place on earth."

"In the gayest place on earth."

"It's your favorite day of the year. Can you just let it be what it is for a moment?"

I pondered this and poured another sangría from the pitcher.

"Besides," he continued, "I'm flying your lady friend up. She gets here in an hour."

"My lady friend? What the hell?"

"I talked with Ash. She said you two had patched things up."

"Oh Jesus." I choked on my sangría. "When did you talk with her?"

"Yesterday noon when I realized you weren't coming."

"Well, that didn't take long. Twelve hours? Good Lord."

"What?"

"Never mind." I waved him off. I supposed it was good to know that, for the moment at least, she had emerged from whatever dark place she had been inhabiting.

Geoff produced some imperceptible sound of glee and poured another glass. I thought for a moment.

"Wait," I said emphatically, realizing what was going on.

He perked up.

"This entire thing, this entire scheme of yours. This is about me and how you think I'm feeling. You abandoned your boat, came all the way up here, orchestrated a party, and are flying Ash up here because you think she's my *lady friend* now? All because you thought I sounded cranky on the phone three days ago?"

"I said as much."

"I should sound cranky more often."

"It'll be a great story in the end, won't it? Oh, and I'm also going to Sweden with you. Surprise."

"The British Airways morning flight on Friday?"

"Indeed."

"How the hell did you know that?"

"I'm sleuthy. And you're predictable."

"You're a weird guy, Gee."

He looked at me expectantly. He needed to hear the rest.

"But I love you." I smiled. And that was that. We were having a party. Ash was taking off from Boston at that very moment.

Later we sent Wendy to fetch Ash from the little airport out in the sand dunes by Race Point. There was no room for three on the moped. It was a good thing, too, because Ash surprised us both by bringing Erik along. I was not sure where Emma had gone.

Geoff and I wandered about town for a bit. The Portuguese flags that lined the pier when I last visited had given way to the Stars and Stripes, a couple dozen of them stiff in the breeze under the blue summer sky. Throngs of people poured from the ferry dock out into the melee of cabs painted as rainbows, bicycle rickshaws, waiting friends, and the town crier eagerly proclaiming that all was well now that they were here.

We hopped our moped and drove towards the West End where hundreds of men were massing for the afternoon Tea Dance at the Boatslip Beach Club. Euphoria descended on the town. Narrow Commercial Street was jammed, and we turned right up Central Street, the next alleyway.

This strange town wore many faces. End of the earth. Three thousand people in winter. Sixty thousand in summer. Old Portuguese fishing village. Artist colony. LGBTQ haven. Tomorrow, in spite of it all, one might call it the most patriotic town in America.

Geoff wove us in and out of cars and bicycles up Bradford Street in the opposite direction from which we had come—eastward, home.

It was still broad daylight when the throng of revelers began flocking in for the party. I had dozed off in a guest room and had just now grown sober from lunch's good decisions. Ash hadn't turned up, and I assumed Geoff sent her home to the little family cottage where I had hung my hat the night before. Erik had settled in another guest room. There was noise from the hall as the crowd traipsed through, as diverse as the town itself: women from my grandmother's generation, younger women from the generations that followed, cousins and quasi-aunts and uncles, the kind that one couldn't distinguish from family, Brett—a local real estate agent who had sold the house to Geoff's family—and a half-life's worth of friends bequeathed to me from the lifetimes that my family had lived here. Jamaicans and Egyptians and Portuguese and Swedes, and the Canadians and their guitars and the folks from New Jersey and New Hampshire and everywhere else that was once new but was now Old America. And it was a jumble of people and hors d'oeuvres and wine and Armenian food from my grandmother's friend down the street whose prolific cooking was itself the reason that Geoff had felt emboldened to throw a party on short notice and then not prepare for it in the least.

And then Ash appeared in the door. She was beautiful in her sundress and lopsided smile. I had again drunk just enough wine to be enraptured by her appearance and managed, "Fancy running into you here."

"I'm always fancy." She smiled as she kissed me on the cheek.

It wasn't long before the crowd had swept us apart. Ash wandering the room, having the last few days transformed herself back into the cosmopolitan socialite who inhabited about a third of her life. This town of many faces was the perfect place for her next coming-out.

I took up a conversation with a pair of Mainers who kept a cottage in the neighborhood. We spoke with disgust about their governor in Augusta, and of satisfaction in all that their recently adult children were accomplishing. They were some of the most decent people I had ever met.

We laughed a lot.

I moved on when I saw Erik through the window on the patio.

"This is great!" He hugged me.

"Hello, old friend. Pour me a vinho verde?"

"What you guys get these for?"

"I'd say about four dollars a bottle; isn't it great?"

"Vinho verde and the Fourth of July in my favorite Portuguese fishing village."

"That's it."

Our Canadian friend played his guitar and filled the terrace with music. Twilight had wrapped us in its veil. A cool, salty breeze blew in from the harbor. We looked at one another and knew we were only a glass or two away. Surely that's why he had come.

"Where's Ash?"

"God if I know."

He looked at me questioningly, probing for details that I couldn't provide.

"She'll be around."

"Off shedding the last remains?"

"Something like that."

"It's her way."

"It is indeed."

The party went on like this. No conversation for long, but every meeting of two people meaningful.

Scott, the Canadian, began singing again.

Hey, momma rock me
Rock me momma like the wind and the rain
Rock me momma like a south bound train. . .

I began singing in the crowd.

Oh, north country winters keep a-getting me down
Lost my money playing poker so I had to leave town
But I ain't turning back to living that old life no more. . .

Ash joined us.

"You're not thinking of getting up there?"

"Of course we are!" Erik could barely contain himself.

She looked at us skeptically.

I hear my baby calling my name and I know that she's the
only one
And if I die in Raleigh at least I will die free!

We liberated the microphone and the guitar. Scott found a glass of water. He looked relieved.

Erik played the guitar. I stared into the microphone. We gathered our wits. Geoff grinned like a man who knew he had, for a moment, accomplished his mission. Erik and I took a deep breath.

A long long time ago
I can still remember how
That music used to make me smile
And I knew if I had my chance
That I could make those people dance
And maybe they'd be happy for a while. . .

This was going well. We rolled on for a stanza. Erik picked at the guitar.

Bye, bye Miss American Pie
Drove my Chevy to the levee but the levee was dry
And them good ole boys were drinking whiskey and rye
Singin' this'll be the day that I die
This'll be the day that I die. . .

It was time. Erik knew it. Everyone knew it. Now we had to stick together.

"Did you write the book of love?"

We picked up the tempo. I began moving awkwardly on my feet. Oh well.

"If the Bible tells you so."

We believed in rock and roll.

But who could save our mortal souls, anyway?

Wine and adrenaline and music and the moment that I had needed for months converged like a wave. Ash smiled at me whilst she danced with a fellow in the center of the room. This was it. I had only an instant to thank Geoff in my mind before we began again.

"Now, for ten years we've been on our own!"

Who was the jester? The king and queen?

I wondered if it had ever been as great as he claimed, when the jester stole his thorny crown.

The courtroom was adjourned
No verdict was returned.

Oh God, oh God, the wine. How clear it was.

We were busy with our books on Marx, here in the summer swelter on the Fourth of July. The birds and their fallout shelter. Good God, it all made sense.

We sang on. Thank God for the wine.

'Cause the players tried to take the field
The marching band refused to yield
Do you recall what was revealed
The day the music died?

We were really wound up with the crowd now. Erik was cool and calm on his guitar, but Geoff danced with Ash. The party rollicked on beer and wine and music and drunken conversation.

It seemed we had become the generation lost in space, with no time left to start again. Fire was the devil's only friend. Born in Hell, though there were angels amongst us, none could break that Satan's spell.

We slowed our tempo together.

I met a girl who sang the blues
And I asked her for some happy news
But she just smiled and turned away

I went down to the sacred store
Where I'd heard the music years before
But the man there said the music wouldn't play

And in the streets the children screamed
The lovers cried, and the poets dreamed

But not a word was spoken
The church bells all were broken

And the three men I admire most
The Father, Son, and the Holy Ghost
They caught the last train for the coast
The day the music died. . .

Erik and I finished the song. My grandmother seemed pleased. Perhaps I was the only one who had thought anything of the words. It was a party, and everyone was happy.

I stumbled out to the veranda. The air was heavy, and I was dripping. I longed to be washed clean by the breeze from the sea. Lights on the patio hazed into one another. Everything was beautiful now. I loved all the people here. It was good that we sang when we did, not a moment too soon for this contemplative fellow.

"You are a drunken fool!"

Ash approached behind me, wrapped her arms around my neck as I turned around.

"But you're a beautiful fool."

She kissed me.

I told her that I was happy she was here.

She seemed happy, too.

It was starkly quiet when we walked down to the beach. The tide had rolled out and was nearly low. We heard the music from the party up the hill. The smell of the sea and the sound of the music wafted together, cool breeze swept us over, and it was dark but for the waning gibbous moon. She wrapped her arms around my neck again. We fell together into the beach grass.

Euphoria had descended on the town.

Chapter Ten

We awoke at noon. It was too late to go see the parade in town. I was mixed up about this. The parade was, on one hand, a reminder that patriotism comes in many forms. Several years earlier it had featured three men dressed as the three women Supreme Court justices. A banner proclaimed one of them to be a *Wise Latina*. On the other hand, I didn't much like parades. They were like concerts, and I didn't know how to act at them. Move about excitedly? Take in the entertainment on display? Make myself part of the spectacle?

Sun filled the room. Ash rolled over to face me, that broad, lopsided smile on her face that I'd spent months longing to see again. I was both glowingly happy and full of anxiety. I wanted to be nowhere else, but knew we'd soon be other places. I hated to waste this moment.

We spoke idly and said little. She wiped a lock of hair from her face and kissed me.

We tumbled out of bed and out of the house a bit after one o'clock. I thought the day would continue like this, but after lunch Ash told me that she was leaving.

I asked her why, perplexed and suddenly filled with sorrow. It was no use. She would do what she pleased.

"I have business back in Boston."

"Business back in Boston. It's the Fourth of July."

"You know how stupid I think this holiday is." She had a way of twisting the knife, even in the best moments.

"It's my favorite holiday."

"I know it is, so enjoy it. I don't want to ruin it for you."

"It isn't really about you thinking it's a stupid holiday."

"Oh?"

"You don't want to be too predictable."

"It makes me uncomfortable."

"You are predictable in your erraticism. I can always predict that you'll break my heart."

"Oh, well, I don't want to break your heart all the time. I've told you that."

"And you just don't want to like anything with too much red, white, and blue. It's that other passport talking."

"I like my other passport just fine."

"It's an odd thing."

"I'll trade you for it."

"Wonderful."

She kissed me again. I felt all right about it. It was as if my singular animating thought was the notion that I got to wake up and live every day under the same sky as her.

"I'll send you a message and tell you where to meet me tomorrow," she told me as she said goodbye and went to the airport. I had no idea where she was going.

To hell with Ashley Maria Luciano. To hell with her.

⁓

I walked down the street to find Erik or Geoff. It did not much matter who I found first, just that I found someone so as to not sit alone and stew about it. The water was too high for a walk on the tidal flats. There were none left.

We three went to happy hour at the Red Inn in the far West End. I loved the Red Inn almost as much as I loved Joselito. It was important to have a haunt in every town one thought of as home. I had a complicated relationship with the idea of home. Was one's home fixed at birth, an immovable birthright for better or worse? Was it ancestral? An inheritance beyond our ability to change? Something chosen? Some place that chose us? Did it matter?

I cared where people came from, cared far more about that than what they did for work. I always asked. I was interested in what they thought of as home. Perhaps it was because I was so conflicted about a home of my own.

Was I Virginian? Was Provincetown my hometown? Swede or Swedish-American? Was there any such thing? How many generations did that last? Did the very notion insult someone who actually had come from someplace else? Someone whose life was far worse than mine, perhaps, or who hadn't been allowed to think of this country as their home. Did they even care?

I thought this an important question. How good must one's life be before it becomes unseemly to feel any angst about it? Particularly when none of it really matters to where you'll rest your head, eat your next meal, or make your next dollar. There were many places in the world where these sorts of questions hinged on those sorts of answers for many people.

It was all quite unsuitable for happy-hour talk. It was summer's biggest day. We had come to drink and celebrate America.

Warm summer breeze whisked across the deck into the garden. It was an authentically Provincetown late afternoon. Cool air kicked off the harbor, lapping gentle waves against the seawall below. Here in winter, I was always happy to step through the white-trimmed door, out of the snow, and into a room warmed by a fire built in the one-of-a-kind brick fireplace whose chimney twisted up the wall. A haven for all seasons in a town that lives for summer. The Red Inn was one of my favorite places to draw down a bottle of wine alongside some of the most exquisitely prepared meals any of us had ever eaten. We ordered lobster sliders and carried on with our meandering talk.

A wine writer friend in Bordeaux had once asked her legion of followers to share the most amazing restaurant to which they'd ever been. Interesting reading in the responses listing bistros, taverns, and dives from South Africa to Hungary to Russia and the United Arab Emirates. California, too. Virginia got a mention from an admirer of the Inn at Little Washington. In America, at least, I'd have given the award to a trifecta in the Northeast: Joselito in Washington, Chimichurri Grill in New York, and the Red Inn.

I made my first reservation here years ago whilst riding a train out of New York one afternoon. It had been a splendid evening for Ava and me.

The place was no secret, well regarded by over a century of Provincetown visitors that once included President Theodore Roosevelt. I had never stayed at the inn, but the restaurant was the object of my great affection. There were four distinct parts to the space itself. We filled ourselves up on oysters, shrimp, those lobster sliders, and sparkling wine as we sat in rocking chairs atop the outdoor deck along the narrow beach leading down to the harbor. The bar area inside was split between two rooms; each possessed of their own personality, both with a fireplace. One beneath exposed wooden beams is where I'd spend a rainy day or a winter's night. The white clapboard ceiling in the other conjured summer. Both filled with revelry whenever the place was open. Both featured sweeping views of the harbor beyond.

Everything was deliciously prepared. The wine list, just a page, was consistently excellent. Blindfold, the white wine cousin to the Prisoner, by Orin Swift, had been my favorite bottle here for years. However, the festive yet elegant feel of the place begged that we begin with sparkling.

We rode our bicycles and chained them at the wharf. No hope finding a parking space. Our friend had a boat there from which we had decided to watch the fireworks. It was another party. Smaller than the night before, but a party nonetheless. We passed snacks and fruits and sweets. We cracked open beers and poured wine and had a grand time until it grew dark and the raucous town grew briefly silent as the first rocket soared to the heavens.

It exploded with a bang and rained red light down into the harbor. Burst after burst showered us in hues familiar to anyone who has ever celebrated this day. The crowd was particularly taken with the shimmering gold starbursts that sparkled in the sky like tinsel on a Christmas tree.

I sat there watching fireworks. The air glowed because of them. They glowed all the greater because of the wine.

And as the flames climbed high into the night
To light the sacrificial rite
I saw Satan laughing with delight
The day the music died
He was singin'...

And the town abruptly exploded with celebration once again, the boats and bars and cafés disturbed expectantly from skyward enchantment by the deafening silence that follows the last rockets.

Just own the night
Like the Fourth of July...

Hundreds of men dancing at the beach club just onshore filled the night with song.

'Cause baby you're a firework
Come on show 'em what your worth
Make 'em go "Oh, oh, oh!"
As you shoot across the sky-y-y

Euphoria was alive and well in town.

Somehow, my bike found its way home. I was glad to have found my way to bed sooner than I expected, and woke early to get in a full day's work at the kitchen table. Today required the internet. I planned to devote tomorrow's hours across the sea to a paper I had spent weeks putting off writing. Geoff had disappeared even earlier that morning, hastening back to New York for Caroline's rare day home from the hospital where she worked. He promised a return to Boston later that same evening, so we'd not miss our flight in just twenty-four hours' time. Nearly everyone in my life was incapable of staying in one place for long.

I kept my head down most of the day, happy to not have interruptions. Nobody really seemed to grasp what I did for work. Just as well. Only Erik would have understood. He joined me to work at the table for several hours, and later we met to take the late-afternoon ferry back across the bay.

The boat was much less of a party than the one I had taken the opposite direction three days earlier. Both of us were tired from the celebrations. We said goodbye at the dock. Erik caught a plane back to Washington, and I was just off to another friend's apartment when I received a message from Ash.

I figure your ferry's in. Meet me in the bar at the Parker House?

I rode the inbound Silver Line to South Station, transferred on the Red Line to Park Street, and walked a few blocks up Tremont.

Ash sat at the stately old wood-paneled bar with two glasses of Champagne.

"I'd have ordered cava, but they didn't have any."

"Nice greeting. What's this all about?"

"You didn't think I'd abandon you on your favorite holiday for no reason, did you?"

"Actually, that seems very much in character."

"Stop!"

"This was your business in Boston?"

"This was my business in Boston." The girl had gone soft. She went on. "I just hated that you're leaving so soon. I wanted to surprise you."

"There's more?"

"There's more. Now sit and drink this with me. I just want to be here for a moment and think about how proud I am of myself for doing a good thing."

She was beaming, radiantly happy from head to toe. I couldn't tell if she was pleased to be there with me or pleased with herself. We drank our Champagne and listened to the music and the low din of *after work* happening in the bar.

That's what they called it in Sweden, where I was going. The Swedes quite literally referred to happy hour as "after work." They are very straightforward folk.

"I suspect the bartender thinks you're paying me to be here." She spoke softly.

"Paying you is all I have to do?"

"I should slap you for that."

"On the bright side, if you slapped me, the bartender wouldn't think I was paying you."

"Would he not?"

"I'm mostly just surprised you made small talk with someone."

We laughed.

She touched my hand and asked if I was ready for our next stop. Up in the room I found clothes that she had brought for me from home. I stepped out of my travel wear and emerged a bit more upstanding. Linen coat and a buttoner.

I asked her how she managed to get the clothes from my apartment.

"I'm very charming . . . and years ago, you left a permanent permission for me to enter. God knows what else I've stolen from the place. The people at the desk are *so very helpful* and fond of me."

I laughed as we walked down the street and through Downtown Crossing, stepping in after a bit to a newish wine bar called Taste.

There was a lovely unique wine list there. We were on the move again after a couple of glasses to Yvonne's, a quirkily decorated lounge known for its excellent cocktails. I would have rather been sitting on a dock somewhere, but I was mostly just happy to be sitting there with her. We disappeared to our room somewhat early. I had a morning flight, and we didn't want to waste any time. I don't recall if I called my friend to tell him I'd not be spending the night at his place.

Chapter Eleven

Geoff and I flew to London in the morning. After all these years there was still a certain magic to flying on the 747, aboard the great jumbo jet of a past era's romance of travel. The seats in the back were cramped. The seats in the front, where one had to fly if he expected to be treated like a human being, were expensive.

I preferred to fly in the morning. The local time would be eleven or twelve hours onward after landing, so the day was ruined, but our day would have been ruined anyway had we flown at night. We drank tea and flew miles above the sea.

Terminal Five at Heathrow Airport is a remarkable place. On these promenades walk representatives from every corner of humanity. Every color, every language, every faith, every idea and notion about the world converges here in a daily dance of beautiful chaos, scurrying about and bumping into one another as people pass day and night to duck through the door of whichever new place to which they are scurrying off.

Our flight to Stockholm didn't leave until the next morning, so we caught the express train into the city and unpacked as little as possible at our room just near Trafalgar Square. It was not clear to me where Geoff had thought he'd be staying, but in any case, I asked at the desk for two beds. My cousin seemed pleased enough with the arrangement.

"I'll buy the drinks," he promised.

"Damned lot of drinks," I told him.

He pointed out that I would have paid for the room anyway, without him, so the arrangement was fair enough.

We marched off into the evening towards Charing Cross. There we found a little wine bar, Lady of the Grapes it was called, that had recently opened. Carole, the proprietor and sommelier, greeted us cheerfully and began pouring from a bottle of bubbles that had grown up in the south of England.

Tess, an old friend of mine, stood to greet us. She hugged and kissed me on the cheek.

Geoff marveled at the coincidence that we should run into her here.

"Oh, it's no coincidence," she told him. "Chris and I had made plans."

"You sneaky fellow." He looked at me.

"There was no sneaking. You just didn't ask." I grinned, happy to have surprised Geoff for a change.

I could already see that they would get on well.

Tess was softly mannered but clearly confident enough that she could be sweet without coming across as weak. Her tongue was sharp, but her wide, deep brown eyes settled your senses and invited you in for more. One of those profoundly interesting people who had seen far more of the world by thirty than most would in a lifetime. We had met years ago, she in the Australian navy and I in America's Coast Guard. Afterwards she had preferred to stay in London rather than to return home. She was one of the most beautiful women I knew, but not outlandishly so. Brown hair fell to frame her warm smile. The twinkling of a single candle on the wooden-plank table danced across her face. She went on with the kind of Australian-sounding—or was it British?—things that make boys from America melt. In a previous time, I might have sought more. Tonight I felt content to sip wine in the company of an old friend. We three laughed together and spoke of wine and politics and sex and love and Europe and America and the world turned upside down.

Others came and went. Above our heads hung a crooked metal light fixture upon which glowed eight filament bulbs bent in on one another in perfectly right angles. They cast beams in every direction. Bottles of wine waited their turn on the shelves that covered an entire wall at the long end of the bar. It was a small place, and Carole moved about sharing her unique tastes with the guests. She returned and asked if we wanted more English sparkling. I asked her where she was from, surprised to learn that she was a French sommelier pouring English bubbles. Part of a new generation that cared more for craftsmanship than for esteemed labels from ancient houses, she explained. She was one of us. We four were the future we had always dreamt of. In my head I counted at least five passports amongst us. None of them was British. And there we sat, drinking English sparkling wine.

It was slow and our new friend Carole closed early. She took us to Terroirs, a nearby wine bar where she knew the staff. There we drank with Ola, who came from Poland. She knew many things about wine.

"I'm Gee Gee; good to meet you." Geoff introduced himself to Ola and another girl named Svetlana, and entertained this makeshift band of new and old friends. Good to his word, he kept buying drinks.

Ola laughed at the ease with which he could transition between talking Arabic miles a minute and the manner of a fellow who had been educated in New England boarding schools. Svetlana rolled her eyes and smiled. We told them we were off to Sweden in the morning.

One enters Terroirs at street level and finds the bar down some stairs. We sat there. A large clock hung on the wall. It was unclear to me at first if the clock worked at all, and after a moment passed it didn't occur to me that I should look again to find out. Time meant nothing here. I love the sound of a ticking clock. That *tick, tick*. Glass of wine in hand, low light hanging down over a simple table. The sun went down. Not light. Barely dark. Cool breeze piercing the summer's heat. Perhaps it all just happened in my mind. And in my mind, I was swept out on the sea of time and all that had come before and all that lay ahead.

There was a chest of drawers and cabinets along the wall near the stairs. Paint stripped in places. Shelves bowed downward under the weight of glasses. Also, a drawing framed on the wall. White fists thrust into a field of red, glasses in fist.

Terroirists.

That's what it said. Rooted in place. Shared amongst the world. Keenly aware that there was something more that made all this beautiful. A call to arms for our generation.

It was a splendid time until they closed. Geoff and I wandered off into the warm summer evening, back to our hotel. The fountain in Trafalgar Square glowed with blue light. What a city; what great swaths of the world gathered here.

⌇⌇⌇⌇

There is a Red Sox bar in Stockholm's Arlanda Airport. Everyone disembarking on flights arriving via British Airways from London must pass by on the way to passport control. It made me giggle every time I walked past. There was, quite literally, no great moment in Red Sox history unaccounted for. Relics of past Bruins, Celtics, and Patriots glories, too. I wondered if the Red Sox would win again this year, but I suspected not. It seemed improbable that fortune would smile a fourth time in fifteen years. I was happy that we had arrived in Stockholm in time for Sweden's quarter-final game against England, which was to be played that day. Luck of the underdog.

We cleared the passport check. The fellow spoke to me in Swedish as always. He spoke to Geoff in English. There is an express train that whisks one from the airport to Stockholm's Central Station in twenty minutes. Stereotypically Swedish—efficient, prompt, clean, expensive. There are profoundly uncomfortable but stylish benches in the chilly underground station upon which one might sit whilst waiting for the next train. I bought tickets with my phone. A conductor stopped and exchanged pleasantries at our seat. She spoke to Geoff in English and moved on.

We hummed smoothly along the track through countryside and then Kista, the outlying town where technology companies made their home. Then back to countryside for a moment, as if modernity had never been there at all. We coasted into Stockholm's Central Station, and stepped out into the perfect summertime. My own grandmother could not have remembered a more beautiful summer in Sweden, nor could any of her cousins who had remained. There had been wildfires throughout much of the country.

I led Geoff through the train station. I knew it well. He did not. We wove through the food court, where the languages etched in the signs above each establishment could leave a person with vertigo as to which country they were in. Into the main hall, which when decorated for Christmas on the opposite side of the year was festooned with garlands and twinkling lights that kept the days longer than the sun would ever allow. Down to the lower level and off through the long wide corridor to the metro.

"You need a card. Have you got one?" I half expected Geoff to pop out with one and surprise me.

"Of course not."

"Come on."

"There's a machine over there."

"It's oddly difficult. Come on, it's easy enough to just get you a card. Don't you collect them at this point?"

"I prefer to collect catamarans." Geoff sidled up to the service desk and made the purchase, speaking Arabic with the fellow behind the desk.

"You relate naturally to literally no one, and everyone. What the hell is it with you?"

"I'm funny like that."

"Right." I swiped my card through the gate.

Off we went to the train. An older set of cars pulled up next to us, but they weren't going in our direction. Then a much newer set pulled up heading south. We glided for three minutes, one stop, to Gamla Stan, and stepped off. Down the stairs, up the stairs, onto the narrow cobblestone street of Stockholm's old town. Then over a block, past a produce stand, and left onto Lilla Nygatan for a block or so until we stepped into the Victory Hotel. I stopped inside the door, and must have looked intent on taking it in, but in truth I was preparing to speak English with my friends behind the desk. They would be happier to not deal with me in Swedish. And I would be ashamed that my grandmother had not taught me better Swedish. And I would amble up the spiraling stone staircase feeling badly yet grand at being back in this place.

We went in, and it unfolded just as I had expected.

There are not many one-of-a-kind places in the world. We sometimes toss about words like *unique* and phrases such as *one of a kind*, but we surely don't mean them. Once, whilst walking the streets of Valladolid, I had told Ava that the city seemed unique, like Boston. Amsterdam reminds me of Copenhagen. I have spent delightful mornings tapping away at the keyboard in a café on a charming street corner, sure that this was as good as it could get, only to find myself weeks later tapping away at the very same keyboard in the very same café on the very same charming little street corner in a similarly unique city thousands of miles away. Paris is Stockholm on the Seine. Perish the thought I might say so to a Frenchman.

Situated on Sweden's east coast, Stockholm is a city of islands perforated and interconnected by canals that ultimately flow to the Baltic Sea. Its maritime identity informs its aesthetic, a city whose urban geography reflects its national flag—brightly colored buildings atop a sea of beautiful sparkling blue. It's a gem of a European capital, ever as charming, historic, and regal as those to the south, and connected to the sea as few others are.

A sight to behold, but unique?

Yes. Perhaps.

Oh well; if I were seeking the unique, I'd come to the Collector's Victory Hotel—truly one of a kind. Paintings of sailing ships hung from every wall not otherwise decorated with models of sailing ships. My brass room key noted the captain for whom my room was named. *Kapten Jönsson*, room 204. The same name was emblazoned on the heavy door, as if the captain himself made his quarters here. His picture hung inside. I wondered if he had sailed the model ship in the lit display case above the bed. Or perhaps he had captained the ship whose old painting hung above the television. What attention to detail that would have been.

An ornate glass chandelier cast bands of light on the ceiling, like crystal shards radiating from the sun itself. Summer's brilliant glow shone through my window, framed by old curtains and open to the frolicking of people on the narrow street below. It was Saturday, and there were many people walking about. I kicked off my shoes at the door to my room. It was unseemly to wear shoes indoors in Sweden. A few moments later I had set up my workshop upon the long desk next to the ornately upholstered armchair. Laptop upon a folding stand, keyboard, mouse, a European plug to charge my phone and watch, notebook and pen. I disconnected the telephone and placed it in the closet. I filled the small wooden chest with keys, passport, and spare change that I'd not be needing here. I was still jingling around with kroner I had withdrawn from the bank years earlier. Here would be my office for the next little while.

I hadn't the internet connection to keep up with my messages the day before on the airplane, and the previous night had been spent reveling around Charing Cross. There I sat, engrossed in my little office for who knows how long. It was Saturday in summer, and I wanted to go outside.

A knock at the door. A girl from the hotel handed me a bucket with a bottle of Jaume Serra cava and a note.

To enjoy amongst cousins. See you when I see you. A.

I smiled. Ash had sent cava. Or had it been Andrew Jefferson? I suppose it could have been Andrew Jefferson. No. He was cheap, and I had left Ash in a far better mood. She had wanted to drink cava in the bar at the Parker House two nights earlier. I wondered if Andrew even knew where I was. Ash would surely turn up somewhere unexpected. *See you when I see you.* I smiled.

It was nearly four o'clock and time for the game against England.

Geoff and I stepped out onto Lilla Nygatan. He read a message from his mother. She had gone up to Provincetown and was watching the game on television, drinking akvavit at ten in the morning. We found a bar and went in. I wondered what the Englishman Billy Grant was up to and couldn't decide if I was happy to not be sharing this moment with him. It was unclear whether anyone in Sweden expected a win. They kept it close throughout the game but were never really in range. There would be terrific parties in England that night.

Suddenly this chapter of our summer was gone. It had been a good show for a country whose population was roughly equal to North Carolina.

Chapter Twelve

Gamla Stan—literally, "Old Town"—is a small island in the center of Stockholm. Narrow alleys and stone streets weave through the island, along which there are little shops and restaurants. Many are for tourists, but Swedes congregate here as well. Up the hill is Storkyrkan, the city's principal cathedral where sits the Lutheran bishop of Stockholm. Walking up the hill along Storkyrkobrinken from Stora Nygattan, itself up the hill from Lilla Nygattan, there is a three-level building that appears in softly muted orange against the gleaming blue sky. The church's oxidized green bell tower rises high above the orange building. This part of town shares its aesthetic with other old towns throughout Europe, and is recognizable for its brilliantly colored buildings and stone streets.

Just steps away is Stortorget, the town square, along which sits the Nobel Museum. There are a great many museums here. Stortorget hosts the Julmarknad, Stockholm's Christmas market. Kungliga Slottet—the Royal Palace—is just on the church's north side, across a small canal from the Riksdagshuset, Sweden's Parliament House.

Geoff and I walked through the town that evening after we had a nap. It was nearly eight and bright as day. We had walked up Västerlånggatan, which runs nearly the north-and-south length of Gamla Stan, crossed under the red stone arches that link the old and new sides of the Parliament House, and stood upon the Riksbron bridge that links Helgeandsholmen—"parliament's island," more or less—with Norrmalm and the main part of Stockholm's north side. A few clouds dotted the still-blue sky, and a train passed over a bridge across a stretch of inner harbor just to the west. The water rustled quietly under the bridge. Here we were.

"Where to, boss?" Geoff asked me to lead the way.

"I think we drink our cava back at the Victory, then go to Gaston?" I turned left onto Strömgatan.

"So, the opposite direction of the Victory?" He laughed.

"More or less." I sighed happily. "It's our first night here, so let's go walking. It's not far. We'll be cracking the cava soon."

We walked and talked and passed ducks and idle teenagers camped on the waterfront and after a few moments came to Strömbron Bridge. From there we continued to the Grand Hotel and then doubled back over the water to the palace's northeast side. Tour boats came and went, loaded with people, meandering through the canals and hidden waterways that linked the many islands to one another. We crossed the bridge.

Back at the Victory we settled in with the cava down in the wine bar. The Burgundy, it was called, was attached to the hotel lobby and was as festooned with maps of French wine regions as the hotel proper was with paintings of ships. My friend Ludvig, who ran the bar, brought us two glasses.

"You're so damned happy to be here."

I looked back at Geoff. "Yes I am. It feels—"

"Yes."

"Miss your boat?"

"Eh. I always miss my boat."

We took a sip.

"Ash send you this?"

"Yes. Well, the note was signed with an 'A,' so I suppose it could have been Andrew Jefferson."

"That guy."

I chuckled.

"It wasn't Andrew Jefferson," Geoff assured me.

"How do you know?"

He handed me his phone with a message on it.

About 8:30 there at Burgundy. Hope you boys are enjoying your cava.

"How in God's name does she do that?"

"Doesn't take much, Mr. Jakey. It's Saturday evening and she knows you have a bottle of cava whose ice is getting warm."

"That's true."

"Cheers."

"Cheers." I raised my glass just a bit.

Burgundy was paneled in wood. Dark but for the small lights that ran the length of the ceiling to the back, a little lamp at each small table, rich carpets, bottles of wine lined up where they could find space. It felt as if we had stepped from summer to winter. It was pleasant to curl up here in colder months. Where the wine bar ended began Tweed, the adjoining cocktail bar. It was possible to spend an entire day and never walk outside. Breakfast in the hotel's cellar in the morning. Work upstairs during the day. Wine and cocktails and a bit of dinner in the evening. I'd never tried it.

Ludvig offered the Ribera del Duero on special, but we had finished the cava and were off again.

Just down the street we stepped into Gaston. It was Saturday night and there was a crowd, but we found two stools at the common table, in the center of which the stone had been cut and filled with ice to chill the bottles. Our friend Lars, the sommelier, said hello. Janni and Carey were working as well.

"You know all the sommeliers," Geoff laughed.

"And you know all the pirates and Caribbean barkeeps."

"Together may we loot and pillage and drink in both class and ill repute."

Carey looked bewilderedly at Geoff.

"He used to live in a bar," I said nonchalantly.

"Untrue. I used to live on a boat. Still do. I just received my mail at the bar." Geoff giggled.

I asked Lars and Carey what was new.

"For wine, or for life?"

"Both?"

We surveyed the list.

"Lars, you know I'm just going to drink whatever you suggest," I said.

"Perfect." He returned a moment later with a bottle.

Geoff was reading the back of the menu.

"Our Philosophy: Bla bla bla bla red wine bla bla bla bla Champagne bla bla bla bla rosé bla bla bla bla balance. . . "

It went on like that. Signed, *Team Gaston*.

"Eloquent, sir," I told Lars as he poured two glasses. He walked off to help someone else.

Geoff asked me what I was doing the next week.

"Working by day, taking walks, drinking wine in the evening? Making good talk with my cousin? What are you doing?"

"I thought we were on vacation."

"I work for money. More or less."

"I have logistics in the islands." Geoff had been leading a makeshift operation of fundraising and supplies and rebuilding for more than half a year.

"God knows America won't." I was exasperated and bitter.

"Why are you so down on America?" Geoff asked.

"Why are you so up on it?"

"I'm not . . . not really."

"Then what's your story?"

Geoff thought for a moment before he answered. He was usually quick witted, so I could tell that a thoughtful answer was important to him.

"I speak from a position of confidence."

"But why? What makes you so confident?"

"Listen, I'm not confident in America. I'm confident of where I stand in the world."

"Easy for you to say."

"It's not about the money. Sure, I have plenty. But I didn't grow up in places that were hospitable to my beliefs."

"Egypt and liberal northern cities?" I tried not to sound sarcastic.

"Have you some idea of how isolating out-of-the-closet Christianity can be in places like that?"

"Like being an Arab in Sweden?"

"Something like that."

"Is that why you don't come here?"

Geoff thought for another moment.

"No. No, we all have our things. Being Swedish was yours. I had others."

"Like being an elitist prick from New England?"

He laughed and admitted, "I never exactly looked the part."

"That's for damn sure. A proper haircut here and there may have helped."

"I got better now."

"I think I've become more Swedish recently."

"Since, oh, just throwing a dart at the calendar, any old place, since November 2016?"

"It's deeper than that. Goes back further."

"And we're back to where this began."

Carey filled our glasses. He was an American, too. Married a Swedish girl.

"I wish I had your serenity about it all, Gee Gee, I really do."

"I pray a lot."

"Ha!"

"I do! You'd pray more too if you'd ever had to outrun a hurricane on a sailboat."

We sipped our wine.

Geoff continued, "I'm confident because I have an anchor. A good anchor, and you're less likely to get tossed about. Storms pass."

"I'll drop mine here."

"In a bar?"

"Perhaps." I smiled from the top of the wineglass, and took another sip. "Besides, it's not any bar. It's a wine bar."

"Four wine bars in two nights. Coming in a little hot, don't you think?" Geoff changed the subject, content that he had at least for now made his point.

"Glorious, right?"

"What are we doing tomorrow night?"

"Maybe we'll add cocktails to the mix?"

"What a terrible pun."

"Accidental."

"Ever wonder why Swedish ships have barcodes on their hulls?"

"Nej," I groaned expectantly.

"Because when they return to port, they have to . . . *Scan da' Navy in.*"

Geoff grinned that Cheshire-cat grin. I laughed out loud and told him, "Now *that* is a terrible joke."

"It's a great joke."

I looked around hoping that no one else had heard.

There was a glass of port sitting on my desk when we returned to the Victory. The hotel staff dropped these in every room each evening whilst the guests were out on the town. I drank a nightcap and read my book, *For Whom the Bell Tolls* by Ernest Hemingway. I had been inspired to it one day after work sitting at Joselito back in Washington.

Chapter Thirteen

I slept late Sunday morning. Seven days and I had slept at least one night in Washington, Provincetown, Boston, London, and Stockholm. So, that had been three nights in Provincetown, one night each everywhere else. That is, if one could really characterize the night of Geoff's party as "sleeping." I had spent the evening alone with Ash at Joselito just a week ago.

It was afternoon and Geoff was nowhere to be found. I walked up to Storkyrkan. Inside were immense brick columns, like the granite and marble varieties that rise from the floor of less northerly, less Lutheran cathedrals. Mortar between the bricks gave these a patterned look as they rose and arched when they reached the white ceiling into which other bricks had been laid in patterns that at once invoked flowers and neural pathways in the brain. Grey wood with inlaid carvings painted in gold lined the balcony where the organ pipes stood. The place was nearly empty. Geoff sat in an abandoned pew, quietly absorbing it all, looking forwards and upwards.

"Services this morning?" I asked as I sat beside him.

"Our people aren't a particularly religious bunch, you know."

"I'm impressed to hear you referring to them as *our people*. Tasteful architecture, though."

"Hmph."

"What is it with you?"

"I believe we discussed it last night," Geoff said excitedly, as if he was happy to be revisiting the topic.

"I am sure that Swedish Lutheranism is what your Egyptian father hoped for when you were growing up."

"Well, my mother certainly didn't hope for much of anything in that regard."

"Our mothers," I corrected, squeaking out a laugh and quickly piping down.

"You just sort of sit here, right? Someone built this. Someone thought this through."

"Fucking incredible, isn't it?"

"Enough."

"I once was here just before a wedding. With our mothers, ironically enough."

It was Geoff's turn to let out a little laugh.

"It was rather splendid, actually. The groom was in the Navy. Might still be, for all I know. Had one of those immaculate Scandinavian beards. Like Erik, but blond. Paired with that dress uniform."

"Odd sight for those American eyes?" Geoff said.

"That's right."

We walked out into the sun making shadows of colored buildings. Quintessential Gamla Stan.

"We've crossed a threshold," I said as we walked.

"What's that?"

I asked Geoff where he was from. The facts of his origin were not particularly relevant to my question, but he didn't know that.

"You know good and well where I'm from."

"Yes, but where do you *believe* you are from?"

"Didn't realize it was a matter of belief."

"A matter of the heart, then."

He considered this for a moment. We walked along Slottsbacken, parallel to the palace.

"I suppose that's a tough question," he finally admitted. "My first instinct was to say Cairo, or Boston. Now I live on a boat. It used to be anchored next to a bar. Or do I live on the Upper West Side? But then I thought about Provincetown."

"But you didn't *live* there as a child, didn't graduate from Provincetown High School?"

"That's right."

"That's the dilemma in the way we think of these things."

I had always found it difficult to say exactly where I was *from*. How indeterminate. It only begged more questions. Was being from a place about having been born there? Having grown up there? Having one's family roots there? Was it the place one chose as an adult? I had once heard an author, Taiye Selasi was her name, sort it a bit. She suggested that the question *Where are you local?* was far more meaningful than the question *Where are you from?*

We tend to form deep relationships with the several communities that we would each describe as being fundamental to our identities and how we experience the world. We visit new places, but we often value equally the roots that ground us in places that are particularly meaningful. Wine lovers might think of this as the terroir that gives each person—like a fine wine—such unique character.

I wondered if this was often on the minds of those who traveled regularly or were meaningfully connected with family and friends in different places. Perhaps it was often on the minds of those raised somewhere so different from the places with which they had come to identify. It certainly made for good small talk at cocktail parties. Certainly far better than the dreaded urban-dwelling rat-race inquiry: *So what do you do?*

Geoff and I discussed this as we turned onto Skeppsbron, walking along the thoroughfare that separates the palace from the harbor.

"So, what threshold was it that we had crossed?"

"Oh, yes." I got back on track. "When you travel, you want to make the most of it. See everything. Do all the things. Waste no time doing that which you could otherwise have done at home."

"But?"

"But then you cross the threshold. Where the place you are seems as much like home as the place from which you started. When you go someplace not to experience something new, but to relocate, temporarily, of course."

"And Stockholm?"

"That's right. That's the threshold."

"Not for me. I haven't been here in years."

"Well, then don't let me keep you from seeing the sights." I grinned. We crossed the Strömbron, walking the opposite direction of where we had come the night before.

"Meh. I have plenty of adventures."

We stepped into the Grand Hotel and then the Cadierbaren. It was a grand place. Columns and an elegant silver chandelier hanging from a tall white ceiling into which had been laid patterns of ropes and flowers. The inner bar was wood paneled, dark tabled, with leather chairs the color of milk chocolate and spruce fastened together by brass studs. A long stone bar extended the length of the room, and interspersed upon it were wooden columns into which gold flourishes had been carved, like in the balconies at Storkyrkan.

The host led us to a small round table by the long windows that faced out into the harbor beyond. It was terrifically bright.

A girl named Tamara with a pretty smile brought us each lattes with a piece of chocolate. We spoke in English, and I briefly pondered her name tag before Geoff interrupted my thoughts as she left.

"So, what makes a person local?" he continued.

"Well," I began, "the author I mentioned suggested that it was the combination of rituals, relationships and restrictions."

"Restrictions?"

"I don't think I'd be much welcome in Tehran. But you might, that Egyptian passport of yours, and such."

"Ah, yes." Geoff understood now.

Tamara returned.

"*¿Te escuche en Español, también?*" I asked if I had just heard her speaking Spanish with the folks at the next table.

"*¡Sí!*" she replied, surprised.

"Where are you from?" I asked her, not oblivious to the irony that I should ask that question in the midst of my current conversation with Geoff. I assumed that she'd be confused had I asked "Where are you local?"

She explained that she was born and raised in Sweden, but that her family was Chilean. She did not look particularly Swedish. I felt enamored by this chance meeting.

"Well, I suppose that makes me local in. . . " Geoff trailed off, back into momentary contemplation.

"Most of the places you suggested, I think?"

"Well, Provincetown, the Upper West Side, and Red Hook, certainly. Cairo. Oddly less so Manhattan than the first two, but I suppose I sometimes live there."

"The fellow selling bagels knows your name?"

"He does. And oddly I know the guys down the street at the shop whose sign out front says that they buy gold, sell diamonds, and give haircuts."

I laughed heartily at that one and choked out, "I'm surprised you don't own that place."

"Indubitably!"

"I'd say that counts. Don't let Caroline hear you even contemplating whether you have relationships there. How is she, anyway?"

"I went to see her the other night."

"I know you went to see her the other night, but how *is* she?"

"My misadventures suit her schedule at the hospital. And then when she *does* get away, I've always a place for us to get to."

"That's true."

"I'll spend the rest of the summer with her there, or in Provincetown. *After* I leave you, and *after* I move my boat."

"Bound to the land. Whatever will you do?"

"It will be terrible."

"You really are one of a kind. You know that, right?"

"So where are *you* local?"

"Stockholm now? I suppose that was the whole point earlier?"

"Well, the bartenders know your name, that's for damn sure."

"At least I don't get my mail at any of them."

"You probably could, come to think of it."

We laughed.

Geoff asked if there was anywhere else I felt local.

"Well, Arlington, of course. I *do* live there."

"For whatever living *somewhere* is worth."

"And Provincetown. Definitely Provincetown. That's my hometown." I thought for another moment. "Madrid and New York are the outliers. And London, perhaps?"

"Outliers? How so?"

"Well, I feel *so very* local in the first three. Less so, but still more so than anywhere else, in the other three."

"Our grandparents started taking us to Madrid when you were ten. Not entirely sure why, but it's certainly been part of your life for a long time."

"That's true."

"Do you still take those silly pictures sitting on those concrete balls on Calle Cava de San Miguel?"

"I do. Every time."

"A ritual if I ever heard one."

"Alright, I'll take it. Local in Arlington, Provincetown, Stockholm, Madrid, New York, London."

"You're a wee bit of a white fellow, aren't you? A liberal-coastal-elitist-prick of a white fellow, I'd say." Geoff grinned and licked latte from the top of his beard.

"I"—pause for emphasis—"am *not* a prick."

"You're very nice."

"You're not exactly a man of the people yourself."

"I'm a local in Cairo. And Red Hook."

"You shot a man for breaking into an apartment building that you *own*. In Cairo. On an island, no less. And in Red Hook you live on a yacht."

"It's a *boat*, not a yacht. And I didn't shoot anyone. I threatened to shoot someone. There were riots."

"Protests. Pro-democracy protests."

"And you can see how well that worked out for them, for us." Geoff paused. He went on when I said nothing. "User error. We were not responsible with our new little democracy. We did not play well with others, like children. So we got our toys taken away. Maybe we'll get them back in fifty years."

"Hell of a long wait."

"Twenty-five, then. Listen, I was there. I almost shot a man."

"You're a weird guy, Gee."

We paid and left. Then we hopped a boat tour that was leaving from the dock just out front. I hadn't planned on this, but hadn't taken one of these in years. It was a beautiful day, and this struck us as the straightest path to be out on the water.

⸎

It was splendid out there. We plied the harbor up into the Nybroviken, whose waters lap up on the Strandvägen neighborhood. Sunlight reflected on every fleeting geometric side of the chop of passing boats, as if God had scattered thousands of diamonds on the carpet of the summer sea. Hotel Diplomat rose above, its white Victorian towers, awnings, and dormers framed by a pale-yellow building to its side and the white of the few clouds that mottled the otherwise brilliant blue sky.

Off a bit were the marinas, and the masts of the Vasa museum ship and the tops and spire of the Nordiska Museet near the Djurgården, and beautiful Skansen park, lush and green and filled with families and lovers and people out running. Summer Sundays. We were lucky to have Stockholm.

This went on for an hour or so, and we were lucky to have been there, out on the water.

Later that evening we ate at a little Gamla Stan restaurant called Kryp In. It was small and cozy, and the food was delicious. A young woman, probably in her early twenties, served our drinks and meal. I found her interesting. At some point a fellow at the next table began talking with her as well.

"You know, your accent is very good," he said to her.

She thanked him, and was gracious. He was very nice about it. He had intended it as a compliment.

"Is that condescending?" I asked Geoff, softly.

"Is what condescending?"

"Shhh," I admonished. "Just that fellow telling our server that her accent is very good. Do you think that's condescending?"

Geoff thought for a moment.

"How do you mean?"

"Well," I went on, "he is clearly American or maybe Canadian based on *his* accent. Is it condescending for him to tell her that she has a *good* accent? You know, as if being American or Canadian and speaking English gives you a monopoly on *good accents*."

"Leave the Canadians out of this." Geoff chuckled. "There are any number of Brits who'd tell that guy *and* our server that they both have terrible accents."

"Exactly. And don't get me wrong, I'm not suggesting that the English have a monopoly on them either."

"They'd suggest it."

"That's true. But really, how universal does the language need to become before the British or the Americans or the Australians or the whoever-else native-English-speaking bunch loses the rights on it? You know, at what point is it just *English*, and the Swedes speak it with a Swedish accent, the Dutch with a Dutch accent." I paused for breath.

Geoff picked up. "And our cousins in Boston speak it with a Boston accent, and they carry on finding it hard to understand Southerners, and the kiwis sort of squeak about it, and God knows the Australians do what they're going to do to it."

"Yes, that's right."

Whatever Geoff's answer to my original question, it would have to wait for another time. The girl returned and we paid. She really did have a good accent. She must have watched plenty of American television, or for all we knew she was herself American. Or Canadian. The Swedes really do speak impeccable English either way.

Afterwards we met our friend George for cocktails, a Greek fellow who was a master bartender at Tweed, the cocktail bar in the back of the Burgundy. It was largely of a piece with the lushly warm décor, but inside Tweed there were rich leather armchairs. Burgundy's hardwood gave way to green carpet upon which were arranged little leather-topped low tables for glasses. We sat at the bar and talked with George as he gleefully handled cocktail shakers and flames and all manner of bottles, producing brilliance in a glass as an artist might impress his patrons. He was a whirlwind of movement and had profound things to say.

I snapped and posted a picture of the beautiful thing he had made. Sometime later I was surprised when Simon—cousin of Emma Cuevas—walked in. He had returned to Stockholm a few days earlier. He saw the photo I posted online and surprised us at the bar. I had grown fond of him.

George torched little sprigs of rosemary and dropped them into gin tonics he had made for us in large glass goblets. We toasted Simon's arrival and carried on like this for what must have been hours. Afterwards, Geoff and I decided together with Simon that we would meet in Gothenburg or Uddevalla or someplace on the west coast in about a week so that we could drive down to Skåne County in the south. It was a good plan, and reminded me that I needed to be online in the morning to firm up plans for the group going to Spain.

We said goodnight. I went to drink Port up in the room.

Chapter Fourteen

A pattern had been quickly established. I would wake in the morning and work in my little makeshift office. Everything that I'd have had in my office back home was there—except for the distractions. I would begin at eight or nine o'clock when it was still two or three in the morning on the East Coast. I'd have an hour or so with my colleagues on the West Coast who were still trying to get things done with our colleagues in India.

Late in the morning I would walk with Geoff to the Grand Hotel for coffee, though on several mornings I was eager for a particular pastry at a café on Södermalm to the south. There we also found a restaurant called Meatballs for the People. They served meatballs, and they were delicious. I preferred those made from elk. On another day when I was feeling adventurous, I tried the chickpea edition. I think we went twice.

We would in any case drink coffee whilst I waited for the East Coasters to wake up. This was of course after the West Coasters had gone to bed, and at a time in the Indian afternoon when the folks there weren't used to having any American to work with. These were good hours to get in touch with a coworker in Vilnius, where there were talented software developers. My late afternoons usually started with the morning routine in Washington and New York. I felt so accomplished by this point, having finished most of my work and needing only to help others get started with theirs. Some evenings

I would step out during dinner to take a phone call with them. The world turned, and its people went about their business. I was just another link in the chain.

Meanwhile life was good in Stockholm. It was the height of summer, and there were people everywhere, so the bars were open. One evening I sat alone with a glass of wine at Gaston. Geoff was on the phone out front—it was of course still daylight—hashing out details with an investor to his hurricane recovery effort down in the islands. Janni had just refilled me with a Hungarian white. I looked into the glass as I often did, watched it bend the light of the small candle into a constellation of twinkling stars, and had the notion that perhaps this was the life that the old fellow had intended when he sent me off to college with a free oil change. I wasn't sure.

He could never have imagined the details of what my life was to become, of course. Wireless internet was a novelty then. *Smart*phones? Forget it. In high school I had subjected my mother to great inconvenience as I drilled holes in baseboards and pulled thick blue cables through conduits I'd hung in our basement, all in the name of being able to share a single dial-up connection throughout the house. How self-impressed I had been. My uncle could connect his laptop when staying in the guest room! It was as if in proving that it could be done, I had vanquished every sense of insecurity I had in my feelings of apartness from the boys my age who were learning to wire for electricity, or lay bricks, or fix cars, or any other vocation from the established lineup of things that men ought to do.

Perhaps the old fellow at the garage had seen some future in that, even if he couldn't have imagined it. I wondered if he'd have thought his small investment in my future, his vote of confidence in my plans, to be worth it if he could have one day sat and drank with me in the country from whence my family had first come.

Geoff had returned. He stared at me, but I hadn't noticed. I was lost in my thoughts and swimming in the liquid constellation held in my hand.

"All well?" I finally asked.

"Indeed. One dollar at a time. Or several million. Take your pick."

I found it difficult to reengage. Finally, I managed a question, no particular question, just a way to absently punt the conversation so I'd not have to work hard at it. "Why are you doing all this?"

"I don't know. Charity? Humility? Faith? Perhaps I just like the place and want it picked back up so that business won't be so bad."

Geoff was the on-again off-again proprietor of a charter yachting business in the islands.

"It's your home," I suggested.

"You might say that I'm *local* there." He smiled.

"Your stab at changing the world?"

"Changing the world is for elitist fools," he said, stopping abruptly as Janni was about to pour him another glass. He held up his hand, choking a bit on his last sip and then asking, "It's still beautiful out there. Want to go down and sit out beside the Burgundy?" We paid, said goodnight to Janni.

Ludvig poured us glasses at a small table out in the cobblestone alley that links Stora Nygatan with Lilla Nygatan.

"Changing the world is for elitist fools, hmm?" I picked up where we had left off.

"It's an elitist idea, really ridiculous if you think about it."

"How so?"

"Well, think. First of all, how arrogant you must be to actually believe that you have the power to change the world. The notion of it is the preoccupation of people who don't have enough real, everyday problems to deal with. Or who are just delusional."

"Says the guy with a sailing yacht."

"Sailboat. *Boat.* How many times do we have to go around about this?"

I piped down.

"Listen, are you going to criticize me or listen to what I have to say?"

"Alright, alright." I promised to not be rude.

"That someone has so few problems that they've the intellectual free time to sit around imagining how he might change the world is in itself a fundamentally elitist concept."

"You might say they're dreamers?"

"And you're not the only one."

"Cheers."

"Cheers."

We raised our glasses. I took the initiative next.

"Or they might be gifted?"

"Yeah, yeah, like that Steve Jobs business: 'The ones who are crazy enough to think they can change the world are the ones who do.'"

"Yeah, trivial little business like that." I held up my phone for good measure. "I've been working here for days. The world has definitely *changed* in the years I've had on it."

"I'm not saying the world doesn't change, nor that individuals can't move it along, or, hell, even change it from time to time. That's not my point."

"What's your point, then?"

"Think of it this way. You take all those people who talk about changing the world. Often they have one of two notions about doing it. Either they are so self-impressed that they are convinced of their own destiny, or they're donating money."

He looked at me expectantly. I decided to just let him roll.

"And they live in this subculture that revels in being impressed with itself over all their generosity. I know it. I live in it. I can't stand it. That's why I ran away to a place where I could be a poorly shaven yacht pirate."

"*Boat* pirate," I corrected him.

"Yes, yes!" He was really worked up. "You know what I'm talking about, Jakey. You live it, too."

"The galas and the dinners and the institutes and other things where educated people get together and tell each other what a good job they're doing?"

"Exactly. And we wonder why half the country hates us, why half of any of these countries hates the other half." He looked around at people cavorting down the street. "And then in our self-righteousness we write checks and donate money and pretend that it all feels right. But how often do you hear any of us actually stopping to consider that perhaps it's the systems we built and nurture just now that created the problem that our donations are trying to solve in the first place?"

"So, you're suggesting, I think, that a little introspection is needed?"

"We are way, way beyond introspection. See, what we've done is created a system that rewards the behaviors that cause the ill in the first place. And we nurture it in our kids, too. Well, I suppose I would nurture it in them if I had any. But the rest do."

"A new generation of self-deluded elites?"

"We send them to the same colleges where they spend years with their own kind. And we make ourselves feel better about it by inviting outsiders in so that we can assimilate them, too. And they're good kids, a lot of them, dreamers, but we convince them that their dreams of changing the world will be better served if they first learn to make slides and spreadsheets, speak the language, be a consultant or a banker or doctor who cares for consultants and bankers."

"Or a software engineer?"

"You people are the ones who pull the thread that makes it all possible."

"Thanks," I replied sheepishly.

"And before you know it, we've put our dreams of changing the world on the shelf. And we've changed our view. Now we're not going to change the world because we're dreamers, we're going to change the world because we know best, because surely the world needs someone as smart as we are."

Ludvig brought us more wine. I sighed in relief. Geoff seemed
to settle down a bit as we talked with Ludvig about new wine bars
that were sprouting up all over the city. This seemed promising, and
I decided that Geoff and I ought to go visit them soon. *Not tonight.*

Ludvig left.

"You don't get along with many other Christians, do you?" I had
no idea why I asked this.

"American Christians? The ethno-nationalist sort?" he asked and
went on without waiting for me to answer. "No, they're crazy people.
If they actually cared about doing God's work on earth, they'd pay far
more attention to the actual lives of the least among us."

I raised my glass again. "To a world made just a bit more righteous
because you are in it, sir."

"Changing the world is for elitist fools," he reminded me.

Silence followed, and my thoughts drifted back to the fellow at
the garage. The whole affair back then would have cost me $20 had
I paid for it. Somehow, in fate's odd way, it had come to pass that I'd
dedicated my life to making that fellow's investment worthwhile. It
was important that I not let him down.

Chapter Fifteen

One day I took the metro—the *Tunnelbana*—up to Kista, the Stockholm suburb where tech companies congregated. There was a company there with which my company partnered, and with whose people I sometimes worked. Geoff and I had been wandering around the city for days, and it felt strange to leave it. The blue-line train hummed smoothly and quietly, as if floating on air above the tracks.

There was not much to see in Kista unless one were a connoisseur of the architecture associated with nondescript office buildings. I heard that some of the companies nearby planned to move into the city center. I worked the day there, and it felt good being amongst real people.

I returned to the city on the blue line, changed to green at Fridhemsplan, and met Geoff at Odenplan for "after work." There was the new wine bar that Ludvig had recommended. The plaza where the busy streets Odengaten and Karlbergsvägen came together felt like a real city. Cars and people zipped about in all directions. A somewhat majestic domed church, Gustaf Vasa Kyrka, stood at the head of the plaza.

Geoff asked me what *Grus Grus* meant as we walked through the door under the sign bearing the name.

"Gravel Gravel, I think, though that doesn't make much sense, does it?"

"*Grus,*" he suggested, "is Latin for *crane*—you know, the bird."

"Odd," I said. "If the Latin word for your bird of choice means *gravel* in your language, maybe pick a different bird?"

"What about *crane* in Swedish?"

"*Trana,* I believe." I thought for a moment. "Wait. The old restaurant next door is called Trana. Clever bastards."

"They do this so the common man won't get it, and the sophisticated man will feel even more sophisticated, no less." Geoff laughed at himself. "Oh well. I suppose I won't be forgetting how to say *crushed stones* in Swedish."

"Suppose not."

We went in.

It was a glorious place. People crowded around the marble bar up front. A chalkboard behind the bar proclaimed the house specials. There was a buzz from the dining room and a common table up just a few stairs from the bar, above which hung a web of filament lights, and around which friends reunited after some length of time apart. A long leather piece the color of cappuccino stretched across as the tabletop, soft and full of character, made beautiful by the wine stains of evenings past. In the center of it all were three marvelous chandeliers. Two layers of wineglasses hung upside down in layered circles on each, a solitary filament bulb in the center, shining out through the glass as a thousand points of soft yellow light. It was one of the most beautiful pieces of art that I had ever seen.

The wine list reminded me of the one at Taste in Boston the week before. It was rather magnificent, though I was disappointed by the omission of a gewürztraminer from Alsace. I'd been dreaming about one of those for days. It was truly the most divinely inspired of all the world's whites. A delightful pairing with spicy curry, I might add, as if the French had invented panang or the Thais were the ancient inhabitants of Alsace. I was not quite sure.

"Where in God's name is *ÖST*?" Geoff asked about one of the countries printed on the menu next to several of the wines.

"That would be *Österrike*, good sir. Austria, in Swedish that is."

"I suppose *TY* is Germany?" he asked, pointing to a riesling from Mosel.

"That's right. *Tyskland*. As in fuck *Tyskland*."

"Pardon?" Geoff was bewildered.

"Sorry, it's just what I said to Billy Grant after Sweden lost its round-robin game to Germany last month."

"Well, we really showed them."

"Good God. It's an accursed thing to be the reigning World Cup champion." I cracked up laughing.

"What is it?" he asked.

"Just something Billy said that night," I said, "something about how it was hard to be British and not be nervous at the sight of vast groups of Germans waving flags."

I ordered a natural red wine from Czechia, made by a fellow called Nestarec. Jason, the sommelier, was excited to serve it. We spoke animatedly about it for several minutes. I sent a photo of it to my friend Lucie in Prague. I was always attracted to strange wines, though given a few years these types of bottles might feel mainstream. Geoff ordered a rosé. Such a pity that more didn't realize that *real* men drink rosé.

"Why don't we ever drink beer?"

"Because we're in a wine bar."

"Yes, but why don't we ever go anywhere else?"

"We go to Tweed with George."

"I suppose." He trailed off. "I like George."

"He's a lovable nut, like you, and come to think of it like Billy, too. Come to think of it, you'd have made a hell of a good bartender." Geoff really would have been good at that. These were three of my favorite people.

"Does it ever strike you as odd that different languages cook up different words for other people's places?" I changed the subject.

"Why the hell not just call them as the locals do?"

"Exactly. I mean, what makes any of us think that Germany or Tyskland is better than Deutschland? If they wanted their country called *Tyskland*, they would have very well called it that, right?"

"Seems reasonable."

This went on for several minutes. I looked at my phone and found a new message.

"Interesting," I said.

"Oh?"

"Ash tells me that there is a surprise waiting for us at the hotel."

"More cava?" Geoff perked.

"Could be, but that doesn't seem right. Why just a random bottle of cava tonight?"

"Maybe she misses you?"

"Ha!" I had picked a hell of a time to be away. She was doing so well lately.

"When are you two going to get married?"

"Probably never, the way it goes with her."

"Shame."

"Yeah."

"What's she doing with herself right now?"

"You mean in the immediate sense, at this moment?"

"That."

"Well, she's rented a flat in Madrid; I know that much. Recently she was on about how she wanted to leave Washington. Some nonsense about taking a little money to a place where she didn't need much."

"Somehow I don't think Madrid fits the bill."

"You see my point. The whole bit about a little money was nonsense to begin with. She's by far that richest person I know."

"And that says a lot, considering you hang out with a guy who lives on a sailing *yacht*." Geoff winked at me.

"Anyway, she told me that she was waiting there in Madrid for the rest of us. Are you coming, by the way?"

"Probably not. At some point I need to go save my boat from the hurricanes."

"Right."

We decided to investigate the surprise waiting at the Victory. It was a direct train ride on the green line back to Gamla Stan. The train passed through Central Station and over the harbor on the Centralbron bridge. Another paradisiacal evening, sun hanging on in the west. Soon it would light the harbor as if it were a lake of fire, like the Reflecting Pool in Washington when I last flew away from home. We stepped out into the sun and shadows on the narrow Gamla Stan streets.

Ash sent another message. "Says the surprise is waiting at the bar—with Ludvig, I assume, though she's never been here so wouldn't know Ludvig."

"I mean, I don't think you need to know Ludvig personally to order up a bottle through the hotel. Be a hell of a bad business model."

"Or Ludvig would be a hell of a well-known guy."

"Or that."

We turned right up the alley into the Burgundy. Ash was sitting at the bar.

I blurted out something unintelligible, genuinely surprised at her turning up for the second time in as many weeks.

"Well, she definitely knows Ludvig now." Geoff smirked.

"Surprised to see me?"

"Never thought I'd see the day."

"Which one?"

"The one where you made an actual honest-to-God appearance in Sweden."

"Afraid your other lady friend might see me?"

Oh, that lopsided grin.

"Surely you're not calling yourself my lady friend?"

"Of course not."

"His other lady friend is a dirty pirate captain," Geoff quickly reassured her.

She kissed me.

There were two glasses waiting for us on the bar. Bless Ludvig.

I asked her what she was doing here. She claimed to have come to see Geoff.

"Seriously, I've been in Madrid for days and I had no idea when you were going to turn up, so I flew here."

The two cities weren't exactly close to one another. It was like flying from New York to Denver on a whim. What's a girl with all the whims in the world to do? Geoff suggested that it was not as if she had much of anything else happening.

"I have plenty of things to do in Madrid, thank you very much."

I asked her how long she'd been here.

"About an hour."

"In the Burgundy?"

"I've been making friends with Ludvig."

"I already like her better than I like you." Ludvig grinned at me.

Ash was staying only one night. This was just as well because Geoff and I had already decided on taking the train the next evening to meet Simon. Stockholm was beautiful, but the bill at the Victory was mounting, and the rest of the city wasn't cheap. We debated what we ought to do with our last and Ash's only night in town.

Geoff asked her if she liked meat. She told him that it was fine. He suggested Svartengrens, but they were booked. Instead, we went to Hornstull, a neighborhood just a few metro stations to the south on Södermalm. Miraculously there was space for three at the end of the long rough-plank table in the tiny Hornstulls Bodega. A fellow who looked like a white Jesus served us wine and took our order for dinner. The table was blackened and streaked with the grain of the wood. A line of glasses hung above, and there was no discernible bar. The table was the bar. This place was tiny. Little candles dotted the table and set the mood as the sun made its long descent through the evening. There were others at the table, too, an American and a Brit and a Swede we befriended. We six drank glasses and ate Brussels sprouts, and Geoff flirted with Ash until dusk.

With twilight waning I realized that we might miss Gaston altogether if we didn't move along. I sent a message to Carey, who agreeably let me claim a table from three train stations away. So we stumbled laughing and giddy out of Hornstulls and back to Gamla Stan.

At Gaston there was the usual music.

"What song is this?" Geoff asked. "I can't quite place it."

"'Dreams.' The Corrs," Ash answered quickly.

"No, it's Fleetwood Mac, though you got 'Dreams' right," I corrected.

"No, 'Dreams' is a Corrs song."

"Nej."

"In English, please."

I snorted. "The Corrs covered 'Dreams.' This is the Fleetwood Mac original. There's nothing Irish techno about what we're listening to now."

"Well, theirs is better." Ash sulked for a moment.

"You two are adorable."

The song changed to "Jolene." Dolly Parton. I asked Ash if she knew it.

"I'm begging of you please don't take my man," she replied.

Geoff told her that I wasn't pretty enough for him anyway.

Carey and I struck up a conversation. His attitude about Sweden's wine was different than what we had discussed in years past. He told me about Ästad Vingård and the sparkling wines on the west coast about a third of the way from Gothenburg to Malmö. And a mysterious wine called Pegasus that was supposedly produced in the town of Flyinge. It was allegedly the best in Sweden, but short of driving to Flyinge I'd not yet be able to get my hands on a bottle. Gaston did not serve Swedish wine.

He made the last call. After a few more minutes we tripped out onto Mälartorget, the street that bounds Gamla Stan's southwest corner. City lights blurred in the air and twinkled off the water. Everything glowed. It was a beautiful moment that I felt I might never forget.

Ludvig was just putting things away at the Burgundy. We fetched the Port from our rooms and drank our nightcap on the big leather couches in the Victory's lobby, surrounded by relics of the sea.

That was Stockholm in the summer of 2018. Ash returned to Madrid the following afternoon. We spent the morning playing in the city, walking through Skansen park, drinking lattes at the Grand Hotel. She was in a haughty mood and immediately proclaimed them to be inferior to any café con leche in Spain. Geoff giggled and sipped his tea without comment.

She kissed me goodbye, and we promised to meet in Madrid.

That evening we boys took a sleeper train from Stockholm to Malmö. This was a change of plans, since we had first arranged to meet Simon in Gothenburg. He had gone down to Malmö, though, and it would have wasted time.

Chapter Sixteen

Simon met us at the train station in the center of Malmö, Sweden's third-largest city. Together we drove into the countryside, which wasn't far off. It was terrifically flat here. Everything was green except for the white houses with red roofs.

I wasn't entirely sure any of us knew where we were going but was quite excited about this detour to a vineyard in Klagshamn, Skåne County. It had been arranged for weeks. When we arrived, Lena and Murat were waiting, guiding us to the garden of Vingården i Klagshamn.

Wind rustled through the garden. Soft from afar, then flapping quickly like a rain stick or a far-off waterfall as it met the bowed green branches of the trees. Vines crawled up the arbor, the open door to the vineyard beyond. Breeze and the rattling of leaves mixed delicately with soft conversation and the sound of dogs playing in the yard. Rows of meticulously trellised vines stretched flatly beneath cloudless blue sky until they met a line of houses a ways off. White-walled, red-roofed, encircling the vineyard in which grew the curious rondo and solaris grapes.

I lifted my glass so that the sight of those branches refracted through its contents. Watched it swirl like translucent gold that softened every detail of the world around me.

"White wine is not easy to make good quality," Murat said, asking me what it was I loved about wine. I told him how I so often found

good wine to be the perfect reflection of where it was made. *Terroir.*
I told him that it was the lens through which I preferred to view the
world. It was a good conversation. Some of the best conversations
are had in vineyards.

Of course, this wasn't a vineyard in Bourdeaux, or Ribera del
Duero, or Sonoma, the North Island, or any of the other places that
one would know because of its history in wine. That's why I had been
so excited about it.

Sweden's winemaking community was still tiny, constrained by
cooler climate and fairly restrictive laws concerning the sale and
production of alcohol. So small, in fact, that Swedes themselves
seemed to laugh off the notion that the country would make wine at
all. They preferred wine from historic European producers in France,
Spain, and Italy. I thought this foolish. At least, in Klagshamn we had
found wine similar in style and quality to the cool-climate whites
produced along the South Coast of Massachusetts or New York. I
wished that the wine was exported such that I might find a bottle in
the United States, and so that others around the world could share
in my surprised delight.

"I haven't yet released 2016," Murat told us as he rolled a cigarette.

Lena poured us some glasses. "There are about a thousand
bottles of that one," she said.

Murat suggested that their alcohol content may be too high to
ever release in Sweden.

It was, he explained, a very different vintage than the year before.
I remembered that vintage to evoke pineapple, apricot, maybe some
frosting like on a cinnamon pastry? Yellow apple, cream? That was
the last vintage Murat and Lena had released of the wine we were
now drinking.

Lena added, "It was very warm, maybe twenty-six Celsius in
September of 2016, when we harvested this one."

This wine called Inkognito had been partially aged in oak barrels.
They had made it entirely from the solaris grape. It was a beautiful

mid-gold color in the glass. Its nose was floral with fruit notes of lychee and kiwi, and a bit of sea air, like low tide. I was pleased with myself for having recognized this when Murat explained that he had fertilized it with seaweed. We were near to the coast there. He mentioned having paired it with a dish of asparagus, mozzarella, and fried egg.

I wondered if Geoff or Simon even cared. They may have been bored, but they indulged me. I wished that Ava were there.

The next wine was uniquely multi-vintage. The bottle we drank was blended in the barrel from each of the five harvests from 2012 through 2016. It was the fourth edition. I imagined it might have gone well with smoked duck. Murat explained proudly that this was the best seller of all the Klagshamn wines in restaurants. He sought for it to be less fruity and more mature than its cousins from the same vineyard. It was a striking darker gold color in the glass, with notes in the nose of cedar, wooden embers, butter, and a touch of apple. It mingled with notes of gently toasted brown sugar, and I was reminded of the sophisticated qualities of a Port wine.

We sat in the garden drinking the latest vintage of Inkognito and the latest bottle of the multi-vintage Ego4 white wines with our hosts. Lena and Murat's wines were on the forefront of what was happening in Swedish viticulture. I was so grateful that they shared their work with us.

I received a message from Peter Dean. "How's Klagshamn?" he asked. I must have told him in passing that we had planned to come that day.

We left when I sensed that our hosts wanted to get back to work. Copenhagen was a thirty-minute drive west across the bridge that spans the Öresund, the strait that separates Denmark and Sweden. I fell asleep in the back seat, but Simon woke me as we crossed the bridge. Blue sea beyond skipped by through the breaks in a rather ordinary-looking railing until finally we were on the suspension. I suppose I should say we were crossing Øresund since we had passed into Denmark. Saltholm, a nearly unpopulated island whose name literally means "salt islet," was just to the north. The bridge turned into tunnel when it came to Peberholm, an artificial island whose name literally means "pepper islet." The Danish were witty people.

It was just early afternoon when we arrived in Copenhagen, which in Danish is called København. Simon had been making jokes all day about the accent with which many people spoke in Skåne.

"*Skauna*, that's what they call it, like *sauna*," he had said. "Sowna!"

He began making jokes about how the Danes pronounced København—in his telling, dropping letters and running together sounds. He seemed quite silly. Geoff and I supposed that these were things only true Swedes could understand. It was all quite the same to our American ears.

First we drank coffee at a nondescript place near Tivoli Gardens, a fabulous amusement park that we decided not to visit. Then we walked, and after a short time came upon Christiansborg Palace where the *Folketing*—Parliament—met. There were bicycles everywhere in Copenhagen. One clipped past me, under the colonnaded and vaulted promenade that encircled the central courtyard. It all seemed very peculiar, such casual riding up to the nation's seat of government.

"The people here are so chill," Simon said.

At Nyhavn there were the famous colored row houses lining the little harbor inlet along which throngs of tourists gathered for food and beer at mediocre restaurants. It was a beautiful sight. Silly folk snapped selfies. I wondered to what extent anyone could truly take in what surrounded them whilst photographing themselves in it.

We found a dock bar where I struck up a conversation with a Latvian girl named Rūta. I decided then that one day I should visit Latvia. She poured us wine and we sat in Adirondack chairs at the end of the pier. Throngs of shirtless men and women in bikinis lined up sunbathing and jumping into the water along the dock on the opposite side of the canal. One particularly odd boat—a sailboat deprived of its mast, outfitted with an ill-suited motor, and driven about by a couple of thrill-seeking bros in T-shirts—passed several times back and forth in front of us. Ferries, tour boats, and pleasure craft zipped along through the shipping channel, creating an air of celebrating nothing in particular but the beautiful summer as I swirled rosé in my glass and kicked up my feet on the bench in front of me.

Airplanes lofted up from Kastrup, the airport, some distance ahead of us.

"Norwegian airplanes look like dicks," Simon laughed tipsily.

"Pardon?"

"Yes, you see it, that's what they look like," he insisted.

Another flew overhead.

Geoff giggled and suggested that Simon didn't much like Norwegians.

"That's nonsense. I love Norwegians. They're like little brothers that we Swedes need to take care of. But goddammit, they make terrible pizza."

"What the hell, pizza? Is that a Norwegian specialty?"

"Well, they have no food culture," he said, "and they're always stringing their goddamned flags all about, bringing them on vacation and such."

"Those two things seem related."

"If I see one more Norwegian with a flag sticking out of her things."

"I'm telling you, he doesn't like the Norwegians," Geoff cut him off.

"Nonsense," he continued to insist. "Our ancestors fought a lot of wars with these Danish over Norway. It's a lovely beautiful place. But they do make awful pizza."

"You're drunk."

"Of course I'm drunk! Isn't it grand?"

"Come on," I said, "let's go to Ved Stranden 10," a wine bar that I wanted to try.

We came upon another wine-serving establishment called Den Vandrette. They had set up a bar in a sort of tiki hut just across the street at the waterfront. I stepped out to cross the bike lane and was almost hit by a girl whipping past. A makeshift beer bar was just next to us, and we made friends with a Faroese fellow pouring pints. He pointed to an old tug tied up to a bollard on the dock and told us that the rest of his bar was there. It was filled with people carrying on. A girl named Eleanor at Den Vandrette poured us a glass of natural wine, a white made from the tsitska grape and grown in the town of Terjola in the Republic of Georgia. I thought I might like to visit Georgia. What a terrifically out-of-the-way place to explore. It was cloudy and mysterious-looking in the glass, as natural wines are. Eleanor showed us a strange animal horn that the Georgian winemaker had sent as a gift in thanks for serving his wine.

An Asian couple sidled up to the bar, ordered something in English, and then resumed speaking a language that I couldn't identify. It was something they alone could share. I thought that if Ash had been with us at that odd urban beach bar, we might have spoken Spanish with one another, and then had something that we alone could share. And Simon could speak Swedish with passersby and Geoff could speak Arabic to nobody in particular, and it would have been like the whole star-crossed world had come together in one beautiful Babel on the beach.

We walked off to find Ved Stranden 10. It was on a cobblestone street called Ved Stranden, which runs parallel to the canal that separates the rest of the city from Slotsholmen, upon which Christiansborg Palace is situated. The rear side of the palace rose up above the water. Busses and bicycles intermingled in a plaza.

Number ten faces southwest on the corner with Boldhusgade, and bright sunlight pours in from windows on two sides in the afternoon. I recognized it soon as we walked up. A picture of its front door had hung on the wall at Grus Grus in Stockholm.

"*Grus Grus*," proclaimed Simon, "is a nonsensical name. It means 'gravel gravel.'"

Geoff suggested to him that it was likely intended to mean "crane crane" in Latin. We discussed this in idle passing for a moment.

"Personally, I like speaking English," Simon offered. "It's quite expressive."

"Thank you?" I asked.

"Oh shut up. You didn't create the thing, don't take credit. It's not yours."

We laughed. Simon went on.

"It's impractical to have too many languages."

"And you Swedes are so practical." Geoff grinned.

"And you Americans are so impractical," Simon shot back.

"I," Geoff said, "am Egyptian."

"That's nonsense. You're as American as they come."

"This," I explained to Geoff, "is one of Simon's favorite topics."

"I did stir something up at brunch the other week, with Ash and that guy Peter, didn't I?"

"You did indeed."

"They're both fools." Simon stopped and looked at me as if I might approve or disapprove of him having called Ash a fool. I moved on without comment.

Tired wood planks in the floor and dozens of small wooden drawers on the wall behind the bar gave the place the feel of something crossed between an old library and a charming pub. A tall, blond Englishman pouring wine at the bar reminded me of Billy Grant.

One instantly knew why Ved Stranden was said to be the best in the city. The place was full of energy. Some girls walked in from across the street. One of them wanted a glass of water. Another was irritated that there was no air-conditioning. She leaned in close at the bar, and smelled of cigarettes. She was quite sexy. Then, abruptly, she turned and walked away to the washroom, shaking provocatively in her floral-print denim skirt. I realized she had come in only for the washroom. I wondered if any of her carrying-on had been genuine.

A group of people shouted merrily at one another around a table in the corner by the window. The Englishman opened a bottle and tossed the cork into a pile strewn atop the bar. It had a beautiful gold color, unlike anything else I'd ever seen. We drank a glass. He was profoundly knowledgeable about wine.

The place hummed with the life of a Byzantine café talking of politics, blended with the excitement of happy hour, the ongoing promise of a weekend that showed no sign of ending, the warmth of summer in July, and passion for sharing wine—and all the world—with everyone who darkened the door.

A Sikh man walked in and asked for a glass of something natural, something "interesting," he said. The Englishman popped him a taste of a white from Hungary.

"Very, very local grape," he explained.

The man loved the very local grape. He ordered a glass, and also two cups of water.

Two girls walked in. They were looking for glasses of white, an escape from the heat. "Something," the Englishman asked, "light, fresh, aromatic?" He paused. "Or something fruit forward?"

The girls lit up at the notion of something aromatic, and paid 420 Danish kroner for two glasses that they drank outside.

A Danish fellow walked in. Straightaway he asked for an orange wine.

"Haven't you got anything more special?" he asked after tasting a sample. He was very serious about something good, or otherwise very serious about appearing knowledgeable to everyone at the bar. He was also a bit crusty, a cantankerous old fellow. He paid for the wine with a tap of his phone.

Now we were drinking something from Østrig. That's *Austria* in Danish. It was a blend of chardonnay, sauvignon blanc, and welschriesling that had been made near the Hungarian border. So the Englishman told us.

Two others walked in and asked for something in Danish. The bartender replied in English. For an instant I could almost see the gears shifting in their heads. They began chattering in English.

We were drunk, and it seemed a fabulous place, number ten on Ved Stranden.

"I'll need a nap," Simon finally confessed.

"Now?" Geoff asked him.

"Yes, now; what do you think? Or otherwise we'll never get out tonight."

So we returned to our hotel in Vesterbro. It was a rather long walk, so we arranged a taxi.

The Englishman had recommended we begin our evening at a place near our hotel called Ancestrale. It was a tiny little place whose walls were half white clapboard and half old exposed bricks bent in arches around the windows and doors. A simple candle sat upon an empty table. Its wood planks were grainy, interlocking streaks of light and dark well defined, but very smooth to the touch.

A French fellow named Arthur told us about his wonderfully explorative wine list. We settled on an unfiltered riesling: gold clouds in the glass, grainy pear and apple notion when we drank it. The food was simple yet profoundly delicious. I wondered if I had ever had tastier bread and butter. Scandinavians love bread and butter. There was hummus, burrata, and veal fricassee for us to try. Ancestrale was so small, so intimate. Rap music played quietly on speakers somewhere in the room.

We talked about our afternoon, and Ved Stranden and Den Vandrette. Arthur knew the people at both. He told us about a place called Bæst, just north in Nørrebro. *Crazy pizza*, he wrote on a napkin next to the place's name. Beneath that he wrote *Slurp ramen joint*. He also told us about a place called Falernum just up the street, which we decided to try because we hadn't had proper sleep in a proper bed for days, and had already been to a vineyard and three bars that day. It wasn't far, and we liked that.

Up the street at Falernum there were people drinking out on the sidewalk. Large windows opened into the night and overflowed with people. Atop the menu card was a drawing of a pudgy bald man in jailhouse pinstripes sitting on a barrel of wine. He grinned and cast his eyes to one side, as if checking in on the shenanigans that his barrel would inspire. Our server was a brunette girl wearing an apron and a cutely inquisitive smile. She introduced herself as Nanna.

That's actually an overstatement. She did not introduce herself as Nanna, but we asked her name and introduced ourselves. She then told us that her name was Nanna. And, to be specific, Simon had no part of this. It was Geoff and I who introduced ourselves, and then introduced Simon, and then she told us her name and laughed as each of our words tripped over the words of the other.

"Why do you introduce yourself to everyone?" Simon huffed.

"Simon. You disappoint me," I answered.

"How is that disappointing? Most people don't care who you are."

"And we'll never determine which unless we introduce ourselves to everyone. Then we find out who our friends are."

"You are strange, strange people, I think."

Nanna returned and we drank orange wine. We were happy to know her.

"What is *orange wine*, anyway?" Geoff looked at me straightaway. He suspected Simon had no idea what orange wine was.

Simon told him that it was white wine made without removing the grapes' skins.

"Ah! Mister Jakey, your monopoly on good information has been broken." Geoff cocked his eye at me. "Wait, is he right? Is Simon right? That's what orange wine is?"

"More or less."

"Good. I'll take my wine advice from Simon from now on."

We ate exquisitely grilled cod and drank wine with Nanna for hours. She didn't drink anything, but she poured everything. Falernum had turned out to be filled with energy.

Simon asked us where we planned to go in the morning.

"Where are you going, anyway, Geoff? I don't think I have any idea."

Geoff told Simon that I was going to Spain in the morning.

"Yes, but where are you going?" I asked him. "Coming with me to Madrid? How the hell have we not determined this yet?"

The two of us had been together for nearly two weeks. The next day it would be that long since I had gone up to Cape Cod and this whole strange adventure had begun. I thought about this for a moment. Somehow I'd only managed to take two days off, Independence Day included. The world waited for no one. It was just as well. Scandinavia was expensive.

"I'm going back to St. Thomas in the morning to save the boat," Geoff finally admitted. "I suppose my luck has run out avoiding hurricanes. Caroline is meeting me there. Remarkable thing."

"Can't be a man of mystery much longer, hmm?"

"Mystery? Me?" He scoffed. "What about you? I'm just a guy with too much money. Who the hell are you, wandering around and working *remotely*. What's that?"

"I'm just getting it done for myself."

"A twenty-first century everyman?" Simon's eyes twinkled with curiosity.

"Something like that." I sipped my wine.

"He really does work hard. Everywhere we go, he's doing something." Geoff cut me some slack. "You know I love you! You know I'm just screwing with you."

"My dear cousin."

"Actually, I'll miss you. I'll miss our talks. But you seem better than when I found you."

"Oh?" Simon knew now that he has missed part of the story.

"He was a mess when I found him."

"I wasn't a mess. I was tired and you surprised the hell out of me showing up in Provincetown."

"You were a moping little mess. And it was your favorite holiday. You wouldn't even come with me to Bermuda."

"Ah yes, will he or won't he sail to Bermuda? The yardstick by which we all must measure happiness. Hell, I've never even been to Bermuda."

"Don't be a prick. I came to see you because I love you."

"You did, and I will be forever grateful for that."

I really did appreciate what Geoff had done for me. He'd reset the clock on the whole thing. That silly party, bringing Ash and Erik. God only knew if Ash would have turned up in Boston without Geoff's meddling. He was completely unrelatable in nearly every way, but he was a uniquely good soul.

We went on like this for several hours. Falernum closed and we went to bed. In the morning Geoff flew from Copenhagen to Amsterdam to Atlanta and on to St. Thomas. I'm not entirely sure where Simon went. I flew to Spain.

Chapter Seventeen

Standing alone in Madrid's Barajas Airport I was reminded of the moment nearly a month earlier when I stood in the great hall of Washington Union Station waiting for Erik Webber to arrive by train. Terminal Four was modern but not less majestic. Steel trusses tower like California redwoods from the polished concrete floor to support the rolling wave of a ceiling. Each truss is painted a slightly varying red, yellow, orange, blue, or green such that when lined up down the great hall, which goes on for nearly a mile north to south, they appear to form a gradient of color gradually changing hues. Thousands of gently bowed wooden slats that form the ceiling convey the beauty of a gently rocking sea under which an unbroken wall of massive floor-to-ceiling glass bathes the great hall in natural light from east or west no matter the time of day. A cathedral monument to the modern age of the world coming together, welcoming travelers to a country from whose stone cathedrals of old the great heroes of the Age of Discovery once set out to explore the vast stretches of their unknown.

I wandered for a bit, having never grown tired of the marvel that was this place.

Then I caught the Cercanías train into town, to Atocha, the central station. *Puente Aéreo*, the air route between Madrid and Barcelona, had once been one of the world's busiest before the high-speed rail began here at Atocha. It was too hot to walk with a suitcase up the hill along Calle Atocha, so I took the metro two stops to Antón Martín.

Walking in the shade of the Barrio de las Letras I was reminded of Gamla Stan, though I was surrounded by the sprawling millions of Europe's third-largest city. Children played in the street as well-behaved dogs and intrepid taxis slid past. People and the melodic rhythmic thrumming of Spanish filled the alleys. Two o'clock, just lunchtime on a Sunday at the cafés. A cacophony of weekend tourists on the move. Once, I imagined, these streets had echoed with the sound of horses' hooves on the pavers. Now Europe's predilection for cobblestone streets had turned the *rat-a-tat-tat* of suitcases bound for their next Airbnb into the defining urban soundtrack of the twenty-first century. Calle de las Huertas sloped again down the hill towards Paseo del Prado and the train station. After a block or so I stepped up to the front door and rang the neighbor through the call box. The door clicked open, and I walked up a few stairs and through the unlocked door of the apartment Ash had been renting.

I noticed a garden on the balcony above the street, and a note on the table.

Out. You should do the same and meet me later at Champis. When do the others arrive? AML.

I was disappointed, but I'm not sure why. Perhaps I had thought she'd meet me. No matter; she was no doubt playing the girl-about-town in this city just the same as the last. She was happy here, and I smiled contentedly, falling into the chair by the open balcony door. The sounds of Huertas wafted up from below. Somewhere an accordion played.

⌒┌ℓ°ɔ°ɔ⌐

There is a small plaza just up from Huertas, across the street from which sits the Congreso de los Diputados. There is a café out front where several people sat drinking with the occasional menacing of young men skateboarding around a small monument. It seemed a great contradiction, drinking and playing just off the steps of the country's stately parliament house. I found it intriguing, so I sat and had a drink. There was the grand old Palace Hotel back across the street. A bellman greeted arriving visitors and shuffled suitcases of the departing into taxis. I had always wanted to stay there, but each time felt it too expensive and anyway enjoyed the sense of locality one gets from staying in an apartment that opens through any ordinary door onto the street.

Good God it was hot. I was happy to be sitting under the umbrella, but when the last of the godello had been drunk I decided against a second and didn't want to hold the table. On I walked, crossing Paseo del Prado onto the promenade that straddled the wide boulevard which formed the center city's principal north-south artery. Traffic raced around the circle that joined the Palace Hotel on one side to the Prado art museum on the other. An old man sat on a stone wall in the promenade, painting a hand fan, his previous pieces arranged for sale upon a blanket on the sidewalk. There was a crowd as always out front of the Prado, and horse-mounted police officers looking on. Then up a small hill to Los Jeronimo where well-dressed folk filed in past an immaculate old car that would within the hour whisk away a bride and groom.

Parque de Retiro is just a few moments on from all this. King Philip IV had constructed a palace here in the seventeenth century, a predecessor to the Palacio Real on the opposite side of the old city. The park's regal origins were evident, though, in its broad walking avenues lined with all manner of statues, trees, and gardens.

I entered through the Plaza del Parterre and tacked to the right through a flower garden encircling a fountain. A single bird bathed in its pool. There were flowers everywhere. A groundskeeper trimmed perfectly manicured bushes. He smiled at me when he stopped to wipe the sweat from his brow. I loved how quiet it was in this little corner set apart from passersby heading directly to the lake in the park's center. Some meters away a lively band played atop a grand staircase at the opposite end of the garden plaza. A bass, a trumpet, an accordion. Six or seven men dancing and laughing as they played. A pile of change at their feet. I was unsure if they played for the money or for the enjoyment of one another's company. There is a great difference between work and vocation.

There was a bench beside the fountain where a beautiful girl sat reading a book. It was an honest-to-God book. Not a tablet, but a book. With paper and pages and, I imagined, that quiet satisfaction one finds turning from one to the next in the shade of the trees on a warm summer's day.

I sat next to Ash.

She asked me where I had been.

"Looking for you?" I asked.

I had not expected to find her here.

"Good."

"You could have met me."

"It was more fun this way. I wanted to see if you'd come here. I've had a lovely time reading my book."

"Have you been here long?"

"An hour."

"You must have left just before I arrived?" I looked puzzled.

"That was the idea."

Now I felt as puzzled as I looked.

She went on. "You don't remember, do you?"

"Remember what?"

She laughed and placed her head on my shoulder, her book folded now around her finger.

"You once shared your location with me, on my phone. We were looking for one another in Washington."

"Wait." I was dumbfounded.

"Yes. I think you only meant to share it for an hour. I'm sorry, but it's been too fun for me."

"Like the permission to enter at my apartment?"

"That's it."

"Good Lord."

She kissed me.

"So," I went on. "That night at Joselito, with our crowd? What did you say, 'Hello, boys'?"

"You practically ignored me, left me to Erik. You were so enamored with your new Swedish friend. I almost left."

"But you knew we were there, didn't you?"

"Oh," she giggled. "Yes. But not just because I could see so on my phone."

"And that time when you sent me a message soon as I was off the boat in Boston?"

"That too."

"And the two glasses of wine, on the bar at the Burgundy? You knew just when to order them, you little sneak."

"Christopher Jacobson, a beautiful blue dot cutting a nice little line on the metro through Stockholm."

She smiled at me. Good God, why that half-cocked smile?

"You're a creeper," I choked out through my laughter.

"I am a resourceful lady."

"You are such a bitch."

I instantly regretted saying that. I didn't mean it. I wondered how she would react.

Ash smiled wryly.

"My mother," she began, "has a sign hanging in a frame in the house she shares with that Luciano fellow."

"Your father?"

"My *adopted* father."

"Yes, him."

She continued, "I'm not *a* bitch. I'm *the* bitch. And I'm *Miss* Bitch to you."

"What?"

"The sign. That's what the sign says." She laughed.

I was relieved.

"You are damned lucky."

"Why's that?"

"Because if you weren't so goddamned pretty right now, I'd be furious."

"I always look"—she paused, sat up straight, and enunciated properly—*"goddamned pretty."*

I kissed her and lowered my head onto her lap, back flat upon the bench, as she continued reading her book.

This is how we began our time together in Madrid.

Another bird joined the lonely bather in the fountain. The air was warm. The shade was cool. The company was intoxicating. I took a passing wonder at where our friends were, having arranged the date but having no idea where anyone was staying. It had been easy for me just to arrive at Ash's apartment. She was fully ensconced, like she lived here. I had a notion that she might never come back home.

I don't know how much time passed like this. After some length we stood to go for a walk. Ash smiled and thanked the fellow tending the bushes. I dropped a euro for the band that had played the soundtrack for our first moments together in Madrid.

Beyond the stairs at the head of the promenade there is a broad pedestrian avenue lined with trees. Paseo del Paraguay, it is called. At the end of the avenue there is a circular plaza with a fountain in its center. Trees bow over the Paseo de Venezuela beyond. There is a large lake to the left where rowboats, ducks, and strange fish compete for primacy. Street performers lined up along the west side of the lake where we stood. An enormous koala bear. A fellow painted gold. A strange goat-like creature adorned in shiny ribbons, all colors of the rainbow. A woman clucked and tapped together the wooden jaw of her mask, frantically dancing up and down for a silly fellow and his girlfriend passing by. I looked away, not wanting to feel duty bound to drop change in her jar. It was a strange sight.

Ash draped her arm around mine and pulled herself in. Two

cats, a mother and a kitten, played in the grass just past the lake. We walked off beyond the next fountain to a place where the crowds were thin, and turned up a smaller path over which trees bent and alternated with lampposts on the ground. We didn't say much until we came to a clearing with a strange monument. A stone woman stood on a balcony gazing down at a bronze man on a horse, a grown Romeo summoning his statuary Juliet, forever cursed that she not come down from her perch.

I didn't much care when the others would arrive.

"When do the others arrive?"

"Clueless to that," I told her.

"Just as well," she said.

"They'll be along."

"You talk funny, you know that?"

"Have I always"—pausing for emphasis—"talked funny?"

"Since the moment I met you. I think. Or some moment just after."

"Then at least you knew what you were getting."

"I was getting nothing."

"You have been crazy about me since the moment you met me."

"You are a dirty cradle robber."

"Nonsense."

"I thought you were in love with Ava then."

"I was in love with Ava . . . *then.*" I paused again. "Probably still am."

"You most certainly still are."

"Something else you knew you were getting?" Smiling at her.

"It's part of what I like about you." She trailed off.

"What's that?"

"Goes to show you'll never let me go, either."

"Wrapped around your finger for life, hmm?"

"It would be fabulous, wouldn't it?"

"I'm not so sure."

"It's true. I am a miserable little wretch to you sometimes."

"Sometimes?"

"It's not my fault, I promise. Well, it is my fault, but I don't mean to be."

"Hell. I knew what I was getting, too."

"Something like that."

We had doubled back. Now there was a throng of people by the docks waiting their turn to hire a rowboat. We considered this for a moment before deciding that the line wasn't worth the effort.

Back at the fountain in Plaza de Nicaragua we angled just to the right down another wide avenue towards the grand Puerta de Alcalá and the city streets beyond. Every city needs a triumphal arch. Puerta de Alcalá was Madrid's.

A few moments later we came to Plaza de Cibeles, above which loomed the magnificent spires of Palacio Cibeles. I believed it to be the city hall. The white of the towers matched the white of the clouds puffed out in the blue sky overhead. Flowers encircled the fountain in the center of the plaza around which cars raced up and down Paseo del Prado. Spanish flags shimmered as they waved in the breeze, a most patriotic sight for a most patriotically shy people. A large banner conveyed a simple message from the building's façade. *Refugees Welcome.*

"I love it here," Ash said.

"I know."

"I can't wait for Peter to get here and see that banner."

"You might consider not being such a witch to him."

"You know I love him. And you also know that he deserves it."

"He is a man of deep feelings."

"Stupid feelings."

"Come on."

"That's it?"

That cocked smile.

"Come on"—I considered—"Miss Bitch."

"That's better."

We turned south into the promenade along the center of the Paseo. Passing the fellow painting the fans.

She suggested we have a drink at the Palace Hotel.

"High roller!"

"Oh, I thought you could buy *me* the drink."

"Good thing you let me stay in your apartment, then."

"Good thing."

We went inside.

It really was a magnificent place. A chandelier hung like palm fronds beneath a fresco in the entry lobby. People moved all about and chattered expressively with one another in that distinctly Spanish way. We climbed the carpeted staircase to the second lobby encircled by elevators, a luxury luggage shop, and the entrance to the bar and rotunda. We looked at one another, torn as to which we should choose. It had somehow turned to late afternoon.

We were evidently standing too close to the door, which occasioned a waiter to usher us into the bar and take our order for glasses of cava that were too expensive. I exhaled, contentedly sitting at a little table alone with Ash.

"What is it?" she asked.

"Oh. What a place this is."

"How do you mean?"

"Well," I began, "both dripping in luxury and wrapped in history."

"It *is* wrapped in history. Or better that history is wrapped up in it."

"Is there a difference?"

"I suppose not."

"Hemingway liked it here."

"Hemingway liked it everywhere in Madrid."

I laughed and a fellow at the next table quizzically looked over.

"What is it?" Ash asked.

"Oh, it just occurred to me what a strange coincidence this is."

She stared at me.

"You know how Geoff calls me 'Jakey'?"

"Like your last name, yes."

"I just think it's funny that you and I, of all people, *Jake* and *Ashley*, should be sitting in the bar at the Palace Hotel."

"Jake and Ashley sitting together in the bar at the Palace Hotel!" a voice behind me exclaimed from the door.

I turned to see Peter Dean and Ava Murray standing there.

"Why the hell does everyone get this but me?" Ash hissed.

Ava didn't understand either.

Peter explained that it was in the last chapter of Hemingway's *The Sun Also Rises* when the principal characters, Jake Barnes and Lady Brett Ashley, shared wine in the bar of the Palace Hotel.

"Hope it works out better for you two," he said with a sly grin.

"Don't be a dick."

"Hey, I was just saying I hope it works out for you two. Just being kind."

We moved to a place where four of us could sit together. Peter ordered a bottle of Rioja.

"Of course you'd order Rioja," I chastised him with a glance over to Ava. She smiled knowingly.

"What's wrong with Rioja?"

Ava explained to him that there was nothing wrong with it. She and I just found it typical, like the first thing that everyone thinks of when they think of Spanish wine.

"You should try something from Toro," I suggested.

"Why's that?"

Ash complained, "It's too early in the day for Toro."

"It's a big red," I elaborated. "Tempranillo grape, like Rioja, though they call it '*Tinta de Toro*.'"

Peter ventured that this seemed rather provincial.

"You're one to talk," Ash quipped.

Ava snorted with laughter. "Tempranillo, *Tinta de Toro. Tinta del País* in Ribera del Duero." She went on. "*Tinta Roriz* in the north of Portugal. *Arragonês* in the south."

"All the same grape, more or less." I finished her thought. She and I chattered excitedly.

"Don't you two ever talk about anything other than wine?" Ash asked pointedly.

We looked at her.

Peter laughed and picked up where Ash had left off. "But seriously, in all your years dating, how many times did you two have a discussion that didn't somehow involve wine?"

"Once they talked about beer," Ash giggled and smiled.

"Huh." I thought about this for a moment. "Maybe we did, once. Talk about beer, that is. I don't recall it, but I'm open to the idea that we might have." I smiled back.

"You talk funny," she reminded me.

We four laughed together. Somehow in all of this Ava had ordered godello. So we drank white from Galicia.

"Godello!" I snipped at her with the cadence of how an ill-informed American might stereotype an indignant British fellow bidding someone a "good day."

"That's not funny, Chris." Peter peered out at me over the top of his glass.

"Oh well."

"Seriously, it's a god-awful pun."

I looked at him and asked, "Do you ever wonder why all Swedish ships have barcodes on their hulls?" He stared back that empty stare that one gives when they are stumped.

Ava erupted in laughter, exclaiming, "So that when they return port they can *Scan da' Navy In!*"

"That one was better," Peter admitted with a chuckle.

"Nautical people humor," Ash groaned.

"They were in the Coast Guard, or something. I bet you lay that one on everybody you meet."

"Actually, that was my first time, but better believe I'll do it again. Hey, Ava, how did you know it?"

"I'm quite smart, you know."

It was an exquisite little bar. Rich carpet. Elegant wood paneling lacquered to a shine. Black-and-white photographs of old Madrid hanging under museum lights. We sat on a plush blue velvet sofa piped in gold next to which stood illuminated glass cases showing off silver pitchers and bowls. A television inlaid in a wooden column at the back of the room cycled through quotes and photos of the world's famous who had visited. The bar itself was surrounded by books. The room was lit by small lamps mounted along the wall.

I was staring at the intricately patterned white ceiling when I heard Ash.

"Chris has had a small world kind of day today."

"How do you mean?" Peter's eyes twinkled.

"Well," she continued, "he ran into me by chance, reading at Retiro."

"Truth be told," I pointed out, "you staged that whole thing and had it on good information where I was at the time."

Peter erupted in laughter. I thought he might spit wine from his nose.

"What's so funny?" I asked.

"Did you just find out that you've been sharing your location with Ash all this time?" He sputtered and laughed some more.

"How the hell did you know about that?"

"Everyone," Ava joined in, "knew about that."

"So he was in on this?" I looked at Ash.

Ava went on. "They two were the masterminds of it."

I frowned at Ava.

"Have you ever noticed how Peter sometimes sends you messages and asks how you are enjoying whatever location you're in?"

"Good Lord."

Ava explained that this had been going on for a couple of years.

Sometimes Peter would send a message and ask Ash where I was. Sometimes she would spontaneously offer the information. I smiled thinking of this twist in their relationship.

"And then ran into you two, right here," Ava added.

"Peter, what are you two doing here, anyway?" I asked.

"We're staying here. Got in and took a nap a little while ago."

I chuckled. "You're staying here?"

Of course they were.

"Too lowbrow for you, Jakey?"

"Yes. That's it. I'm staying at a much nicer place."

"Ash's apartment on Huertas?"

"Did I tell you that?"

Peter handed me his phone. There was a message from Ash a few hours earlier.

He just left my apartment on Huertas. Walking past the Palace Hotel. He might run into you.

About to nap, read his reply.

I groaned. Scrolling up a ways there was talk of he and Ava staying there, and of my being at Vingården i Klagshamn the day before. Good God, it really had just been the day before. Somehow the world seemed less small and more as if I were a hapless creature being toyed with. It also seemed that Ash and I sharing a drink here was not accidental. I wondered what the two of them would talk about now their jig was up.

The bottle ran dry. I needed to get off some work to people on the East Coast. I also needed a nap. It was unclear which would come first, but both were required before evening commenced.

Peter ordered a bottle of Toro. I offered to pay for Ash and me. He told me that splitting checks was for losers. I winked at Ash, and left the three of them to it. The apartment on Huertas was just a few minutes' walk away.

Chapter Eighteen

The sun had nearly set when I awoke hours later, wiping away exhaustion as if it were a tangible object as I ran my hand across my face. I had not meant to sleep so long. Two days filled with the train to Malmö, midday at Klagshamn, walking everywhere about Copenhagen, the flight, and drinking at the Palace had finished me.

A message from Ash glowed back at me from my phone.

Now you can see me. I guess this is true romance nowadays.

I smiled. She had shared her location with me. *Permanently?* I wondered. It was so unlike her to do anything permanently.

Her blue dot pulsed on the screen just up Huertas. I showered and went out. Ten past nine o'clock. I'd arrive for dinner as planned. The air had cooled a bit.

Peter had somehow marshaled the crowd, and Ash had led them to Alimentación Quiroga, a popular neighborhood haunt that doubled as a fine market and typically overflowed with people in the evenings. It was a modern place: colorful painting on the wall, exposed ducts hanging from the ceiling, cheese cases, an island bar in the center of the room over which towered a rack of wine bottles for sale from the market. I loved it there.

I was astonished to find them all in the back, loosely mingled and celebrating around a set of tables that they had claimed as a basecamp. Ash, Peter, Erik, Emma, even Billy Grant.

I came first to Peter and asked, "How in God's name did you get these tables at this hour?"

He grinned, red wine on his lips. "We've been here for hours. Where the hell have you been?"

"Good Lord."

"Napping! He's been napping!" Ash pecked my cheek and put a glass of cava in my hand.

Emma ordered a new glass from the waiter. "Spanish, Chris, Spanish. I'm just set up here speaking my trashy island Spanish."

I laughed. She was so genuinely witty, even with the wine.

"Trashy island Spanish? Where are you from, anyway?" Billy looked at Emma.

"My father is Cuban. My mother is Finnish. I grew up in the Ohio."

"Oh, I see."

Emma asked Ash how she had come to speak Castilian rather than whatever brand of Colombian dialect Emma assumed Ash's long-dead father must have spoken.

Ash replied that she was a "proper sort."

"Oh, go to hell!" Emma snapped. "But seriously, you sound like a fool when you talk like that." She made a long, hissing *thhhhhh* sound and took a sip from her new glass. "You could learn something from my trashy island Spanish. English in school, trashy island Spanish on the street."

Erik piped, "My love. Your grandfather would say 'Swedish in school, Finnish on the street.'"

"Fuck off," she said, and then they exchanged a lingering kiss.

She was clearly carrying on about this because of some earlier discussion before I arrived. I realized that Emma and Ash didn't know each other well. Ash explained to Emma and Billy that her father had bought property in Spain, and left it to her when he died. There had also been money to send her to school. She had lived here with her mother for a time as a child.

Billy asked her where she had found the rest of us.

"Weren't you studying abroad?"

Erik finally broke away. "Hello, sir!" We hugged.

"Wait, wait." Billy laughed. "You're telling me that you met these people while you were studying abroad. In the United States?"

"No, you idiot. I was studying abroad in Spain."

He laughed even harder.

"So, you're an American who lived in Spain, then went to the States for uni, only to study abroad back in Spain?"

"We moved back to the States years earlier, before my stepfather," Ash clarified.

"That's hilarious."

"Why?"

"Well, consider it another way. I have an American second cousin or something, he's in uni now, studying 'abroad' in DC." Billy paused for comprehension and quickly went on. "And it just cracks me up that the kid can do a year abroad in DC. That Southern Confederacy thing still sticking around. 'Oh, goin' up to a foreign country! Goin' up north! Wonder if I need to change my money?' I mean, it's designed to give you a new perspective."

"An Englishman lecturing me on new perspectives?" Ash cocked her smile in Billy's direction.

Erik, ever reasonable, said, "Well, I mean, he did move from England to work behind a bar."

"Joselito has a hell of a nice bar," I suggested.

"I've been in the country ten years and I am still not a permanent resident. I'm a provisional-permanent resident. Kind of oxymoronic, like *Great* Britain or *Ultimate* Frisbee or Make America Great *Again*." Billy abruptly changed the subject. "Alright, so you met these people studying abroad. Which one?"

"Chris and Ava. Then Erik shortly thereafter."

"Jesus, they were all in Spain? Who the hell are you people?"

"Chris had just gotten out of the Coast Guard," Erik clarified.

"He putzed around Spain for a month. Ava came to visit him, then I came sometime later, just to visit."

"I wouldn't say that I putzed. Hey, Peter, where *is* Ava, anyway?"

"She's sleeping."

"Sleeping?"

"Yeah, she felt terrible. The flight over was really hard for her. Says that her side is really sore."

"That's no good."

"She'll be fine in the morning. Just needs to sleep."

Erik asked what we should do the next day.

"Let's have an easy day."

"An easy day? We came all the way here to have an easy day?"

"We've got time."

"Speak for yourself. I've got to get up to London to visit my mum."

"You'll stay. You'll not be able to help it."

"We'll see."

It was ghastly hot in there. We ordered more cava and vino tinto and all manner of things, including *tosta de aguacate*—avocado toast—which was quite expensive. I wondered whether avocado toast was the reason I hadn't bought a house back in the States. But then I also considered that I didn't need much. If the suitcase out of which I spent most of my life living was, well, good enough for most of my life, what need did I have for more things?

The colors of the big painting on the wall glowed with the halo of the lamps and the twinkling Christmas lights wrapped around a bush in the corner. And the evening went on and on until I thought Erik might fall asleep. Billy had been drinking coffee for at least an hour. Peter wandered back to the Palace Hotel, the rest of us to some or another place on Huertas.

And there it was, a night that we might replicate again and again as if every night were just an extension of the last. There we were, in the continent's second-largest city, the city that never seemed to sleep until after sunrise, the city that had once ruled an empire to rival all the empires the world had ever known. Madrid, big and beautiful, old to American eyes, young to Europeans. Its beautiful little cobblestone alleys filled with Spanish chatter and motorbikes delivering sushi. Madrid. The global capital to the country that had made right after all those years. My head hit the pillow in that little top-floor flat, and I was filled with all the excitement in the world just to be falling asleep in Madrid.

Chapter Nineteen

There was a point in the midmorning hours sometime after the sun had come up that my arms emptied as Ash crawled out of bed. In Sweden I'd have felt compelled to be up hours earlier, but it felt unjust to wake so early only to sit at my computer and work in the pitch black—the sun didn't rise in Madrid until after eight o'clock—whilst my colleagues back west slept soundly.

I asked Ash where she was going.

"Oh, lover, I'd not trade a thing for our night last night."

"So, don't trade, and come back here."

"Hmmmm," she mumbled noncommittally, as if she had someplace to be.

"We never did make it to Champis last night?"

"Is that a question, or do you really not recall?" she giggled.

"No, I recall. We never made it to Champis."

"No, we didn't. Tonight, maybe."

I felt bad. Perhaps this was the first time in my life that I had not spent my first night in Madrid in that little tavern.

Ash milled about pretending to do things and then crawled back from whence she had come. It was after nine o'clock. We rolled around a bit and said things to one another and then eventually parted ways. I went down to El Diario at the corner, my favorite place to drink café con leche and write. Could have been email, could have been a novel. I didn't much care. I was getting something accomplished, and that seemed good enough. Ash stopped by and we talked about what our friends were up to. It was without conclusion, and she rode off on a bicycle she had purchased days earlier. We'd find our friends eventually. The longer from that moment the better, because God knew I had work to do.

So, I worked feverishly until one o'clock when a message came in from Erik. We went to lunch on the little terrace just across the street from the Cortes. It was the same place at which I had drank that glass of wine alone the previous day, before finding Ash in the gardens.

"Quite a night last night!"

"You're always exclaiming something, you know that?"

Erik laughed. "It was an exclamatory night."

"It's always an exclamatory night when Pete's around. Who paid, anyway?"

"Peter."

"Of course." I felt badly, and decided that I meant to take him out to something special whilst we were here. He really was very generous.

Sounds of laughter and skateboarding and wineglasses wafting through the plaza cheered me.

"Let's walk up to Plaza Mayor," I said. "I've been sequestered away working all morning, and I can't believe I've not yet been up there. Have you been working, too?"

"Yes."

"What is it with us?"

"It's what we do."

"Always working and never working at all?"

"How the folks back in West Virginia would scratch their heads at us."

"They're good folks," I said.

It occurred to me that Erik was my oldest friend. We'd followed such similar paths over more than a quarter century together. That small country town. Each to one of America's two oldest colleges. The Navy and the Coast Guard. Software. And here we sat drinking wine on a plaza in Madrid at half past one in the afternoon on a sunny Tuesday in July.

Peter and Ava came out from the Palace Hotel and saw us sitting beneath an umbrella across the street.

I asked Ava how she was feeling.

"Better," she said.

"But still hurting a bit," Peter jumped in. He sounded almost tender. He really did love her. In that moment seeing him put his arm around her as they stood in front of us, I felt truly happy for the way it had all worked out. She forced a smile, and I could tell that Peter was right. She was still hurting.

"Chris and I were just about to walk up to Plaza Mayor."

"What are you two up to?" I asked.

"Futzed about a bit this morning, thought we might have some lunch."

"Or some coffee," Ava elaborated.

"Or both."

"Well, we've already eaten, but I suppose we could eat again."

"You two walk up; we'll find something."

Ava asked Erik and I if we were working this afternoon.

"Probably."

"Tapas and such after work then?"

"Let's do it."

"Where's Ash? And Emma?"

"Hell if I—"

Erik cut me off. "They're together, actually."

"Out speaking trashy island Spanish?" Peter laughed.

"Or bickering about it, that's for damned sure."

We laughed. Nobody knew where Billy was. It was nice having nothing to do and not having to worry about everyone's whereabouts or plans.

Erik and I doubled back down a few blocks and took the walk up Huertas to Plaza Mayor. There were people all about. Huertas slopes gently up a hill, westward from the Paseo del Prado down by the train station towards the two grand plazas at the city's center. Quotes and profound things once said by various famous Spaniards were etched in brass into the cobblestones. I commented on one, and somehow that brought Erik and I back to our conversation before Peter and Ava had turned up.

It conflicted us, having left that old town behind. Neither of us came *from* there, and I suspected neither of us were *local* there any longer. Like a ship in a bottle placed upon the mantle of our collective recollections, experiences that informed our thinking about the world, yet felt completely foreign in the world we now occupied. Billy Grant hadn't gotten it right; Washington and New York and Boston and all the great American cities in which we ran about were as foreign from that little West Virginia town as that little West Virginia town was from Madrid.

We wondered if we ought to be dismayed by this.

"How to sort it all out?"

I thought about Erik's question. "Go ask Peter," I chuckled. "Pete's got an answer for everything."

"I'll bet."

I asked, "Why sort it all out, anyway?"

Erik looked at me quizzically.

"Seriously, what makes you think it's within our power to do?" I thought of my discussion with Geoff, about elites and changing the world.

"Aren't you the one who has always felt that it wasn't just some empty gesture that time the old man fixed your car?"

"You've got me there."

We detoured onto Calle del Príncipe.

"Do you remember when we discovered this place together?" Erik asked as we entered the small plaza.

All those years coming to Madrid as a child, and it had not been until my twenties that Erik and I had stumbled upon Plaza de Santa Ana.

"That was the time we told Billy about last night."

"The time we met Ash."

"Yes, well, we didn't meet her here. But yes."

"No, but we were in Spain."

Now there was a Five Guys in the plaza. Time marches on, and if you're not careful, the most hallowed places will blend in with the terrain over which progress has run amok.

"I tend to be both very into feeling important yet rather disdainful of people who think that they are important." I jerked us back to our meandering discussion as we walked on back up Huertas.

"Sounds hypocritical."

"Sometimes hypocrisy can be considered in a different light when its nature is reversed."

"How do you mean?"

"Well, it's a thought experiment." I paused. "Consider the idea that one person can change the world."

"Yes?"

"Well, that's pretty absurd, isn't it? It's totally elitist to be so arrogant to imagine that you can change the world. As if just because I'm educated, and in with the crowd, somehow that makes me capable of shaping events of which I only understand a fraction."

"Or can control." Erik was such a rational fellow.

"Yes, yes," I hurried on. "All hail the upper middle class. Graduate of elitist places. A straight, white man in America."

"And yet?"

"And yet," I said hopefully, "I aspire to change the world."

"How is that not hypocritical?"

"You're the one who put me up to it." I looked at him. "How the hell did you turn this around on me?"

Erik laughed.

"It's all about perspective, Erik—the humility of knowing that you are small. Dreaming that you might overcome that smallness is a different story entirely from being so arrogant to think that you are large. That's what separates self-entitlement from the meaningful acts that really move us forward."

"Is that why you're going to go back to work in an hour?"

"Maybe."

We walked in silence for a moment.

"I don't know," I admitted. "I hadn't expected all this to come out."

"You were just waiting for a moment alone together?" He grinned wryly.

"That's right," I said most sincerely. "That's actually exactly it."

"So, is this what's been bothering you?"

"I don't know."

It just seemed such a waste that we should have come from that little town and wound up here with nothing to show for the privilege.

"Harold Macmillan, the British prime minister, had a notion about miners being the best people."

"Now that sounds like something you'd say." I laughed at him, but I got the point. "This is about loving your countrymen for who they are, for the blood and sweat that they've given to a country they love just as much as you do."

This seemed about as satisfactory a conclusion to the discussion as we'd find today. I really loved our talks, even when they had nowhere practical to go.

We sloped down just a bit and entered Plaza Mayor through the towering archway in its southeast corner. Roaming street vendors launched silly little helicopters and spit out strange chirping sounds as they tried to sell the flying toys to the parents of children running about in the square. Tourists gorged themselves on lunch at the mediocre terrace restaurants that lined up under the arcade encircling the old rectangle of a space. The equestrian statue of King Phillip III in the center contrasted with the azure sky above the plaza's spires. What an unremarkable ruler he had been.

This had once been my favorite place on earth. Before the sound of old men and their accordions had given way to the sound of young men selling toys. Before I was old enough to know how mediocre the food was. Back when I meandered about the square with my grandparents, discovering the city for the first time. I still smiled at the thought of it. Erik and I walked about the perimeter and out the southwest *puerta*, down the stairs to Calle Cava de San Miguel where I'd once snapped the picture of my grandfather sitting atop the concrete orbs that kept cars off the sidewalks.

We turned the sharpest of rights, doubling back up the street. Mesón del Champiñón—*Champis*, we called it—was on the right. We didn't go in, though I promised myself we'd return that night. These little taverns, the *mesónes*, lined the street. We stepped inside Mercado de San Miguel. Vendors inside the fully glassed-in market took orders from the counters of well-appointed stalls as people milled about mixing and matching their lunches. A *croqueta* here, a piece of fish there, a glass of sangría from that place over yonder, then ambling off to fight the crowd for a table in the corner.

We had a drink and some early tapas. It was a lovely time with my old friend, and I had no desire to return to work. We promised each other that we'd take a few days of proper vacation now, the kind where we diverted our work email to special folders to avoid interruption.

"Like my *dicks* folder," I said wryly.

"Pardon?"

"I have a rule in my email that diverts messages from people I don't like into a special folder, so they never touch my inbox. The folder is called *dicks*."

Erik choked on his wine in laughter.

"Swear to God," I promised him.

"That's brilliant."

"Thanks."

We finished our wine and returned to work in our flats.

Chapter Twenty

I worked torridly through the afternoon, eager to squeeze days' worth of productivity into hours. Hours seemed like days and nothing at all. I had come to Spain determined to have a proper holiday with these people I had dragged here. The invisible office corridor that linked Madrid to Washington to Stockholm to Hyderabad and Seattle and Singapore hummed with life until around six o'clock when I decided it had to be good enough. I put up an out-of-office message alerting all who might try to find me that I was missing. It felt liberating to step out on Huertas having just deleted my entire work account from my phone, like a rocket or plane having slipped the surly bonds of earth. Huertas was my path to freedom, the vast expanse of this glistening city, and my unexplored beyond. *Goodbye to all that.* I smiled.

I retraced the steps I had walked with Erik earlier that day. Up Huertas. Through Plaza de Santa Ana. One of those fellows delivering sushi zipped past on a motorbike. Then into Plaza Mayor. Under the archway of the same puerta through which I always entered. There I stood, exalting in the light of the golden hour in the center of the centuries-old square that had been my favorite place in the world for much of my life.

It is unclear how long I spent there, looking up at the statue and the spires and the silly little carnival toys floating down. The light of the long summer evening shining radiantly on my face.

I walked on, back down the steps to Calle Cava de San Miguel, back past Champis. I lingered at the door, and for the second time that day contemplated whether to go in. Cheerful music from Juan's electric keyboard and synthesized tracks wafted out from the inner tavern just onto the street. It was otherwise still quiet, so I went in. Jose worked behind the bar counter. He lit up when he saw me, as he always had. Year after year, it always astonished me that he still worked here.

"*¡Hola! ¡Mi amigo! ¿Qué tal?*" Always this was his greeting, firmly shaking my hand from the other side of the bar.

We spoke in Spanish for a moment. He plunked a glass of sangría down on the bar in front of me. It had become too sweet for me over the years, but I drank thirstily. Nostalgia for simpler times or respite from summer heat? I could not tell which. I promised him that I would return later with friends, and left again when my glass was empty.

A message from Ava.

Tapas?

Yes. Where?

Peter doesn't want to go back to Quiroga tonight. Wants something else.

Lavapiés?

Bien. Veinte minutos. Te veo.

I walked to the crest of the hill where Calle Cava de San Miguel meets Calle Mayor, at the corner upon which sits the *mercado* where Erik and I had walked about that afternoon. It all seemed new again, looking with eyes made fresh by the notion that I'd not be returning to work for a bit. Calle Mayor sloped back down again to Puerta del Sol. Throngs gathered here, bright lights like Times Square in Madrid, the figurative center of Spain. A bronze plaque inlaid in the sidewalk in front of the old post office marked the point from which the Spanish roads and highways marked their ascending kilometers emanating out from the capital.

I thought forlornly about the Iraq War protests I had seen here in the aftermath of the train bombings at Atocha fourteen years earlier. I recalled angrily the moment years later sitting with Peter on a train at that very spot, listening in mortified horror as he pontificated on the power of his American passport. And I remembered the exasperated glances I'd once thrown at the protesters I'd seen here demonstrating in support of a Spanish republic and the downfall of the monarchy, and the pride in my quasi-adopted country at seeing its people fill the streets, rediscovering their sense of nation and waving their flag in defiance of Catalan separatism.

"You have bizarrely certain opinions of Spanish politics for someone who never actually lived there," Ava had once told me.

Looking back to the square, I was happy again, remembering cold winter nights galivanting with Ava under the twinkling lights of the enormous Christmas tree that was erected here each year. Time was short. I walked beneath the street and hopped the metro's *línea tres* one stop south to Lavapiés.

In Lavapiés there were more people out on the street, crowding onto terraces and overflowing from little restaurants and bars. Some years earlier this would not have been a place around which my grandparents would approve me walking. Now it had become a place where hipsters and immigrants and old-timers folded in on each other, like waves washing over one another and rolling down the proverbial sands of the oddly steep city streets and gentrifying tenements.

Ava and Peter were waiting for me at La Fisna, a little wine bar on Calle del Amparo. I poured something Galician from the bottle into an empty glass they had waiting for me. There was an empty stool at their table.

"How did you find this place?"

Ava shrugged.

"We went walking," Peter offered. "Couldn't stand to see the love of my life cooped up in the hotel for another beautiful evening."

"I do feel better with the air," Ava suggested. "Actually, I've been feeling better and better."

"Nasty jet lag?"

"Something. Nasty way of sleeping on the plane."

"That says a hell of a lot. How'd you ever make it back in the day when you had to fly in the back with the peasants?"

"The proletariat," Peter corrected, dripping with disdain that he didn't even recognize.

"You're a Marxist prick, you know that?" I joked in response.

"I'm very lucky to have what I do," Ava clarified, casting a disapproving glance in Pete's direction. "But I still don't sleep well on planes."

It was a lovely place. Wooden shutters covering large doors were open wide to the warm evening. It felt as if we were outside. I was happy to be there just the three of us. It seemed possible we'd not have another moment like this.

"You and Erik solve all the problems of the world this afternoon?" Peter helped himself to more wine.

"As is their wont," Ava laughed.

"Indeed. Though I'm not sure what. We didn't accomplish anything."

"You've been working like a fiend since we showed up," Peter admonished. "I hope you accomplished *something*."

"Well, surely at work, but nothing of the likes Erik and I talked about. Besides, I'm done. I've quit for the duration. Now I'm on vacation!"

"Damn time."

"Seriously, though, what *were* you two talking about so intensely?" Ava asked.

"Do you have to ask?"

"Will I regret it?"

"Probably." I paused. "Either because of me. Or because of him."
I gestured at Peter.

"Oh God," she groaned.

"And?" Peter grew impatient.

"Changing the world stuff?" she asked.

"Liberal do-good nonsense, hmm?"

"Well, at least we agree on the nonsense part," I retorted, attempting bridge building.

"You two sound like socialists when you talk, you know that?"

"Please no," Ava pleaded.

I laughed it off.

"Too much time in Sweden." Peter grinned and poured himself more wine.

"I fail to see the connection."

"They're all socialists there. Damned Scandinavian socialists."

"That's factually untrue," I said. "Though I am impressed that you know where Scandinavia is."

"Go to hell." For a moment Pete's eyes betrayed that he was considering the idea that *hell* might be a bridge too far for his best friend. "Don't go to hell, but for Christ's sake get a grip on yourself, man. You're too smart to be one of those damned *millennial socialists*. And that's what they are. They're crazy."

"They're coming for you, you know that, right?"

Ava cast her piercingly cold eyes in my direction, silently pleading with me to end this before it went any further.

So I ended it. Happy coincidence it was that Ash should pull up on her bike that very moment. She leaned in through the open doors.

"Hola!" she greeted us, ordering a glass of something she'd been craving whilst she dismounted her bike and left it to rest upright against a brick wall. Ava told her that she'd not have imagined being happier to see her.

"Oh?"

The girls looked at one another. Ava, knowingly, until a look of feigned horror formed on Ash's face.

"Oh, oh God." Ash glared at me. "You are stupid! Why the hell would you say things like that?"

I giggled. "You're the one who loves to goad him on."

"Well, that's true." Lopsided grin forming. "It's fun."

"Go to hell, Ash." Peter fidgeted and looked the other way.

Ever so briefly I mentioned Pete's accusation of millennial socialism to Ash. She snorted with laughter.

We drank more wine.

"Where have you been all day?" I asked her.

"Emma and I were off with *my* friends."

"Your friends?"

"A fellow named Bustamante. He has a tea company up in Malasaña."

"That's only one friend," Peter goaded.

"Well, he has friends. Emma and I went to see him, and there were others."

"No invitation for us?"

"I didn't feel like speaking English."

I laughed loudly. "That's a hell of a lot more charitable than you were being to Emma last night."

"My friend is from Venezuela."

"I see."

"You'd like him."

"Let's meet him, then!" I suggested.

"You'll do—you and your trashy imitation Spanish."

"I try hard."

"You do, you really do. I'd not be with you otherwise."

"Well, will you look at that," Peter jested. "She's finally admitted to being *with* you."

"Is it hard being such a reliable jackass each day?" Ash glared, eyes narrowed.

Our phones vibrated in unison on the table. Ava sighed in relief. *Quiroga!* From Erik.

"I really do enjoy you three," I said. "I'll actually be sad to break up this little group for the evening."

Peter returned the message. *I don't want to go to Quiroga again tonight.*

Erik shot back, *Here with Emma and Billy. We have table space. Come quickly.*

The other three of us stood. Peter had lost this round. We trudged up the steep hill back to Huertas. Ash walked with her bike, and left it inside at the flat.

⁕

At Quiroga it was as if nobody had ever left the night before. A beautiful girl from South America brought us *tostas* and chatted idly with me about how she'd like to go to New York. I picked several bottles of wine from the rack in the center of the room, insisting that I'd pay tonight.

Peter proclaimed loudly, "Well, at least one of you isn't a complete freeloader!"

"Peter accused you and Chris of being *millennial socialists* earlier," Ash flatly said to Erik.

"They are!" Emma shot back.

Ava glared that hateful glare at my girlfriend. I cracked up laughing, awestruck by Ash's capacity for manipulation and catty backstabbing. It was less than an hour ago that she had seduced Ava into thinking they were allies in the interest of keeping Peter from blowing up the evening. Though Ash had just wanted to delay the action until more could join it.

"Why are you so obnoxious?" Billy asked her.

"It's sporting."

"Socrates would push arguments and keep pushing," the Englishman went on. "So annoyingly that rightly in the end he was put to death because he was, in fact, quite irritating."

"Ava and Peter have got a dog named Socrates."

"Interesting?"

"I'm hardly a socialist," Erik exclaimed matter-of-factly. "I'm barely a liberal."

"We call them *progressives* now," I corrected. He looked at me skeptically.

"Bullshit," Peter said. "You're just like that crazy girl who just got herself elected in New York."

"Please, *girl*, she's only five years younger than you are. Hell, she's older than Ash."

"And just as obnoxious," Peter said.

"You're like a lawn mower, you know that?" Peter looked at me, dumbfounded and waiting for me to elaborate. "It's true," I said. "Just pull the cord and you'll start right up again."

"Why do you let her get the best of you like that?" Ava asked her husband. "She's just trying to provoke you into saying something foolish."

Erik returned to the point. "You're aware that *you* are the one who created that *crazy girl* from New York, right?"

"Now, wait." Emma tried to jump in.

"You too," Erik told his girlfriend. "Hell, maybe I created her, too."

"I see where he's going," I said.

"Right."

I continued the idea. "Listen, if enough people think the system is broken, then it doesn't matter what good ideas you think you had when you created or perpetuated it. It doesn't matter how you feel about some dead conservative president from an idolized past you barely remember. It doesn't matter whether he or you or anyone in between was right or wrong, then or now. It just doesn't fucking matter."

"But, Jake, we live in a time of abundance because of the system," Peter protested.

"*You* live in a time of abundance. To be reasonable, everyone at this table lives in a time of abundance."

"I'm a goddamned bartender," Billy interjected.

"Well, in fairness, you're a sommelier."

"And just look at how much those get paid," Billy said.

"Valid."

"Listen," Erik began again before Peter cut him off.

"Stop the hell telling me to listen! This isn't a listening problem." Erik barreled on, undeterred now. He was the smartest and ostensibly most reasonable of us all.

"The point is that it doesn't matter what you think is a right or wrong idea. When you fail to create a better vision, when we're living life in our beautiful homes and flying first class whenever we leave them, when we fail to give people any alternative to whatever form of hopelessness they have, then someone, something, some idea *will* emerge. And you might not like it, but *you*, well—not you personally— but you, you had your chance and didn't produce a better vision."

"But it's wrong!" Peter doubled down. "Those people disregard decades of—" He was really getting worked up. Suddenly I became so concerned with his gesticulating and swinging around of arms in these close quarters that I didn't hear the point he was making.

"What sorts of hopelessness," I finally heard Peter ask. I'd have given him credit for asking, but I knew he'd just argue with whatever Erik said.

I jumped in, imagining that I could be reasonable about all this. "The immense debt most folks take to go to college? Precariousness of the places too many people, even educated ones with mountains of debt, find themselves working? The fact that I can't buy a house in my own city?"

"You can buy a house in your own city," Peter insisted.

"I work in software."

Erik cut in again. "Peter, most of these kids have no memory of Communism. No idea why or even that it failed. But we're surrounded by the failures of capitalism."

"And listen," I began again, "I'm a committed capitalist, but the fact is that it's broken. Wealthy people like you—hell, maybe me too—we ruined it. It needs to be fixed if it's going to survive."

I piped down and went back to the thoughts overflowing from my nearly empty glass. Peter and Erik bantered on for a few more moments. Ava looked horrified. Emma sat silently, dejected and muted. Ash and Billy had turned to their own unrelated conversation, like ne'er-do-wells who had just yelled "Fire!" in a theater before walking out the door to let the place roil in chaos.

I, on the other hand, was comforted by the discussion. There was something reassuring to me about the idea that so many people my age—younger, even— should be so committed. The only sense of peace I had with the whole ghastly affair those last couple of years was the sense that great swaths of society were building a world in which they'd actually want to live, rather than imitating their parents, who had even at their best only ever managed to avert the next immediate catastrophe. If I was bitter about anything, it was that at nearly thirty-five years old I was the oldest of the first generation in American history who had been left a country in worse shape than what the previous generation had inherited. Our grandparents had defeated fascists and communists, and our parents had squandered the spoils in smug self-satisfaction.

Then it happened, unfolding in what seemed slow motion to my eyes. I don't even recall what Erik said. Pete's eyes opened wide. His agitation crescendoed. And in a fluid motion he threw his arms to the side, wildly gesticulating once again, and he smacked a passing waiter in the face.

"Peter!" Ava yelled.

He grinned.

I apologized profusely to the waiter. The fellow assured me it was all right. I ordered two more bottles for the group and assured him we'd change the subject. He told me it was too loud in there for anyone to have noticed other than the moment Peter socked him in the face.

Billy nearly fell off his stool, laughing wildly and choking out some British idiom that nobody understood.

I helped the waiter recharge all the glasses.

"Good Lord, did you really need to order more wine?" Ava asked me.

"Yes."

"Why?" she hissed.

"Listen, if we leave too hastily, it will look like we caused a scene."

"He's right." Billy was still laughing. "Just have some more wine and it will all look like an accident."

"It *was* an accident," Peter insisted, chuckling. "I really feel badly. I didn't mean to hit the man."

"Wasn't an accident for Ash," Ava said coldly. "I hope *you're* happy."

Ash flashed her adorable crooked smile and looked away at Billy. I asked her if she could just behave the rest of the night.

"Oh, I'm mission accomplished," she replied.

So, we drank the bottles and talked about what we planned to do the next day now that Erik and I had declared ourselves to be on vacation.

"Time for Champis!" I announced when the bottles were empty.

"Please behave there."

"There will be music and Juan and Jose and it will be great fun," I promised.

I paid the check. We set off in a pack, stringing down the street in little groups. Erik and Ava and I at the front. Then Billy and Ash prancing around behind us. Peter and Emma commiserating with one another in the back.

We paraded through Plaza Mayor. It was the third time I had walked this way that day. Down the steps. Out to Calle Cava de San Miguel. Into Champis, which was now packed with tourists from Asia and a crowd of American-looking people sitting in the corner.

"Pilots," I said to Peter.

"Pardon?"

"Those people at that table, they're pilots. American pilots. Somehow this became a pilot bar over the last ten years or so."

Ava gave one of them a hug. The fellow started talking at me as if I were her husband. It happened that he and Ava had gone to officer candidate school together back in the Coast Guard. He just assumed that she and I were still together. I introduced him to Peter and moved on.

Ash and Emma were out at the bar chatting up Jose. I joined them. Jose hurriedly plunked a glass of sangría down on the bar. He told Emma that he remembered the day I first walked in with my grandparents, almost twenty-five years earlier.

"He's a regular here!"

I looked bashfully at the bar, trying to conceal how happy I was that someone of whom I'd been so fond since childhood would call me a regular. I felt *local*. Life is full of simple pleasures.

"Jose's been working here for, what? How many years?"

"At least a hundred!" one of his younger compatriots blurted out as he sliced *jamón ibérico* from the pig's leg hanging proudly on the wall.

"Forty years?" I asked.

"More or less," he said, pointing at a picture hanging on the wall over the stairs. A much younger Jose stood behind the bar of a barely different Mesón del Champiñón.

I was twenty-one years when I wrote this song.
I'm twenty-two now but I won't be for long. . .

I hummed to myself, wondering if Juan could play us any Paul Simon.

Ava joined us at the bar. Her Spanish was very poor, so she couldn't say much to Jose. She told Emma about walking into the place with me for the first time over ten years earlier. I think she was twenty-two—maybe twenty-three. We were young, then. Time had not yet hurried on.

Suddenly I felt a bit overwhelmed. My eyes welled up thinking about the little bits of life I had happily passed in this little hole cut into the wall below Plaza Mayor.

Ava walked away and beckoned us back into the tavern where Peter, Erik, and Billy had incredibly managed to lay claim to the table just now being vacated by Ava's pilot friends. I ran into Juan at the door. He hugged me as he stepped out from his music to have a cigarette with Ash on the street. She didn't smoke often, and I did find there to be something irresistibly sexy about kissing a beautiful girl after she'd smoked just one. At least, I felt that way when I had been drinking too much wine. She grabbed the back of my head and kissed me passionately in the doorway before giddily prancing off with the older fellow. I sat on one of the little stools around our newly acquired table.

"Do you know Paul Simon?" I asked Juan when they returned.

He did not.

"Elton John?"

He played "Crocodile Rock." Of course! It was a perfect fit.

"Want to come with Peter and me to see Elton?" Ash asked me. "We're going in October."

"Farewell tour."

"Goodbye, yellow brick road," I started singing.

Erik fidgeted on his stool, the two of us unable to resist the same impulse that had summoned us to the front of the room at Geoff's party earlier that month.

"It's a sad year," he said. "Paul, Elton, here at the end."

"Elton's taking his good sweet time saying goodbye," I told him. "I think this is a three-year tour or something. I plan to go see him in Sweden next year."

"I'm happy we were old enough to be part of it all. All these years. You know? Old enough to have been there?"

"Old enough to legitimately claim we were alive when Graceland came out?"

"Barely. Eighty-six."

"I remember eighty-six," Peter insisted.

"You were three!"

He laughed.

"It is true of this generation," Ava began, "that we were young enough for them to have been around our entire lives, old enough to remember them when they were still young."

"Relatively, I guess. Easy to still be young in your late thirties when you're still kicking in your seventies."

"We talking about Elton or Paul?"

"Does it matter?"

"I think Paul is older than Elton."

"Either way." Peter poured more sangría from the *jarra* and raised his glass. "May we be so lucky."

"Cheers." We all agreed.

Time hurries on.
And the leaves that are green turn to brown. . .

I hummed quietly to myself.

Juan played Bon Jovi.

"Juan Bon Jovi!" Emma giggled on her sangría.

A group of Madrileños crowded around the tables in the opposite corner of the tavern, singing and carrying on. The Asians who were scattered all about at the other tables quietly drank their cervezas and sangrías. One of the Madrileños asked Juan to play a song that I didn't recognize. Then Erik asked him for something. It was as if our two groups in opposite corners of the bar were conspiring to make the night last, partners in keeping the party going. A few more songs and we were all up, roaming about the place and singing together, clapping one another on the back and laughing, drinking.

Somehow Peter and I befriended a Spanish girl who told us she had once lived in New York. This intrigued us, for in our state it seemed like bizarre good luck that we should chance to run in to anyone who had ever lived in such a small unknown place as that. She spoke impeccable English. I was slurring my Spanish. Ash joined us at the bar. The girl begged her to make me stop speaking in Spanish, saying that she had lived in Madrid all her life and couldn't understand a damned word that I said. Peter laughed uproariously and dragged me away as Ash consecrated her new friendship over beer and fried mushrooms.

Juan played on back in the tavern. His basket overflowed with euros. Ava was kissing Peter. Emma was merrily dancing about with Billy. Everyone was happy.

"Do you know 'Sweet Caroline'?" Erik asked one of the Madrileños.

"What?" she shouted back, struggling to hear.

"'Sweet Caroline'? The song! Neil Diamond."

She did not know it.

"Juan!" I spoke up. "Do know 'Sweet Caroline'? The song?"

He began to play.

At first it was only us Americans who sang. We knew all the words. Some other Americans near the bar sang along with us.

"Where it began, I can't begin to knowing. . . "

But then we knew it was growing strong.

Those who knew the song sang. Those who didn't know the song drank.

Then spring became the summer
Who'd have believed you'd come along?

I looked at Ash. She seemed oblivious to the notion I had at just that moment—that given enough to drink, almost any song could seem an eerily appropriate description of something important in one's own life. It was as if the key to good songwriting was subtly convincing a throng of borderline alcoholics that you were thinking about them and their own concerns when you wrote the thing.

Hands, touching hands
Reaching out, touching me, touching you. . .

In this instant it occurred to more people that they had at least once heard the words. Some of the Madrileños began to sing, and it seemed the Asians knew the entire refrain.

I'd be inclined
To believe they never would. . .

Then the volume of the room fell by half as the Americans took over for the verse.

A moment later somehow nobody was sitting, and I felt badly for the ruckus of mingling strangers and spilled sangría that we had caused. It was hot, and we were drunk, and that was the night we taught the Madrileños and the Asian tourists the words to "Sweet Caroline." We stumbled off merrily into the night, promising strangers who we'd never again see that we'd look them up again. Good times had never seemed so good.

<hr/>

Erik and I led the procession back to Huertas, singing to ourselves and embarrassing the ladies.

"And then we were all in one place!"

"*The next* generation, lost in space!"

"May your fist not be clenched with rage, old friend," he slurred, though I was mostly all right.

I laughed. "My fist? I'm not the one who assaulted a waiter tonight."

Even Ava cracked a smile at this.

Ash kissed me up the stairs to our flat. We rolled through the door together. Back there, alone, together coming down from the high of our night out in Madrid. Here in Madrid where we had come to pretend that this was a normal life. Come with our friends, imperfect a group as they may be. Come to ignore the news and escape our world back home.

I knew that Ava was still angry with her.

But I didn't care.

In that moment alone with Ash there seemed no right or wrong. All I felt was what there was. One of those moments when you look into her eyes and you see the beginning and the end and all that comes between those two things. And on every other point, not much caring what consequences there may be. You know only that you love her, and she is for you and you are for her and there are no other things or considerations to be had. Consequences be damned. And nothing that either of you have ever done wrong matters. She is the most perfect of all kinds, the one you have sought and labored for, and just be damned and to hell with the rest. This is your moment, your beautiful moment together, and no matter that fucked-up world out there, you both shall have this. And it shall be immovably beautiful for all time. And nothing they ever say can make you give a damn.

This was the moment we had in that little flat in Madrid. And I imagined that it would be immovably brilliant, held in my mind for all time. And nothing the rest of them could say would have made me give a damn. And it was beautiful. And she was beautiful. And for that moment. That beautiful moment in which nothing else mattered; she was beautiful and perfect and none of her imperfections could make me give a damn, for she was what I always imagined her to be. And we were all that either of us had ever hoped we could be. And nothing mattered but the beating of our hearts and the elation of having pulled one another close. Nothing mattered, and there was no one there but us.

Chapter Twenty-One

Ash had run off by the time I remembered anything on the first morning of my proper vacation. Predictably I went down to drink café con leche at El Diario. Ava found me there, and we drank café con leche together. She'd been feeling badly again the night before and had not slept. Coffee, fresh air, and a bit of daylight seemed to lift her up.

"You've become different, you know?" she asked.

"Should I worry?"

"Oh, no. I'm just not accustomed to seeing you drink coffee in a café."

"Good, because this is a bar."

She laughed.

"I always loved that about you."

"What, that I hang out in bars? Because normally too much of things like that could worry a girl."

"No, that you make me laugh."

"Of course I made you laugh. I haven't got much else going for me, so I supposed I'd have to make a girl laugh if she was going to stick around."

"See how well that worked out for you."

We sipped our coffee and existed in this moment of tender fondness whilst Ava felt out how Ash and I were doing together. I knew she was still upset about what Ash had done at Quiroga the night before.

"It's a strange thing, actually."

"What is?" Ava perked up, clearly hoping that I was about to divulge some romantic secret. It is true that I told her almost everything, but in this case I didn't have much to say.

"I worked so hard in my twenties."

"You barely ever seem to work at all."

"Do you really think that?"

"Of course not. I remember all those nights you used to spend with the door closed, working on whatever creation you had when—"

"When what?" I asked softly.

"It doesn't matter." Ava lingered with the cup to her lips.

I must have looked concerned.

"Don't worry about it. All I was saying is that you've done well to appear to everyone else that you do as little work as possible. I'm not sure anyone knows what you do for money, which knowing you is I am sure exactly how you want it."

I chuckled.

"I feel like I missed so much back then."

"In your twenties?"

She laughed. "I have three kids who I left at home to run off to Madrid so we could all pretend together that this is normal life."

I wondered for a moment if we two were destined to share thoughts without words for the rest of time.

"Ten years ago all I wanted to do was work and do well for myself and be the best at whatever I was doing. Guarding coasts. Building software. Leaving some sort of mark on the world."

"You were very serious about it all."

"It was very important to have a pressed uniform. Or to wear tweed to the office and ties out to fancy dinners with the boys."

"To have all the things?"

"All the things."

"And now?"

"Now I'm pretty content to wander the world with a backpack, wear jeans to the office for as much as I go there, and write about whatever comes to me whilst sitting in a café in Madrid."

"Technically it's a bar," she laughed. "But I get it. You looked like you were about to cry last night at Champis when you were reminded of how long Jose had been there and how much of your life you've spent hanging around there."

"What is it with you?"

"What?"

"Why do you know everything?"

"Because I shut up and pay attention, which is more than I can say for most of you."

"Not wrong."

"A little midlife crisis in the age of, well, whatever this is the age of?"

"Something like that. I mean, what the hell are we even doing here? What good does any of it do? How much more aloof to the real problems of the world can we be and do literally *nothing* about any of it?"

We ordered more coffee.

And this was the essence of the days that followed. I passed the mornings drinking café con leche at El Diario. There were visitors each day. Sometimes Ash would come down with me. Sometimes Ava or Peter or Erik or Emma would stop and drink with me. One morning I was surprised to see Billy turn up having heard the night before that this had become the pattern.

In the afternoons we would have lunch and drink wine at Quiroga or some other little café. Afterwards we'd find something to last us until naps in the late afternoon, little duos and trios adventuring out into the city. Ash and I off to little secret places. She had befriended two stray cats we met in the grass by the lake in Retiro Park my first day in town. Later I learned that this was one of her regular destinations by bike, stopping to buy a little can of food from the store just down the street from our flat, then riding over to see her friends in Retiro where she had also made an enemy of a belligerent duck who had grown very fond of ill-begotten cat food.

Billy convinced us to go see Santiago Bernabéu, stadium home to the famed Real Madrid *fútbol* team. Ava and Emma were uninterested. Ash pretended to be disinterested, too. So it was just the boys. We marveled at the trophies piled up in the museum to the world's most successful sporting club, a vainglorious display that would have made the New York Yankees blush with modesty. It would be a lie to say that I was not enthralled. We were all enthralled, and behaved like awestruck schoolboys having just discovered some childhood idol hitherto known only in legend.

Emma, who was new to the city, and Erik, who lived for monuments and museums and all manner of historical and cultural interests, disappeared from time to time, off to see the palace or the Prado or some other thing. One day the three of us went to visit the Congress in Cortes. What a beautiful place it was, bedecked in rich gold and carved wood and red carpets and banners and all the trappings of constitutional monarchy. It really was very striking.

⌒⌒⌒⌒⌒

On Friday evening I went alone to Reina Sofía, the art museum down near the west end of Calle de Atocha, where the road meets the immense traffic circle and its train station. Admission was free on Friday evenings.

I didn't much like art museums, but this was more of a pilgrimage than an art lover's excursion. That's why I had come alone, lest one of the others drag me into some prolonged ordeal perusing every exhibit in the building.

I beelined for the gallery in which hung Picasso's *Guernica* on the long side of the wall.

In it Picasso had forever memorialized the German air force's bombing of the Spanish village called Guernica. The Nazis had done this to support their ally, General Francisco Franco, and his nationalists at the height of the Spanish Civil War. In so doing they had demonstrated the power of their new technology, of fire and chaos rained down from the sky. It was in 1937, end of the calm before the great storm, a terrifying portent of the horror that was to fall upon the world.

There amid the crowd in the center of the room, I stared for perhaps an hour at a painting that I had seen many times but each long stare at which revealed some new secret.

I saw first the woman floating in from the window—or was she the divine, her candle shining light on the ghastly scene? Called down by the nun's cry that absolution be granted to the world shrouded in darkness.

The bull, symbol of its once-great homeland, confused and lost in events that it, though proud, could not control. Protecting the mother, screaming in anguish, her child limp in her arms.

A building burns, engulfing in flames a woman crying out in terror. In her last moment, like the horse in the center, run through with a spear. I had never noticed the spear, never seen it pierce the horse, as if Picasso had added it recently so that I might discover it that night. Such was the nature of *Guernica*; another horror to greet the passerby, another reminder of the world as it was, in its last unheeded moment before the gathering storm.

A soldier, slain and lying upon the ground, his generation condemned. His lifeless expression fixed in fear, gazing to the sky. The sword in his hand broken, a tool of yesterday's battles, useless in the face of today's dangers. And from that hand, a flower, that the world may know new life.

Afterwards I met the group at Quiroga. Each night was a progression of tapas and wine and late dinner. Most gatherings featured some sort of frustrating philosophical debate between Peter, who had long dug in, and Erik, who still held out naïve hope that he might be able to convince Peter to cease his standing athwart history yelling "Stop!" I had, at Ava's quiet request one morning at El Diario, demurred from any further discussions with the two gentlemen. Billy and I drank wine with the girls. We had made quite a sport of trying to learn more about the mystery man we all came to believe Billy was in love with back in Washington. He was not keen to share details aside from that the fellow had gone up to New York and hadn't been seen in weeks.

On one occasion we wandered up to work our way through the cafés and wine bars on Calle Ponzano, near Nuevos Ministerios. It was on that occasion that it occurred to me I had not made firm plans to return to the States, and had no idea when anyone else was leaving, either. It was an uncomfortable realization that we'd have all preferred to stay on in Madrid, though Ava had grown eager to go home to her children. She and the rest had firm plans to return in a few days' time, after we'd been in Spain for around a week and a half. Erik told us he had business in Prague for a few days following our departure from Madrid. This interested me.

"Mind if I join?" I asked.

"Sure!" He was ecstatic.

"How have you not bought a ticket home?" Emma asked. "Don't they cost a fortune to go one way?"

"Jake's got a scheme, no doubt." Peter grinned a wine-stained grin.

"Miles, Emma, miles," I assured her.

Ava rolled her eyes.

"So, are we really going together to Prague?" Erik asked, concerned that it might not work out.

"Why the hell not? I've only been there once."

"How will Ash do?"

"You mean when we're in Prague?"

"Yeah. Isn't she expecting to go home with you?"

"Do *you* think that Ash is planning to go home with me?

"You have a point."

I was worried about Ash. She was nowhere to be found here on Calle Ponzano, and hadn't seemed her bantering self for a couple of days. She'd kissed me the last time I saw her earlier that day, and said she was just tired from all the nights out. Said she needed to be quiet for a moment. But just today she seemed to be feeling worse than Ava, who had felt on and off badly the entire trip.

It was also on this occasion, up here on Calle Ponzano, that Ava and I decided that we were sad to have not been to a winery since we arrived. In truth, none of us had even left Madrid save for the day before when several of us went out to El Escorial. I loved El Escorial. Loved the architecture, the conscious collision of monastery and palace, the splendor of the library, or the crypt where Spanish kings and queens were laid to rest juxtaposed with the austerity of the lonely stone chapel under which it was buried.

Two days later we all took the train south to Méntrida. We barely felt it moving. The tracks gently hummed as they glided beneath us, the rail yard melting into buildings that melted into hills until we had been swallowed by the greens and browns of the Spanish countryside just south of Madrid. We stepped off in Toledo after about thirty minutes.

Ava and I invited the others to come along, but I was happy that they all preferred to wander about old Toledo instead. It was the one-time capital of Spain, famous for its cathedral and its steel swords.

At the train station we met my friends Juan and Caroline, who whisked us off down the road to one of the smaller and lesser known of Spain's winemaking regions. Méntrida was unique in its proximity to Madrid. It reminded me of Virginia wine country, just a short distance from Washington. I wondered why more Madrileños did not day trip here.

We drove about half an hour to the vineyards in the *media alta*, the middle elevations, on winding dirt roads surrounded by lush green countryside where Juan told us hunting deer and other game went hand in hand with tending vineyards. Quiet rows of vines rustled in the wind as they stretched down the gently sloping hills on into the horizon.

Here we met Maite, the winemaker at Bodegas Arrayán. She introduced us to Carlos, who worked in the cellar. Together we walked from barrel to barrel, tank to tank, stopping at each to sample the now-aging vintages first of a white grape called albillo, then of garnacha, syrah, merlot, and petit verdot. I imagined that the albillo might become very popular with the hipsters in the wine bars and cafés of America's gentrifying cities. Carlos asked how we'd compare Méntrida's petit verdot to others we'd had. The wine in our glass here was fruitier, with more blackberry and rich vanilla creaminess than the mineral-laden glasses I knew at home in Virginia. They were cooler and more delicate than those in California that sometimes felt very hot.

I swirled a fresh pour of albillo in my glass and looked out at the countryside. What a beautiful place it was. The land unassuming and unspoiled. We left the cellar to wander about. I looked through the glass at crushed stones along a path obscured by golden hue, out to the proper tasting room in which a spiral staircase led to an exquisite library of past vintages. It was as idyllic a setting as it was a source of beautiful wine.

We finished together with a bottle from 2014 called Selección. A blend of syrah, cabernet sauvignon, merlot, and petit verdot was not something that I'd expect to find in Spain. The bottle was quite a unique fusion of the variety of grapes grown in Méntrida.

I sniffed my glass. "Cranberry," I said, looking expectantly at Ava.

"More complex than that. Mint and nutmeg," she replied.

We swirled our glasses with Juan and Caroline and Maite and Carlos.

Ava went on about how the wine was velvety, but with some mild tannin in the mid-palate. "Notes of black tea mingled with fruits. Far more subdued in the mouth than in the nose," she said. "A bit of plum in the end. Mint persists throughout."

I smiled and took another sip.

After a bit of idle conversation about the vineyards Ava added, "Lovely nose after a few minutes. Fruit medley dominated by ripe raspberries and gentle spice."

We thanked our hosts, and Juan and Caroline drove us off down the mountain about twenty minutes to the small town of La Torre de Estaban Hambrán. A fellow named Juan Alonso greeted us in the central square, next to which, it turned out, was his family's home and winery.

There's magic in the peace and quiet of a small town where wine is made. Midday sun warmed us standing next to the unassuming bodega. I smiled, mindful that there was a barrel cellar beneath my feet. A puppy leapt merrily out the door to great us. Children played in the otherwise quiet streets.

Juan Alonso invited us into his Bodegas Alonso Cuesta beneath the large stone house.

I wondered if one could be simultaneously a traditionalist and an innovator as he led us through the modern production floor and into an exquisite barrel room that appeared as though from another time, built into the foundation of his family's centuries-old home. Here he produced the region's signature garnacha grape alongside cabernet sauvignon, in a combination of old and new French and American oak barrels. Everything seemed part of the storied order of things. There was a quiet desk where I knew I'd have spent hours were it in a cellar beneath my home. Were any of us to even have a real home. Rows of barrels sat in quiet repose under archways and vaulted brick ceilings, lit only by a band of light flowing in from the ground-level window near the ceiling, sunshine casting a blue hue on the stone floor. We signed a dusty leather guest book that reached decades back in time.

Yet he spoke adventurously of exploring new markets and new techniques for his wine, how he planned to renovate the unused portion of his cellar that opened onto the street so that he could welcome visitors to a new tasting room. The mood exuded a reverence for roots and an appreciation for the craft's *plus ultra* that appealed to me.

Our journey through the cellar was a lesson in how different wine develops through time. Our first taste of cabernet sauvignon was all notes of tobacco and surprisingly powerful green pepper, so different from the Californian or even French editions that I knew most would associate with this grape. The garnacha from new French oak had taken on notes of tobacco and baking spice, whilst the same garnacha in new American oak threw us a nose of gummy peach candy, freshly cut pepper, robust raspberry, and licorice root. The garnacha from year-old American barrels moved us into notes of sugar plum candle, retama, and cassis. At last, the three-year-old American oak brought out well-balanced red fruit, pepper, and licorice in Méntrida's favorite grape.

We had lunch together upstairs when we had finished drawing wine from the barrels.

Together we talked of wine and Spain and politics and things in America and in Europe. Someone who had stopped by explained to me that there was not yet a strong national right in Spanish politics because there were still many alive who remembered the dictator Francisco Franco. Fascism was real and palpable and part of the shared memories of those in my mother's generation. But even that was changing.

Time hurries on.

We ate venison sausage and tortilla, and drank from some of Juan Alonso's favorite vintages. One fellow ceased his talk of politics and began playing the guitar. Juan Alonso made gin tonics just like Javier's gin tonics. Several hours passed in this way. After which our friends returned us to Toledo, and we returned to Madrid by train.

I was happy to have spent this time alone with Ava. A weaker man than Peter might have thought me trying to steal his wife, and Ava trying to steal his best friend. I was grateful to Peter for being so good about this arrangement. There was no telling when we might have another moment to do so.

Chapter Twenty-Two

Tuesday was our last night in Madrid.

Each of us found time to revisit whatever we had most enjoyed the last ten days. Ash was feeling much better, so we decided to spend the day alone together. It was gorgeous, a bit cooler than usual and perfect for walking outside. Together we retraced my steps from the very first day when I had arrived and found her reading in the garden at Retiro.

We sat together on the same bench. I dozed off in her lap whilst she read her book. It was as if nothing had been achieved the entire time we were gone. Finally, I had learned how to take a vacation.

We walked on and she smiled as she opened a can of food and fed it to her cats.

"Nicholas, I've decided to call him." She gestured towards the kitten.

"And the mother?" I asked.

"I've not decided yet. I'll have to spend some more time with her."

I felt uneasy about this. Suddenly I knew for certain what I had suspected for days.

"I'm sorry," she said after a silent moment.

I will forever wonder at the different directions things may have taken had I responded differently in this one moment crouched together feeding a pair of cats by the lake at Retiro Park.

She went on. "You knew, didn't you?"

"That you'd decided to stay?"

"Yes."

"I knew. Suppose I knew."

She laughed and smiled that beautiful cocked smile.

"It doesn't matter. You know I'll get bored of it and see you in Washington later this week."

I laughed, hoping that joviality would obscure my sadness.

She rested her hand on mine.

"I'm not staying long. Promise. We'll have a grand old time together in Washington when I get back. I just need a few days to recharge. You're going to Prague, anyway, and besides . . . I still need to get my money's worth from that bike I bought."

We stood and I pulled her close. She kissed me.

"*Adiós, gatos. Hasta luego,*" I said with more confidence than I felt.

We walked hand in hand together down to the Puerta de Alcala, laughing our way through a happy afternoon together. Our siesta back at the flat lasted into tapas time. We headed out for *la última cena*, and found our friends at Quiroga.

They were jovial. Peter passed a bottle of cava. Emma ordered *tosta de aguacate*. Erik hugged me when I came to the table. Billy, who had never gone up to London to see his mother, listened along to some story Peter was telling. He began telling it again when he saw me.

"Ava and I were at a wedding reception, some wedding at one of those wineries-turned-wedding-factory type places upstate. Horrible place."

"How so?"

"Food was terrible. Wine was worse. They served all their own wine. Really tacky stuff. One of the bottles actually said *Pinot Noir* on it. Bet they charged an arm and a leg for it."

He took another swig of cava.

"Anyway, I asked one of the servers for some wine. She brought me a glass, but it was no good. So the catering manager came out."

"I am sure Ava was horrified." I looked about. "Where is Ava, anyway?"

"Oh." Peter broke stride. "She was feeling really badly today. Said she'll meet us for dinner after she gets some rest."

"Are you worried about her yet?"

"Oh, for sure. But she'll be fine. We're going straightaway to the doctor when we get back to New York."

"Good."

"Maybe she's pregnant?"

"Fantastic!" Peter grinned widely.

He took another drink.

"Anyway. So the manager brought me three different glasses of wine. Two Bordeaux style and a Burgundy knockoff. I tried 'em all."

"And?" Billy asked expectantly.

"I tried 'em all, and I looked at the manager and said. . ." He cracked up laughing at himself. "How about you bring me a Budweiser?"

I groaned.

Billy laughed uproariously. "It's doubly wonderful. It's offensive, and it's anti-French!"

I reminded Billy that the wine had been from New York, just French in style. He had missed that detail earlier and seemed sad that his crack at the end had fallen flat.

"Don't you find that the least bit offensive?" Erik interrupted. "Being a bartender and such?"

"Fuck yourself. I'm a sommelier. And of course I find it offensive. I just said as much. But, listen, serve crap wine, get what you get."

We paid and left.

My friend Luis was the sommelier at a place called Triciclo a couple of streets over from Huertas. It was a modern bistro on Calle

Santa María. He was an immense wine geek whose creativity was surpassed only by the warmth with which he shared the latest bottle on which he had gotten his hands. I thought that he was one of the most gifted young wine minds I'd encountered anywhere in Europe or the States. He had a talent for pairing obscure wines to whatever the chef was sending out.

We hugged one another when I walked in. I'd sent him a message a while earlier, and he'd managed to keep enough space clear for all seven of us to eat and drink with him at the bar. I had in the past made multiple friends from multiple countries out of the clear blue whilst sitting at that bar. We'd have come sooner, but Luis had been out of town.

I asked Luis to pour anything about which he was feeling good. He lit up like a Christmas tree and grabbed a bottle.

"Bermejo," he explained. "Malvasía volcánica. . . "

"From the Canary Islands!" Ava exclaimed.

He laughed. "Yes, those. Lanzarote, to be specific."

He continued explaining that the grapes were grown in soil heavy with volcanic ash. I would never cease to be amazed that such delightful wine could be made on islands off the coast of Morocco. They were unique in the pantheon of Spanish, European, and global winemaking.

"Has me thinking of both an albariño and a verdejo." Ava swirled and sniffed, no sign that she'd not been feeling well earlier.

The nose was almost effervescent, with a little grass and orange melon wafting up from the glass. There was a little acidity on the front, but the whole thing was otherwise smooth and round. Flower scents popped out of the glass.

"This is delicious!" Erik practically tripped over himself to say so.

"Good. I'm glad you like it." Luis smiled and went off as if suddenly aware that he had other customers.

"See!" Peter lurched abruptly into the conversation. "They're growing wine in Africa. The world hasn't ended in your fiery doom quite yet."

"Is that climate denier humor?" I asked.

He grinned like an idiot.

"Why do you have to be such an ass?" His wife glared at him.

"What? I'm just saying how happy I am that we have this delicious wine to drink. Your friend Luis knows his stuff."

"Don't be an ass."

We were enraptured by the predictable.

Peter and Erik turned to one another and began debating one or another topic that nobody else felt like discussing. Billy and I frolicked on with the girls. But it was hard to avert my ears from the philosophizing across the table.

"I swear I am going to let him have it if he tries to draw anyone into another debate on our last night here," Ava seethed.

"It'll be alright," I assured her, unconvincingly I am sure. "Promise."

"That doesn't mean any of you have to talk with him if he goes there. You and Erik just get him going. And you." She looked sternly at Ash.

"My mother didn't talk to me for three weeks," Emma said flatly.

"Must've been a mighty pleasant three weeks!" Erik veered back into our conversation.

"Good God, I'd have done anything to keep my mother from talking to me for three weeks," Billy laughed uproariously.

Emma asked him if he'd like her mother to adopt him.

"I don't speak much Finnish." Billy declined the offer.

"Are you actually going to visit your mother?"

"Not this time. Too much time spent with you people. Javier's waiting for me to come home."

"What's a Spanish restaurant to do without its English bartender?"

"Sommelier. I'm a sommelier."

"Don't be a prick."

Billy giggled.

Peter asked Erik and I what we planned to do in Prague.

"Erik has business there, not sure what," I answered.

"Not saying much 'til it's done. There's a little company there that's making good stuff. Couple of Czechs."

"There tend to be many Czechs in Prague."

"What about you, Chris?"

"I'll work during the day."

"What the hell do you actually do, anyway?" Billy asked.

"How is that you've known him for two years and you've no idea what he does for work?"

"And, hence, evidence that Chris has succeeded in that nobody has a clear picture of what he does for work, or that he even does any work at all." Ava laughed.

"I believe the phrase you're looking for is 'digital nomad,'" Peter quipped. "At least that's what I hear the rootless citizen-of-the-world, citizen-of-nowhere types call it nowadays."

"Well, that is the whole point of being that, whatever the hell that is," Billy laughed. "Nobody understanding what it is you really do for work. That, and living an extremely metrosexual lifestyle. Manicures and pedicures. Seriously, let me see your nails!"

I laughed uneasily.

"Alright, so you're working during the day. What are you doing at night?"

"Drinking wine with Erik, I suppose."

"Why do you drink so much wine?"

"Wine is his window."

"Pardon?"

I didn't like being talked about.

"You know, his window. It's his window to . . . you know?" Ash stuttered.

"Perhaps I should ask why you drink so much wine?" Erik winked at her.

She told him that she'd barely had any wine at all.

"No, I get it. It's like food," Ava said. "People connect over food in a way that they otherwise might not be able to in conversation or shared experience. Food, or wine, that is the shared experience."

"Tell me more about this wine."

So I closed my eyes, swirled the stuff in my glass and told them more about the wine we were drinking. I remembered being on Lanzarote, the warm breeze unlike any you'd ever experienced in lands where wine is made. Tropical, wrapping you up inside of that very distinct sense of what standing in the middle of the ocean feels like. Yet it was not what truly thrilled the senses there. Open your eyes to the horizon, where the bluest of skies meets the black, pockmarked, grey-stoned earth as if we had colonized the moon, and this was our vineyard there. Indeed, that volcanic island eighty miles from the coast of southern Morocco—yes, Africa—felt a moon's distance from the cellars where the finest wine was typically made. Yet there I had stood in the shadow of the Timanfaya volcano, amongst the estate vines at a winery on Lanzarote, one of Spain's Canary Islands, grapes in hand, awestruck.

"See? His window."

"Cheers."

"Cheers."

We drank from our glasses.

"Is that the meaning of life?"

"What, wine?"

"Tropical islands?"

"No. To accumulate experiences. Is the meaning of life to accumulate experiences?"

"Going deep, are we?"

"I subscribe to the notion that there is no meaning to life. It's an accident that we exist to begin with." Billy glanced about to see if anyone agreed with him.

"That's nonsense," Erik replied dryly.

"Convince me I'm wrong."

"A little midlife crisis in the age of. . . " I tried to remember the phrase Ava had used when we were alone at El Diario a few mornings earlier. "... of whatever this is the age of?"

Soon as I said it I knew I'd walked us straight back to rhetorical doom.

"Goddamn, it's hard to not talk about this stuff nowadays."

"Is that what's been bothering you?"

Ash took my hand in hers under the table. She kissed me sweetly on the cheek as if to say "It's alright."

"Yes," I admitted. "I think so."

We talked on for a little while about the world and all in which we were caught up just now.

"What's happening in the world right now is not just unseemly. It's a total betrayal of everything our grandparents accomplished, the world they made safer for us."

Peter bristled.

"It's a betrayal of how we've always thought about ourselves when we're at our very best," I started. "And every moment I spend writing software or drinking wine and wandering the world feels like a moment wasted. And I have no idea what to do about it."

We sat glumly.

Luis poured more wine.

Erik thought for a moment. Then he brightened, always one for perspective.

"America is about the quest for liberation, about the revolution. Running away from the tyrant," he said, "about making something new."

"So now's the time to make something new?"

"Well. . . "

"It's about asserting your rights and the rights of your group in the face of those who would deny them."

"This also includes me," Peter huffed. "What about my rights?"

I thought about this. That was, indeed, our story. Perhaps that's what made America great. It was baked into the psyche of the country. It had been going on for 500 years.

"The revolution didn't begin in 1776, nor did it end in 1780." Erik lectured on. "Revolution," he argued, "is part and parcel to the ethos and entire history of our nation."

"Watch yourself." The Englishman smiled up from his wine.

"That's what makes the statues so difficult to take down." I was trying to throw Peter a bone now. "That they are an assertion of rights on both sides of the issue."

"They're a sideshow," Emma insisted. "Who cares about the damned statues?"

And we were back.

Peter brightened a little at the defense of his perspective I had just provided him. I was weary of this conversation and hoped we'd be able to find a way to end it. I was tired of feeling so wound up. We had lived this beautiful lie the last ten days, but always there was the specter of some argument breaking out, some reason to provoke Ash or sadden Emma or enrage Ava or simply frustrate me. Perhaps we could talk more about wine, I suggested. Everyone loves wine.

Instead we talked about the cursed climate. Poor conversational decisions in mixed company was the wont of confused educated folk in those days. This was how we spent the summer of 2018.

On this score even Emma turned against Peter. The mood grew more tense because he felt so outnumbered. Not even Billy's usual humor could turn us back. Being a bartender, he was so very good at pulling us back from the brink. Being a sommelier, he was so very good at giving us something new and interesting to discuss.

I drank my wine and said very little for a few minutes.

Ash was beside herself on this topic.

"Don't you get it?" she pleaded with him as if anything any of us had to say really mattered. "You think we have a refugee problem now? Wait until you've finished destroying their homes!"

This was visceral for her. She knew where her father had come from.

"I can't help everyone," Peter insisted.

I was finished.

"Goddammit, Peter!" I slammed my fist hard upon the table.

We were standing beside one another along the bar. He looked at me expectantly.

I stammered for a moment.

"You are literally killing your children!"

And we were finished.

The panicked sense of free fall backwards took me before I realized how much it hurt. Ava let out a low, startled shriek somewhere in the distance. I was so surprised by the whole thing that I didn't see much at all, and it was not until I landed hard on the floor that I realized what had happened.

It was a clean punch. My best friend. His inane beliefs about the world. My admonishment about his children. His fist. My face. It had all been so clean and predictable. But there I sat, wondering why I had said that. God it hurt. Everyone in the restaurant looked at us in silence. Six Americans and a Brit arguing about the world we had made for ourselves.

"Well," Billy said, "least he didn't smack the waiter this time."

"Not the time, Billy, not the time," Erik said as he fished me off the floor, helping me stand upright.

Ava fought back tears.

I apologized to Luis, paid, and left.

It was a rotten way to say goodbye to Madrid.

Chapter Twenty-Three

Erik and I flew to Prague. It was always such a surreally calm moment stepping out onto Huertas in the early hours of a beautiful morning. The streets empty and washed clean. Very few people about. Time's longing echoes ringing through the narrow streets, mingling with anticipation for what was to come.

Dull the senses of it all. My face was still sore, but I had just shared a long goodbye with Ash, and more than anything I felt consumed by the empty sadness that one feels when the eventuality of their best-laid plans have evaporated or slid through fingers like fine sand. Moments in life are like grains on the beach. You'll never again find the same bits once they have mingled into the sea of time.

A girl at Prague's Hotel Medvidku served us beers in the small lobby as we checked in. Seems the place doubled as a brewery. Real metal keys hung on wooden charms made to look like tiny beer barrels. My room was a cavern, the ornate metal door opening atop a platform with some stairs down into the bedroom, cathedral ceilings arching over the bed like a cloister.

We ate lunch at the nearby Café Louvre. Erik went off to his meeting. I worked a bit in my room, then walked about. There would be so much to love and share about that beautiful city during our two evenings there.

At the Café Louvre we had discussed where to go later that

evening. My friend Lucie messaged that she was out of town but would return the next day. She suggested that we try a place called Veltlin up in a neighborhood called Karlín.

It was a smallish place. Filament lights hung haphazardly from the ceiling. Shelves arranged along the wall displayed empty bottles from both quiet contemplation and revelries past. Light streamed out from behind the shelf, a white glow illuminating green bottles as if to suggest that they had been sent to us from the great beyond.

The main attraction on the opposite wall was a mural-sized map of Central Europe, with borders as they had appeared a century earlier.

We discussed the last evening's events, but there wasn't much to say. Erik felt badly and admitted to having instigated the whole thing out of conviction that Peter could in the end be persuaded. Said that he suspected Peter felt badly as well.

"Ever confident in reason, your reason," I chuckled.

"Does it help for me to admit how naïve I even seem to myself sometimes?"

"We've been together a long time," I told him. "You are idealistic, not naïve."

"That's fair. But this time it got you punched in the face."

"My outburst about the kids got me punched in the face."

"Easy enough for the childless to underestimate paternal instinct."

"I shouldn't have brought his kids into it."

"But you were right. Peter *is* killing his children. He may not live to see it, but in the end, even if the angry and the dispossessed don't come with their torches and pitchforks. . . "

"Nature comes for us all?"

"That's right." Erik nodded.

"I don't know."

That's what people said when they hadn't much left to offer on a topic.

"Beautiful map." Erik motioned towards the mural on the wall.

"Yes."

"Actually, I find it eerie."

"Eerie?"

"It's a modern homage to something that hasn't existed for years."

We spoke of once-proud empires split and scattered asunder, their people enslaved for generations.

"The War to End All Wars, they called it. Then it came crashing down."

"And now?"

I thought for another moment. "Do you remember when we were growing up?"

"We're not that old," Erik chuckled.

"No-no, that's not what I meant . . . I meant that we grew up as end-of-history kids."

He smiled. "Our early childhood playing outside in the tree forts we'd build, pretending that the Russians were coming, and it was up to us to defend West Virginia from communists?"

I laughed out loud. "And then, just like that, it was the end of history. There were no more communists for little boys to battle from their tree houses."

Perhaps I had needed to drink a bottle of wine with my old friend somewhere behind the once-extant Iron Curtain to put my finger on this. Or perhaps it was just that map on the wall. In either case, we sat there and meandered through some explanation of the emotional attachment we had developed—subconsciously as kids coming of age in the 1990s—to the idea that everything would be better tomorrow than it had been yesterday. In a way I was angry that we had been promised the world only to have the world brought to the brink of ruin by the very generation which had done the promising. It was visible yet . . . And, I might add, a visitor from afar might not have known it sitting here looking at us living large and sipping our wine. Every day, though, the idea lingered that the world of our old age might very well look dystopically different from the world in which we were just now sipping our wine. I was angry that Peter didn't understand this, didn't accept this, didn't get it.

But mostly I was sad. Sad like I imagined the children of the Lost Generation might have felt when the promise of the War to End All Wars came crashing down around them. I was sad that the idyllic experience of being an end-of-history kid had slipped through our fingers. We'd never find the same bits of sand again. They had mingled into the sea of time.

And I was sad that I hadn't been able to find it within myself to do a damned thing about it.

"It was all so grand again for a moment."

"Still feels pretty grand," Erik pointed out as he raised his glass to eye level.

"Yeah, still does, I guess."

"You sound unconvinced."

I gestured towards the map.

"Once," I began, "these were the world's great cities. Prague. Budapest. Vienna, locus of intellectual fervor. A multicultural melting pot that spanned across Central Europe. Imperfect, to be sure, but in its time unlike anything else."

"That's probably a bit of a glossing over things."

"We're Americans. We're first-rate glossers."

We laughed quiet, geeky laughs.

"You think Americans might have gotten better at being European than Europeans?"

"Don't say that too loudly!"

"Ha!" I didn't laugh.

"How do you mean?"

"Well, think about it. Fifty states, different people and cultures, figuring out how to coexist and live together for centuries? Seems like we figured it out."

"For a time."

"Yes, that. And now we fragment."

"Now Europeans are better at being American than Americans?" I really laughed this time.

"They have their own problems."

"And finally, I've gotten you to think with perspective!" Erik smirked.

"For all the good it'll do."

"I don't know," he finally admitted. "Perhaps we're the ones standing athwart history yelling *stop*. I just don't know."

Even that discussion seemed inconsequential. It would be some time before I thought of it again, before I figured out what I had really been trying to say.

The next night we went to a place where one entered through a quietly cloistered courtyard whose cobblestones reflected the light that shone down from above, beneath arches and columns both stately and sooted by time. A soft bronze glow of filament bulbs and candles gently twinkled through the phalanx of glasses and bottles. They cast merry shadows on the vaulted walls of a place that we might have thought dilapidated if we didn't know it was a wine cellar. There was community inside, the revelry of young and old both crowded around a common table and the high tops wedged in any alcove not otherwise lined floor to ceiling with bottles. We were inside of Vinarna Bokovka, self-styled as a *decrepit courtyard offering great wines*.

Lucie said hello to us and hugged me just inside the door. We sat in and amongst the crowd at the long table. She told Erik about her country's little-known but delightful winemaking, and the natural wines that clearly owned Bokovka's heart. She paired delectable cheeses with a lineup of natural sparkling and grüner veltliner from Moravia, an "orange" pinot grigio and another natural pinot gris from Italy, and a more classically styled pinot noir. This place's repertoire was as impressive as it was unique. The lineup of cheeses, meats, and freshly baked bread quickly left us feeling as if dinner were a thing of the past. It was one of the most enchanting little cellars I had ever encountered.

She poured us glasses of a natural sparkling wine from a place called Jižní, in Moravia. It was unfiltered, making it stylistically very different from sparkling wine made in the French traditional method for which Champagne and most other sparklers were known. That lack of filtration produced a beautiful, cloudy, shimmering gold color in the glass, from whose center a lonely seam of bubbles emanated. The nose was reminiscent of light cider. It effervesced lightly in my mouth—again, a far cry from traditional method sparklers. Largely apple and subtle pear notes paired beautifully with the mouthfeel and entire visual experience. It's a glass I'd have drank again and again if Lucie hadn't plenty more to share with us.

"I had a message today that made me think of you," Erik said once Lucie had gone.

"Oh?"

"Yeah." He shook his head in disbelief. "So, at work, we offer one of those volunteer time off schemes, *VTO*, it's called."

"Alright."

"Anyway." He cracked up laughing. "There was talk the last few days—I didn't see it until I tuned in on the plane this morning—about a posse of our very junior software developers taking VTO in the Caribbean. It cried of bullshit to me."

"In college," I offered, "it used to annoy the life out of me how kids would try to raise all this money, asking parents and aunts and uncles and such to fund their *service trip*, all so they could go down to an island and paint a school or something."

"Whilst lounging around on the beach?"

"Yes, exactly. And, you know, put up angsty Facebook statuses; well, I guess back then they were Instant Messenger away messages."

"Instant Messenger!" Erik laughed.

"Right. Away messages about how inspired they were by all the kids. The whole thing was a racket to make them feel better about their place in the world *and* get some time on the beach."

"Their impact would have been far greater had they just sent the money and let the school get painted on the local economy. Paying jobs. Painted schools. That type of thing."

"Exactly."

"So, believe it or not, this thing at work was even more absurd."

"Do tell."

"These people," Erik laughed hysterically, "they tried to pass off *taking care of puppies* on the beach as legitimate *volunteer* time off. Anyway, the engineering manager who supervises them asked one of their colleagues who didn't go on the trip. Actually, this kid has been using his VTO to mentor an after-school robotics club at some public school up in the Bronx. Really good kid."

"What did he have to say about it?"

"Oh, he knew it was happening, said it really upset him, but didn't feel right turning in his friends."

"And how is it turning out for his friends?"

"Let's just say that their VTO bank hasn't been debited, but their paid time off balance is hurting."

"Hilarious."

"I mean, at least the kids in college were making some effort to paint a school, or whatever it was they did."

"More than I've done lately."

Lucie returned with a grüner veltliner. This bottle was not at all like what we expected from a typical grüner. Biodynamic and natural, dark and cloudy gold in the glass, shimmering in front of the candle similarly to the sparkling we had just finished. Floral in the nose, with definitive notes of Grey Poupon and tuna. Odd, actually.

"It's distinctly possible that one would have to try this themselves to understand why we like it," I told them both. "Can't imagine my tasting notes would read very well."

"Try me."

"Alright, well, briny," I said. "The fish elements carry through in the palate, mingling with lemon and lime that is typical of a grüner. I'd pair this with poultry, not fish. The wine brings its own fish, like opening a can of tuna, making a sandwich, looking at the cat and saying 'Screw you, Nicholas, I'm drinking this,' and then carrying on with your life."

"Nicholas?" Lucie looked at me quizzically. "You have a cat named Nicholas?"

"That's just what his girlfriend, Ash, named the stray cat she found in Madrid."

She laughed.

Our tablemates alternated between laughter and serious talk with some folks they didn't know on the other side. There was, more than anything, a profound sense of community here as regulars and guests of all ages gathered around tables to explore wine without assumption or pretension. Bokovka exuded a revelry and familiarity that would make anyone long to find it on the corner in their own neighborhood.

Lucie poured glasses of a pinot gris called Youngster, from Nestarec, the same wine producer that Geoff and I had drank at Grus Grus in Stockholm. Another natural wine, it was made from grapes harvested and fermented just the previous year. Many natural wines tended to be young. Its youth was borne out by its other qualities. Very light, pear-juice colored in the glass, a nose of lilies and pear, green and yellow apples with notes of lemon-lime spritzer on the palate.

"*More than you've done lately?*"

"What?" I asked Erik what he meant.

"Something you said a few minutes ago, *more than I've done lately*, I think it was."

"Oh. What about it?"

"Well, the other night Billy said that there was no meaning to life, that it was an accident we're here to begin with."

"He's quite nihilistic, isn't he?"

"The real question is, are you?" Erik paused for effect but went on. "Are you sad that painting a school is more than you've done lately because you think it's all meaningless—like Billy—or is it just the opposite? That you know you could have done more, but didn't?"

"Hadn't thought about that. Guess it was more of a passing comment, really."

Erik asked me if I remembered that conversation we had walking up Huertas to Plaza Mayor the week before.

"Yes, of course. It was like so many of our talks."

"Well, we talked about it in terms of the hypocrisy of changing the world. So imagine there's Billy, the nihilist at one end. He subscribes to the notion that it's all meaningless. Then at the other end there's *impact*, the notion that what one does with their life might actually matter."

I remembered what I had said that day on Huertas, about the difference between aspiring to overcome one's smallness and the arrogant presumption that one was large to begin with.

"Right, right!" Erik exclaimed. "That's the other idea. The difference between *destiny* and *experience*."

Now I saw where he was going.

"Okay." We were such geeks. "So there are guys like Billy who think that we're all *destined* for *meaninglessness*."

"Yeah, that's the *nothing matters* quadrant. They're all nihilists there."

"They have the virtue of at least being less obnoxious than those who think that it's their *destiny* to have a great *impact*."

"Ah yes, the people—how did you put it? The ones who are arrogant enough to think themselves large? The elitists who think they will change the world?"

I suggested we call them the *entitled leaders*.

"As opposed to?"

"Well, those who aspire to make an impact, but who do so because of their *experience*, not their birthright."

"Suppose those are our *servant leaders*?" Erik asked. "You know, the ones who see whatever they've experienced as a gift in life for which they should be grateful?"

"The ones who don't want to throw it all away."

"Yeah."

"And the last quadrant?"

He chuckled. "Those are the fun ones. They're the ones who live for the experience, consequences be damned."

"*Experience* mixed with *meaninglessness*."

"Go big or go home."

"The *absurdists*."

"So, which are you?"

I really wondered.

Lucie brought us back to Moravia with a more classically styled pinot noir to end the evening. A bit of cedar and milk chocolate in the nose was followed up with vanilla bean after some good swirling in the glass. She served it slightly chilled. It was creamier than many other pinots, and overall a great reminder of two things: how great pinot noir could be found the world over, and that Austria wasn't the only Central European country that knew how to be one of those places.

That was all there was for us that time in Prague. The next morning we flew to London and then immediately on to New York.

Chapter Twenty-Four

We touched down around five o'clock in the afternoon. My phone was abuzz about a lunar eclipse visible to almost everyone except for Americans—and Canadians and Mexicans and the rest of North America of course. There were several messages waiting for me.

From Geoff Gamal: *Once again we find ourselves in the same city. Odd, right?*

From Andrew Jefferson: *Heard you're back. I'm in New York. Let's have drinks.*

And most surprisingly, from Peter Dean: *Taking Ava to the doc this afternoon. Stay in the city a night and come over in the morning? Kids would love to see you.*

Erik mused that I seemed to be in high demand.

I was unsure whether to feel hurt that Ash hadn't sent me anything, or worried about Ava. So we spoke of neither as we taxied to the gate.

"Guess it didn't take long for Peter to get over things."

"We'll see."

I shot messages back in reverse order.

To Peter Dean, *Absolutely. Good luck. See you in the morning.*

To Andrew Jefferson, *Meet at the club? Two hours?*

And to Geoff Gamal, *Mind if I stay at your place tonight?*

"Well, if those logistics don't work out," Erik offered, "you can stay at my place."

"Will you be there?"

"No, I'm catching a flight back to Washington. Spend the weekend with Emma."

"However has she survived these two long days?"

"Two days are nothing."

"I know."

We quickly cleared through passport control. Erik headed back up to the Washington flight. I took the train to the city. We hugged one another and agreed to meet at Joselito on Sunday night.

"Maybe I'll meet you at Union Station." He winked.

It had been just over a month since I'd done the same for him, coming down from New York just as our strange summertime odyssey had begun.

* * *

I rode the express Long Island Railroad from Jamaica into Penn Station and hopped the subway one stop from Herald Square up to Bryant Park. I put on a clean shirt in the washroom at the Princeton Club, dropped my bag with the bellman, and found Andrew Jefferson in the bar upstairs.

"Aren't you exhausted?"

"Of course I'm exhausted," I said, "but the best way to get back into this time zone is to stay awake until ten or eleven, and have good, hard sleep until morning."

"It's good to see you, old friend."

He drank gin. Plymouth with a bit of ice and lemon.

I ordered a glass of sparkling as I asked him what he was doing in New York.

He told me that he'd spent the week at the United Nations, but didn't say why. He never much cared to say why.

"I thought I'd stay when I heard you were coming back from Prague today."

"I never told you I was going to Prague."

"You must have told me."

"Nonsense. Wait, are you in on that scheme with my phone location, too?"

He stared at me blankly, clearly having no idea what I was talking about. I explained the business about Peter and Ash using my phone to always know where I was.

"Please," he retorted. "I don't like either of them enough to be part of that. She's a twit and he's a buffoon."

"Tell me how you really feel."

"That is how I really feel."

We sipped our drinks.

"Ah, Jake, I've missed you."

"I've missed you, too, Andrew."

We talked about Spain. It seemed to me that he already knew quite a bit about our trip, and that perhaps he had been texting with or otherwise had seen Emma. I couldn't imagine who else he would have seen. Then we talked about his precarious financial situation, to which he added that he was feeling somewhat better about his lot having perhaps found a man that returned his affections. The last three, he reminded me, had in order not been willing to admit he was gay, knew he was gay but married a woman anyway, and finally was self-assuredly gay but married to another man.

I asked him what he had been thinking over all those years.

"About the men or the money?"

"Both?"

He finished his gin, ordered another, and sighed.

"Well, I suppose all my life I was always just waiting for the other shoe to drop."

"*Which . . . other* shoe?"

"I thought I was going to be dead, Jake, okay?"

I laughed. "That's not very damned funny."

"What's funny is that I'm still here after all these years. East River and a bridge haven't claimed me yet. The trouble is trying to decide on my preferred bridge."

"Well, at least you have several to choose from."

"From which to choose."

"Do you have some small idea what a prick you are?"

"Fully."

We laughed quietly and raised our glasses.

Seams of pale orange and white coursed through the otherwise charcoal stone bar counter. Sebastian, the bartender, brought me a glass of grüner. Suppose my tastes were still in Prague. Bottles were piled up in the center of the bar, shimmering with the light glowing up from the pyramid shelf upon which they rested. Pictures adorned the wall. An old crew shell hung from the ceiling. I felt strange comfort being back in such a familiar place.

"I watched *To Kill a Mockingbird* the other night. Still makes me weep." Andrew took another swig of gin. "Not sure why that's relevant."

I raised an eyebrow, considering for a moment that we might talk about it, but decided to move on, making mostly idle conversation. It was too late. I asked him when he would be back in Washington. He didn't know.

"I actually really like it up here. Maybe I'll stay? Long as someone's paying my bills, that's for damned sure."

I was drinking soda water now. Sebastian brought me another and Andrew more gin.

Later I walked alone to Times Square where I found an express train up to Ninety-Sixth Street, the subway station on Broadway. It was raining, and still terribly hot.

Geoff and Caroline shared an apartment off of Ninety-Third

Street. He had sent me a message earlier telling me to come on up anytime. Joe the doorman was expecting me. I had known him for years, coming in and out of this place most times when I was in the city. We chatted about how the Yankees game had been postponed that day. They were five games behind Boston.

"Geoff tells me there's a Red Sox bar in, where was it? Stockholm? In Sweden!" he marveled.

"It's true," I chuckled.

"Too bad there's not a Yankee bar! You'd love that."

"Guess they're just not that memorable."

He laughed.

"Swedes have good taste, what can I say?"

"Saw you didn't do too bad in the World Cup!"

"Oh, it was really great."

"I'll say. Better than we could manage to do!" He muttered something rude about the American team.

Mostly we were baseball fans.

I went up the elevator with a brass door. Geoff lived on the twelfth floor.

"How's your boat?" I asked when I walked in.

He hugged me. "Boat's fine! Left it in Provincetown. Just got back this morning. Your timing is good."

"You'd have let me stay anyway."

"It's true." He poured me a drink that I didn't want, but it was good of him, so I accepted and drank thirstily.

"Where's Caroline?"

"She's on her way."

"I wish you'd have gone to Madrid."

"Oh. Why?"

"Peter could have used a friend. Hell, I could have used a friend."

Geoff bridged those difficulties in a way that Erik could not. Peter trusted him as being bona fide. They didn't agree on much, but Peter trusted that he was legitimate and sincere in his moral views.

Geoff grinned. "Was he as nuts as usual?"

I laughed and said he was.

"But I love him," I added. "He's a good fellow."

We drank.

"Actually, he punched me," I finally said. "Punched me square in the face. I felt like an ass afterward. I'd said something I shouldn't."

"Endearing that you should get punched and be the one who feels like an ass."

"Suppose so."

"Well, that's exciting! How's Ash?"

"Still in Madrid."

"She'll turn up in a few days when she's had enough alone time."

"Funny, Erik said the same."

Geoff smiled.

The door swung open. Caroline walked in.

"Hello, Chris." She sank into the sofa. I had not seen her in some time.

"Long day?"

"You've no idea."

We sat in silence.

"Jakey got punched in the face!"

"Good God, when?"

"A few days ago."

"Oh. Well, you got better."

"True. Why do I feel it doesn't compare to whatever you've been through?"

"Ah, it's not that. I just feel terribly. Sometimes there are days when you feel like you've really made some difference. Then you have days when you know that you broke someone's heart."

I imagined it was like that at the hospital.

"So today you broke someone's heart?"

"I just had the worst day." She stood up and poured herself a drink. Then she kissed Geoff.

I stood up to pour myself another drink.

"I'm sorry, Chris, I should have—"

"Nonsense," I said. "It's no problem."

"I saw a woman today," she went on. "There with her husband and her kids. Really nice people. Kids were so damned sweet."

She sipped her drink.

"Anyway. She kept herself together. The husband really struggled. Such a sweet man. He was so sweet to her and their kids. It just broke my heart."

"Sounds sweet enough," Geoff suggested. "What was wrong?"

"Oh. I tried to be gentle, but direct. I always try to be gentle and direct. There's no chance this woman will make it. She probably won't live to see next year."

Caroline began to cry. Light, whimpering cries. I couldn't imagine what it must have felt like to go to work and be her. To hold life and death in your hands in such a personal way. To look people in the eye like that.

She wiped away a tear.

"I'm usually so good with this. But it was just heartbreaking. Complete strangers, I'd never seen them before."

Geoff put his arm around her.

"Yeah," she said. "She was so young. Thirties? They had no idea. It just snuck up on her. Tumor grew so large that it cracked her rib. That's how she knew something was wrong. They'd been traveling, somewhere, I don't know where. Thought she'd slept the wrong way on an airplane."

I think all the blood left my face.

Geoff looked at me. He was about to say something, but Caroline went on.

"I mean, we'll treat her. We'll do our best. But she won't make it. And she knows it. Her husband doesn't realize it yet. And those poor kids. Goddammit."

She took another sip.

"I'm sorry, Chris, not what you were looking for tonight. I'll be better." She looked at me. "Oh God," she said. "Oh God, I've made a terrible mistake, haven't I?"

"Her name." I shook. "It was Ava, wasn't it?" I knew. I can't explain it, but I just knew.

"Oh God," she wept. "I am so sorry. I had no idea."

Chapter Twenty-Five

There is a strange serenity in despair. I am not entirely sure how I
spent the moments that passed just after the last one I described,
or how many of them passed at all. The deeper I reached into my
mind, into the pit of my stomach where in that instant I felt something
terrifically awful, the more lost I became. It is as if, as I think of it, I was
floating in a purgatory of misery and sorrow and shame and sickness, a
lost world turned upside down, of fleeting coming and going illness, of
ghostly white face and blood that fills the senses, and, oh God, it feels
so warm, so interminable, so sickly, such a thing that starts and stops
and is punctuated by lapses into reality, in and out of surreal things
that go on and on and yet feel as if they have never started, as if in the
moment you are submerged beneath the waves of horror and elevated
to escapist nothing-at-all. As if nothing seems real, and everything
seems palpable. The weight of your little world lies upon you like a
mine, and you are so desperate for escape that you turn to whatever is
at hand. Self-assuring delusion. Drink. Laughter amongst friends. And
to walk away from all of this, even in dire exhaustion, is to slink away to
a place where time does not pass and consequences are meaningless,
and all there is will be you, and sleep, and a drowned confusion at the
thing you just discussed and felt and mourned and celebrated and
otherwise experienced in a drunken, suspended-of-all-belief stupor
that neither knows much nor suffers much yet suffers greatly and

draws your desperate mind, clinging for something sensible, in and out of cruel reality.

And that was how we spent the evening.

At first there was nothing but Caroline's guilt at having given it all away. She knew nothing, had never met our friends. She was new, and hadn't been there along the way.

Then there was rational talk. A discussion of what she knew, and having already given the first part away, she begrudgingly divulged the rest. Suppose she felt badly having thrown our world into chaos only to say nothing.

At some length I felt warm, warm to the touch, warm to the feel inside me. I wondered if it was the wine, which I had stopped drinking I had no idea how long ago. And I imagined Peter and the children and Ava holding it all together, and I imagined them sitting there at the end of this night that I had passed happily with Andrew Jefferson at the club, sitting there side by side, arms 'round one another. I wondered if they knew, if one of them knew, if neither of them knew. And perhaps Caroline was wrong. Perhaps it was hyperbolic. But to hell with it all. I wondered what there was to be. And at the same time I dreaded that which was to come. Yet I wondered how long it could be drawn out, if even for eternity, forever, for as long as we all might have otherwise gone on.

Or perhaps this was all nonsense. Perhaps it was foolish science. Perhaps we need only to pray.

And suddenly it was nearly done.

I stumbled off to my room.

I had not drunk anything in hours.

My lips were chapped and raw.

I don't remember what we discussed.

If you've never passed out from disgust, then you might not know what it feels like to be so overwhelmed by the moment that you simply must withdraw from it. I had slept well after I threw up. It was a sound, deep sleep, as if my body knew that it would find peace only in sleep. I felt better in the morning. Everything looks better in the morning.

At ten o'clock I caught a cab across the Park. Peter and Ava lived amongst high society on the Upper East Side. I preferred the character of the Upper West Side. Or perhaps I just knew it better. It was more familiar to me after all those years visiting Geoff and talking baseball with Joe.

If the night before had been surreal in its awfulness, the greeting in the door with my old friends was surreal for its jumble of confused emotions. I was the only one who really held all the cards.

In Peter's mind, the last chapter had ended when he punched me in the face. So he picked up there, having no idea that I knew of Ava's condition.

In the minds of the little girls—Catherine and Meghan—there were neither sore faces nor fractured ribs, only the arrival of Uncle Chris, who brought bagels. To Patrick, the youngest, there was little to perceive outside of his delight that his sisters were themselves so delighted.

Then there was Ava, whose intuition I imagined made her more self-aware of her own condition than her husband yet realized. Yet she too had no idea that I knew anything about it.

I had neither anticipated nor rehearsed any of this. So it was in a jumble of hugs from excitable children and a firm slap on the back from Peter that I immediately reconsidered my dour mood and pretended that my only cares in the world were for mending fences and eating bagels.

It felt selfish. Jumping first into my own trivial problems. Assuring Ava that my face hadn't hurt much in the days that followed. Joking with Peter about how it was only a matter of days before we had begun to laugh about it all. Recounting the wine bars in Prague. The big map on the wall. Natural sparkling with Lucie. Things that seemed years ago and a million miles away. But it all felt necessary to not let on that I knew. I supposed they would learn soon enough that the doctor was closer to home than they imagined.

It was only after some time that I casually asked how Ava was feeling.

"Well, I think we found the problem," Peter said between sips of coffee.

"Oh?" I asked, calibrating my tone for what I expected to follow.

He rubbed his hand on hers. "Somehow she fractured a rib."

I almost choked on my coffee.

"Really?" I asked, trying not to seem incredulous that this is where we had landed.

"Yeah, damndest thing."

Ava glanced nervously at the girls. They playfully ate their bagels and giggled with one another at the table. Seemingly oblivious, though children are intuitive creatures.

"That must have been a helluvan airplane ride," I offered, sounding more confident than I felt.

"It was a helluva trip," she corrected. "Remember? I started hurting the first day."

Peter laughed nervously. "Yeah, my first thought was that she had slept a strange position on the plane the way over."

I said that I hoped it had not ruined her trip.

"Not at all. You two and your bickering did far more to *ruin* my trip than any ribs. Besides, I've given birth. So there's that." She smiled beautifully, a lock of hair falling gently over her face.

We talked more about Spain. It was excruciating, sitting there knowing so much, yet having to pretend that I considered the matter of her condition resolved.

Eventually it was noon.

"Time for a beer!" Peter proclaimed when he heard the chimes on the clock.

I looked about uncomfortably, hoping he'd take this opportunity to tell me what was happening. Ava suggested Peter and I go out for something.

So after some debate about how far we were willing to go for midday drinks, we finally decided to go quite far indeed. We took a number six train all the way down to Thirty-Third Street. Then we walked a couple of blocks to a place called Cask where we used to all go together. I was surprised Peter had suggested the place, but he knew I liked it, and I supposed that he wanted to be in a place with warm memories.

We ordered beer, though I wasn't sure why. I hardly drank beer nowadays. It would go well with the lamb nachos we had also ordered.

Peter began laughing and shaking his head. "I'm really sorry I punched you."

More laughter. I was impressed with how he was keeping it together, yet frustrated with how long this was taking.

"Yeah," he went on, "I don't know what got into me. I mean, you're wrong about whatever you were saying. I don't actually quite remember how you put it, but you were wrong. But I shouldn't have punched you. Jesus." Sip of beer. "Jesus, Ava was furious with me."

This was the opening I had been looking for.

"You worried about her?"

"About her? Oh, her rib?"

"Yes." I looked him in the eye.

He looked away back down the stairs to the bar. Gathering his courage.

"A little, yeah." His eyes watered when he turned back to look at me after a moment. He seemed unable to hold back now.

"What is it?" I gave him a momentary reprieve to gather his thoughts. "Don't tell me you've broken a sympathy rib?"

"A what?" He gulped a little courage from the tall glass.

"You know," I explained, "like somehow you've gone and hurt yourself so you can be laid up together, out of sympathy?"

"What would make you say that?"

"Your eyes were watering. I figured you might have hurt something. Sorry, it was a bad joke," I conceded.

He chuckled nervously and told me that he was fine.

Then he went on. "It's a tumor, Chris."

"What, the American right?" I joked, and—with that poorly-timed joke—felt inoculated against any possibility that he'd ever guess that I already knew what he was about to tell me.

"What?" He looked baffled.

"Sorry, another bad joke."

"No, it's a tumor that broke her ribs."

"Excuse me?"

"Alright, let's backtrack. Ava has a tumor; she has cancer, Chris." He let this sink in for a moment. "And apparently it grew and put physical pressure on her ribs until they cracked. I guess they cracked overnight on the plane over to Madrid. Maybe she did sleep in a strange way and that was the final straw? I don't know."

"Jesus." I was startled by how surprised I was to hear this news again. It was only slightly less shocking the second time around, and more so coming from Peter. "Did you have any idea?"

"What, did we have any idea that she had cancer?" He was a little incredulous. "Of course not. We'd have told you straightaway. We've not even known for twenty-four hours, and here you and I sit."

"That's fair." Really I was very grateful that he was telling me now, so soon. Later I would feel selfish about having felt that way in this moment, wondering if at the time it had been vanity, self-satisfaction at knowing that I was the first they had told.

"I'm so sorry," he said.

"Strange thing for *you* to be apologizing to *me* right now."

"Yeah." He sucked in some air. "I don't know. It's—"

"It's what?" I softened my voice.

"It's hard for me to tell what is worse about this conversation," he began. "Having to say for the first time what's wrong. It just breaks my heart for her. Or—"

I cast my eyes down, trying to feel with him whatever it was he was feeling.

"Or," he breathed heavily, "knowing that I was going to break your heart."

His fist had felt better than this. Or at least, I had been more prepared for it. And suddenly it was time for me to hold back whatever I was feeling. He didn't need that right now. Peter seemed to recognize this, and went on.

"She'll be fine in the end. She will fight it. And she will win."

He suddenly seemed confident. I wondered if anyone ever said otherwise in this stage, if anyone ever conceded defeat so early. I suppose not, and there was still a great deal of fighting to be done. His confidence made me confident, and I felt better just being told that it would be all right. Lately I had been feeling so defeatist about the world that it felt good to feel confident about winning something again.

I learned quickly in that moment that if you've never faced a revelation like this, that someone so close to you might die, then you've really no way to understand what these conversations are like. I had not, and would have been unable to understand before about one o'clock in the afternoon on that very Saturday the twenty-eighth of July. Tomorrow it would be exactly one month since Peter and I had hatched the grand Spanish scheme drinking wine at Joselito.

I looked around the bar as we talked. It occurred to me that this was the place where I had first developed an enthusiasm for drinking in the presence of filament lightbulbs. That was years ago. When between us there were fewer responsibilities and no children. Even in broad daylight the place was dark in a way that collaborated with the drinks to slow the senses to a manageable pace.

Somewhat early in the discussion I asked Peter what he and Ava needed. He demurred, but it was obvious that he had something in mind.

"It's a big request, I know."

"Get on with it," I told him. "I promise it's alright."

"Well, she's going to be starting treatment very quickly. There are some tests, but the doctor was adamant that we move with some purpose on this."

I decided not to ask about the doctor.

"Yeah, so. . . " he trailed off. "Anyway, could you come up here for a while? Spend some time with the kids? I know it's a lot."

"It's nothing. I'll manage."

We agreed that I'd return to Washington for a few days, show my face at the office, and then come up to work mostly from New York. I happened to know that Geoff was to be off again to Provincetown, and that Caroline was barely home anyway, so I'd have the flat on the Upper West Side mostly to myself. We consummated the arrangement with another round of beer.

We meandered on, full of talk about Ava's condition and Pete's understanding of her prognosis. At moments it was all very matter of fact. Poor men's understanding of medical science. Treatment. Logistics. Then in other moments it felt quite philosophical. We spoke of the unfairness of it all, randomness, the slipping away of youth. How ironic it was that this had all transpired on a trip filled with youthful abandon and made possible by the adult experience of having money to waste and vacation time to spend. It was as if we had been looking back, trying to recapture a bygone era, when destiny laid its gnarled hand on our shoulder as if to say, "Come along now; it's time."

Suddenly our beers were empty and we felt very old indeed. And we knew that there was never any returning to the way things had been.

⁕⁕⁕

I returned to Washington later that same afternoon. At Penn Station, before boarding the train in New York, I decided that I wanted some wine. Penn Wines and Spirits, Pascual's shop, from whom Peter and I had once bought the Pappy Van Winkle, was off the exit corridor towards Eighth Avenue. There was time now before my train, so I lingered around the rack of Spanish bottles until Pascual appeared. He hugged me like a long-lost friend.

When we first met he had asked if he could help me find something. I had told him no, but introduced myself just the same. I did not realize then how much he would one day mean to me.

Now together again we drank a glass of something that was left over from a tasting he had poured at rush hour the night before. It was a garnacha rosé from Ribera del Duero. I tried to pay for the bottle I'd drink on the train, but he'd have none of it. Then we agreed that I'd return soon.

The train escaped the city and moved south through endless New Jersey. Eventually we rolled along past houses, farms, and fields, and the great stretches, lit by the setting sun, that span the rivers and bay out to the sea through Delaware, Maryland, and down towards Washington. I passed uneventful time unable to do my usual work, growing increasingly contemplative of the meaning of life the more of the bottle I drank. Later I fell asleep as the best alternative to growing weepy and drunk thinking about Ava and Peter.

At some point I realized that I'd not heard from Ash in some time. I felt bad about this and knew that I had been caught up in all that had happened back in New York. She must have been terribly worried about me, but it was bordering on too late in Madrid for her to read the message I had just sent.

Erik waited for me in the center of the great hall when I arrived at Union Station. I had sent him a message asking for him to come, but hadn't said why.

"Here we are again!" he exclaimed, evidently happy to see me.

"Hello, sir. Good of you to wait." I forced a smile.

"Joselito?"

"Just as well I passed out on the train," I said, trying as I might to not let on about what had happened with Ava.

"You're a drunk," he said as we hugged.

And there at Joselito over a glass of wine I told him about Ava, about Peter putting on a good face. But I didn't tell him about Caroline giving it all away. Better he not know, and better I have a friend who knew little enough of the whole thing to not be too defeatist about it.

I'd not seen Billy when we first walked in, but he eventually popped by at the bar.

"Just in from the train, yeah?"

"It went on for too long."

"What, the train?"

"Yeah."

"All alone with only his bottle of wine," Erik mused.

"My mother would put me on the train from one side of the country to visit my dad on the other side of the country. I was eight. All alone. And of course she'd put me in the smoking carriage because it was a pound cheaper." Billy's eyes twinkled with the look of a person who felt he had just said something quite funny, and he pranced away.

We talked into the night, and Billy brought us more wine, and the music played and the candles cast their soothing light on the bar, and it all seemed very nice and normal to be home again.

That song—the one I had thought of weeks ago in the same spot—played in my head as I walked away from Joselito.

Llega tarde a casa con la bruma Del Mar
Llega con la rabia enroscada
Entra muy despacio para no secuestrar
El sueño más bonito que hay.

⁂

I looked out the big windows of my apartment at the river and the Capitol and the Washington Monument and all the sights I had seen from the air in the moment I had last left the city. The moon hung bright and full in the sky, obscured only slightly by a wisp of cloud, the horizon beyond the city lit by its brilliant reflection shining up from the quiet river.

I thought of the last waning gibbous under which Ash and I had made love in the beach grass. Tomorrow it would begin to wane once again.

Sale de la niebla de un bostezo lunar. . .

A chime, and I looked at my phone. It was nearly half past eight in the morning in Madrid. I smiled. Ash must have sent me a message soon as she had awoken to mine from much earlier. I was desperately happy to have her back in my life. Now most of all. She had been so right-minded this time. So happy. I smiled thinking about that night she had arranged for me in Boston. Thinking about how I had so expected her to abandon us again just after Independence Day. But she had turned up there in Boston. And again in Stockholm. And in Spain.

It was then in that moment, all alone in the dark of my apartment for the first time in nearly a month, lit only by the lights of the city streaming in through the big windows. Then I decided that Ash and I ought to get married when this business with Ava was over.

> *Y María le dice que sí,*
> *Dice sonrojada que sí,*
> *Y se esconde en sus brazos.*

I felt suddenly young and that the world was full of promise. Life seemed once again laid out ahead of me. This clear moment changed everything. I knew then that Ava would recover. To hell with Caroline and things doctors say. I was happy and self-assured.

> *Y él contesta que todo irá bien*
> *Que las flores volverán a crecer*
> *Donde ahora lloramos.*

Then I poured some peppermint tea and picked up my phone to read what Ash had sent. I wanted to suggest the idea to her now. I'd not dare share such an important idea over means so cheap as text. I feared I'd break her heart with the casual tawdriness of the thing. Perhaps I'd fly to Madrid in the morning and ask her. Bring her back to New York with me, and there I'd stay for a bit watching the children and planning a wedding that we could have soon as Ava was well again. We'd all be together, and what a happy moment it would be.

You're drunk, I laughed to myself. Thank God I always felt such a happy drunk.

I sipped my tea.

We hadn't had a wedding in years. Peter and Ava had been the last. What an affair that had been! I laughed out loud again, all alone in the dark, remembering how Ash had nearly not come when she realized that the invitation had been sent only to me and that she was *only* to be my date. At the time I had decided not to tell her what a chore it was even to convince Ava of blessing that idea. She had been angry with Ash for having again abandoned us a while earlier.

"When *you two* get married one day, I promise I'll be there," Ava had said sarcastically, believing full well she'd never have to make good on the promise.

Now she'd have to get well soon.

I smiled and had another sip of tea. Then I opened my phone to read the message from Ash.

I really do love you. But yesterday while I was out on my bike, I couldn't help but face the reality that I don't feel romantic anymore.

Then a second message.

There isn't some magical future in which this is OK. Stop waiting for some mythical moment where I'll wake up and be fine. This is what there is, and one day it would destroy you like it's destroyed me.

I looked out the big windows.

And so the moon looked down, as it always had, insensitive to the success or sorrow of the people who live their lives under its waxing and waning glow.

Then I sank into deep sleep without an alarm.

Chapter Twenty-Six

The worst of it seemed over. I awoke with a sense of purpose, as if I had been searching all this time for some great cause into which I might throw myself. In Ava's sickness I finally found that which I had sought. We were going to make her right again. All of us.

Except for Ash.

There is a thing about loving someone like that. In the sad and inevitable end it leaves you empty. It leaves you hollowed out. It leaves you breathless and gasping for air. There is a hole in your stomach that no words can fill. No other happiness, no recompense for that which you poured out to love the unlovable, to salve the emotional wounds that would otherwise be bound up by love. As if love were a thing that made sense. You are alone and adrift. Bewildered as to where it all went wrong. There is nothing you can do, and eventually you resign yourself to that idea. There is no reason, no amount of love that can be poured out to fill in the darkness. She was alone in her own mind, and I was helpless.

Under normal circumstances I would have moved on and quietly waited for her to come back. This one seemed final, though. Not for anything she had said. Rather it had taken me deciding so surely that it was time for us to be together, only for her to moments later break my heart again. That reconciled me to the idea that she would have just gone on breaking my heart for as long as I allowed it.

To hell with Ash.

"Besides," Erik told me later that day, "you know just as well that you were always in love with Ava. And Ash knew it, too."

I sipped my café con leche.

"Where do you go from here?" he asked.

"Back to New York, I suppose?"

"Should we just expect to see you up there from now on?"

"You know how I pour myself into my work."

"Ava your work now?"

"Call it rallying for the cause."

"Try not to be so eager for a purpose in *your* life that you forget that *her* life is the reason you're up there."

Good advice. I would like to say that I spent the time that followed taking it to heart. Perhaps I did. It's a grey thing, caring for someone you love when they are ill. Your conscious mind suggests that your efforts are for them, and that you are pure in your intentions. Yet we are human, and humans like to be heroes. I suppose it does not matter in the end. I lingered another couple of days in Washington. I went to my office, checked on the junior software engineers, wondered if I ought to go up and visit my old pastor friend in West Virginia. God knew I could have used some spiritual reinforcement. Then I tortured myself thinking about the fellow at the garage.

And having thus checked all the boxes of being back at work, I left for New York as quickly as I had returned home. Three nights in my own bed, drinking wine alone and staring at the moon seemed sufficient. There was no telling what awaited me in New York, only that there was an adventure yet unseen, and how good it felt to direct my energies towards something meaningful. It was Tuesday night, and I was off again.

Penn Station in Midtown Manhattan is a ghastly place. A tormentor's lair of odd smells and stale air and a crush of people beneath the street. It is a subterranean mirror of the grandeur that is Grand Central Station across town, reflecting beauty with hideousness. A sensory disgrace, but a marvel of logistics. Through this place runs the spine of *Bosnywashingtonia*, the Western world's great megacity and all its contradictions.

When I walk through the place, down the long Connecting Concourse that spans the distance between Seventh and Eighth Avenues, I am filled with the hope and vigor that comes from stepping off the train and into the city and all its living energy. So conditioned I am in the knowledge that Peter and Ava and Geoff and Pascual and all the others are just moments away. That crush of humanity is my family, and here to them have I come home.

Hours on the train, a few nights drinking wine alone in my apartment, and the dark cloud that Caroline and Ash had unknowingly conspired to cast upon the world had caused me to forget—I think—that it had only been two days since I had last seen Ava. Then she had seemed fine, and she seemed ever as fine when I walked in the door. The children were on the decline towards sleep. Peter shuffled them in and out of their baths. The nanny had been sent out. Ava sat quietly at the counter with a glass of wine. A gnarled cork, stained in deep red, sat next to a bottle on the counter. There were two unused glasses. She smiled when she saw me.

"Screaming Eagle?" I asked.

"Last bottle I'll drink for a while, I suppose?" She shrugged. "Peter wanted to drink something special tonight."

"I remember buying it. Well," I stammered, "I remember when he bought it."

It was a good story. We had been out with Erik the night of Ava's shower when Catherine was on the way. Peter had bought two bottles of Screaming Eagle, one as a gift for his future eighteen-year-old daughter and the other for us to share on a momentous occasion to be determined. I supposed that this occasion was as momentous as any.

Ava poured me a glass.

"I start my treatment tomorrow."

"Tomorrow," Peter exclaimed as he burst into the room, "is the first day on the road to recovery."

"Cheers." I raised my glass. They raised theirs. We were happy to be together.

"What has it been?" She looked at me. "A week since we went to Méntrida?"

"Good Lord."

It was summer, and time had no meaning here. We were like children again.

Peter began giggling uncontrollably.

"I'm really sorry I punched you, man."

Ava raised her eyebrow at him.

"I'm sorry, I'm sorry!" he insisted. "It's just so damned funny."

"Ash and I were not amused," Ava admonished him. "Come to think of it, that's the only time I've ever felt she and I truly saw eye to eye."

"You don't like her much, do you?"

"She is"—Ava chose her words—"not my favorite."

"When's she coming home, anyway?" Peter asked.

I told them about the texts she had sent.

"Now I really don't like her. Back to not liking her at all, in fact." Ava took a sip of wine measured to convey an *I told you so* degree of smug satisfaction.

"She'll be back, Jake. Always is."

"Not this time, I don't think."

I told them about my revelation, about having needed this to happen at the moment I felt committal about the whole thing. How casually heartless it had made her seem.

"Are you scared?" I changed the subject abruptly.

"Scared of what?"

"You know."

"Oh, I'm terrified," Ava shot back without hesitation.

Peter put his hand on hers atop the counter.

We talked about it.

Then we heard the girls bickering about something in the other room.

Peter went to check on them. "They're *supposed* to be asleep," he said, a twinkle in his eye.

"Actually, I'm quite annoyed with Geoff," Ava said once Peter had left the room.

"Oh? Why?"

"He came over here today while Peter stopped in at the office. Wanted to check on me."

"That sounds nice?"

"That wasn't all he wanted."

I looked confused.

"He wanted to apologize."

I almost betrayed an admission of my foreknowledge, but Ava continued without interruption.

"Wanted to apologize for what happened between us back in the day."

"What happened between you? I thought you loved Gee Gee. You said so that day in the vineyard."

"I *do* love Gee Gee."

She sipped her wine.

"Which is why I don't need him coming in here three days after I'm diagnosed, apologizing for spending the night with me, what? Eight years ago? Give or take."

I never imagined that I'd choke on a gulp of $900 wine, but now was that time.

"You can't be serious," I managed, incredulously.

"Oh, I'm serious. Sat just where you sit. Right here at this counter. Told me how sorry he was for having taken advantage of me. Said that he had regretted it ever since."

"What was there to regret?"

"That's the point!"

"Sounds like a wee bit of Jesus talking. Does Peter know?"

"Of course not. He's weird and sensitive about those sorts of things."

"Well, he knows you slept with me."

"Of course he knows that. But we dated for years. And you're his best friend."

"I'm his best friend?" I asked. I was genuinely touched to know he felt that way.

"Of course you are. Why do you ask such obvious questions?" She flashed a good-natured smile. "But this isn't about you, so stop it."

"Right, right."

"I don't know. I just thought he was an ass to say such a thing."

"I felt like an ass today, too," I admitted to her.

"What for?"

"Actually when I walked in just a bit ago."

She waited for me to continue.

"I don't know. I'd just been so depressed, and then yesterday I rolled out of bed and felt ready to take on the world. So I spent two days psyching myself up for what good care we were going to take of you."

She groaned.

"And then I walked through the door and there you were sitting here drinking your Screaming Eagle like it was nothing."

"Surprised that I'm not an invalid?"

"Yeah, kinda."

"You'll have to work harder than that to get rid of me, Chris Jacobson."

"I'm not trying to get rid of you."

"You're trying to pretend you're a hero!"

"Am I that transparent?"

"No." She put her hand on mine. "I just know you too well. You're very sweet to be up here with me. With us. I can't begin to tell you how happy Peter is to have you here. He'll never say so because you're both foolish and stubborn. And because I am, of course, still the adult around here."

I raised my glass. "You're like the incident commander of your own incident."

She giggled. Coast Guard humor.

"No, seriously," I tried to reassure her, "I'm very proud of you and how good you've been. You are incredibly strong."

She stared back at me with glassy eyes.

Peter returned, and we drank some wine.

Ava shaved her head in the morning. Said the night before that she planned to do it. Said that she planned to be in control of her own situation.

"Treatment didn't take my hair. I took my hair. Donated it. Wanted to try on a new style. A new wig. I think I look good as a blonde." That's what she told everyone.

The weeks that followed were an uneventful horror show. She grew thinner, and far more tired. But she laughed. And the kids played, and I played with them. It was a tidy arrangement. I worked in the New York office during the day. Most of those days I had lunch with Geoff, who was rattling around the city like a caged bird. Once when I flew somewhere for a meeting, there was a pigeon flying about inside the terminal when I returned to New York. It darted from one enormous glass window to the other, thinking that this was the moment of great escape. Geoff behaved similarly during the height of hurricane season when he was separated from his boat and his islands. Normally he'd have been up to Provincetown, but his strange guilt about a dalliance with Ava eight years in the past kept him tethered to New York. So we had lunch nearly every day.

Peter sent the nanny away most evenings. He spent quiet time with Ava. I put the kids through their nightly rituals. Bathed them, read to them, then left them at the end when their mother and father came to kiss them goodnight. The little boy giggled mightily at the sight of his mother without hair. The girls tried on her wigs. These were silly and warm times in the long evenings of the long summer.

Some nights we wondered if Ava was going to make it. Other nights she was strong and lively and put the kids to bed herself. Most nights Peter and I shared a bottle of wine after the others had fallen asleep. From time to time he joined me in my cab across the Park, back to the Upper West Side. There we drank sangría at Buceo 95 on the corner of Ninety-Fifth and Amsterdam.

In times long past I had lived a stretch up here in Geoff's apartment. That was before Caroline, and during the winter when Geoff was down in the islands. Ash would often take the train up from Washington, and we'd sit together at Buceo 95 drinking sangría at the little high-top in the corner by the kitchen window. Now it was summer years on, and Peter and I sat on the terrace outside, drinking sangría and reflecting on all the things upon which men in their mid-thirties might have to reflect. We no longer talked of politics, and Ash had not been heard from in weeks.

The days quickly ran together. I accidentally went to my office on a Saturday. One Sunday I stopped in to see Pascual, but he was off every Sunday. The fellow who owned the shop laughed at me and asked if I had really forgotten what day it was.

One afternoon I had a call from Peter. He told me that the nanny had taken the kids off to the Park. It was a beautiful day. Ava felt awful, and was terrifically tired. He was home sitting with her, but wondered if I could break away to fetch her a take-out bowl of her favorite soup.

"They don't deliver. Who in God's name doesn't deliver?" he joked nervously.

"Give me a few minutes and I'll be up."

I fetched the soup.

Peter left me alone in the room with her.

I asked her how she felt.

"Terrible, but if you ask Geoff, he's the one who feels terrible."

"Good God." I was really exasperated with him. "He visited again?" I asked.

"Yes."

"The man desperately needs to go back to the islands."

"Honestly." Ava sat up in bed. "Honestly, Chris, please don't let him come back over here again. I don't want to see him."

She knew that this hurt me. She knew that it was a lot to ask.

"I hate to ask it of you, I really do, but—" She quieted for a moment. "I'm not a thing to be regretted." She gulped back a tear. "When he tells me he's sorry. Who knows if I have much time left. Maybe I'll live forever. I don't know. But I'll be damned if I am going to die as somebody's regret. It's not his place to cheapen me into some moral lesson of his tormented religion."

I took her hand.

"Promise me that you won't let him come back over here."

I promised.

We ate soup together.

I asked her if she remembered eating soup together in Portugal.

"Yes. So delicious."

We talked about the time we'd once spent there.

We had journeyed by car from Porto. It soon became clear that we were dealing with something special as we emerged from behind mountains high above valleys where the land dropped out from under us, chimney smoke and early-morning fog blanketing the open air beneath us, and miles of terraced vineyards stretched out as far as the eye could see.

Perched high on a strikingly steep mountain rising above the winding Douro River in northern Portugal, one of the most stunning sights we had ever seen, terraced rows of vines etched into the hillside led up a winding road to the Quinta do Pôpa winery.

We turned left off the road and up the hill to the winery after about ninety minutes of driving. The vineyard's land stretched all 550 meters to the top of the mountain, where olive trees grew alongside grape vines. Older grapes produced some of the richest notes. The vines closest to the river were over eighty years old, growing younger further up the right bank at forty years old.

I was happy that Ava fell asleep after a few moments of recounting this, closing her eyes to remember it all before drifting off.

Another night and Ava was in particularly high spirits. She stayed up with Peter and I after the kids had gone to bed. We drank tea and talked in circles. She had heard about a gala dinner the Coast Guard Foundation was hosting on a Saturday in August.

"You can't be serious thinking that we should go?" Peter asked her.

She was tenacious. Her husband and I were dumbfounded. Sometimes it seemed that her treatment made us more tired than it made her.

"I think it would be fun!" she insisted.

"Rallying for the cause?"

"Are you surprised?" I looked at Peter over the brim of my teacup. "I mean really?"

"I mean really!" She pattered on, her voice quieter than it would have been in the past, but no less determined. "Are you two really going to tell me that we can't go?"

"Look at your husband." I threw my hands up.

He looked at her, a small smile on his lips.

"Then it's settled." She laughed. "I've lost some weight. So at least I'll still fit in my uniform."

I raised my glass to Peter. "To my favorite arm ornament! May you look half as pretty as the girl who brung you."

Peter asked me if that was humor, or if I actually thought *brung* was a word.

"What?"

"Who *brung* you?"

"Haven't you ever heard that phrase, *dance with the girl who brung you*?"

"No. You sound like an idiot."

"She *brung* you."

"That she did." He put his hand on hers. She smiled.

I called Erik and asked if he'd like to come. He was enthusiastic.

"Who you gonna brung?" Peter asked me, grinning stupidly.

We discussed this for a moment.

It occurred to me that I'd not thought much about women in weeks. There had been weepy moments thinking about Ash. Sometimes I even cried. I was always alone then, usually in the dark of night back at Geoff's apartment. Otherwise I felt so consumed by Ava and Peter and the children and all that was happening.

"Hasn't thought about sex in weeks," Peter giggled.

Ava nearly spit out her tea.

"What about Tess? Isn't she still in London?"

"That's mischievous."

She looked back at me mischievously. Ava always believed that I ought to have spent my late twenties romancing Tess rather than longing for Ash. Our Australian friend and I had, however, never touched one another.

Peter mused, "I love how a girl in London is your idea of a convenient date."

"I'm more interested in his happiness than his convenience," Ava shot back. "Besides, what is it you say? British and American run an hourly bus service between here and London?"

"It's true."

I sent Tess a message.

Love to. Bags packed, she shot back.

What the hell are you still doing awake?

It was ungodly late in London.

Waiting for you to suggest this. It will be great fun!

"That was easy. 'Waiting for you to suggest this,' like she knew ... Wait!"

I looked at Ava. She smiled.

"You sneaky little girl."

"I've had a lot of idle time on my hands," she said, giggling.

I snatched her phone from the counter.

He's going to ask you to come play with us in New York. Sometime within the next five minutes.

Peter pulled out his phone and bought an entire table sponsorship. "Seats for eight. Guess we bring Geoff and Caroline?"

Ava groaned.

"What?"

"Nothing," she assured her husband. "Just Caroline. Too close to home."

"She's been mighty good to us all."

"That's true."

Ava had no problem seeing Caroline at the gala. Caroline was not the problem.

Otherwise, it was decided. The date was set. The Foundation was several thousand richer, Peter Dean several thousand poorer, and all of us one-night-like-old-times happier.

Chapter Twenty-Seven

Erik and Emma came up on the train Friday afternoon before the gala. Pascual was pouring a wine tasting in his shop at Penn Station. We three met there and drank wine with Pascual. He opened a bottle of something special after we exhausted the tasting lineup. Frantic passengers scurried in and out of the shop on their way to the trains. The scene reminded me of the day Peter and I had bought the whisky for Ava. Then, we had followed our stars. Now there were fewer stars in our eyes.

Later we went to dinner.

At the corner of Forty-Third Street and Ninth Avenue, in Hell's Kitchen just west of Times Square, was an extraordinary restaurant called Chimichurri Grill. One of Pete's banker friends had introduced us to this tiny Argentinian steakhouse years earlier. Stunning food and wine, charmingly intimate spaces, and warm-from-the-very-first-moment hospitality from our friends Carlos and Alicia had us in love on the first night. Afterwards it became the site of quiet dinners together, celebrations with friends, and glasses of wine whilst watching the snow fall ever deeper outside. That was a particular night. Before there were children. Snow fell as Peter, Ava, and I rambled on together about how late we could stay and still manage a cab back to the East Side. We waited too long, and later had to get out and push somewhere heading up Third Avenue.

Emma had somehow never been there. Newcomers were always struck, on entering, by how small the place was. Thirty seats and a small bar.

Wilmer, the longtime head waiter, seated us at our favorite four-plate table in the front near the only window. An excellent spot for people watching. The same place we had sat on that snowy night years ago. Things were cozy further back towards the kitchen. The place took one into the embrace of a delightful evening many miles from the stress of the world as the sun went down and the neon god we'd made came to life outside.

Erik gestured in that direction, telling Emma how the long table back that way had once served all the boys at Peter's bachelor party. He was very excited to be sharing this old place with her. I was surprised she had never found her way here with us before. We'd been telling her about it for years.

"I just don't spend enough time in New York," she guessed. "My man's always coming to DC to see me!"

Wilmer told us about the specials. Sweet corn empanadas. A bone-in ribeye. "And, if you like fish," he said with a twinkle in his eye, "we have a delicious branzino." He was self-amused at how well Erik and I knew that branzino was *always* on special.

He returned a few minutes later with our wine.

Erik exploded in laughter.

We looked at him suspiciously.

"Oh my God," he stuttered. "That man is walking around with a parrot on his shoulder. This is fucking New York."

The man with the bird walked past the window. I shook my head.

Emma whipped out her phone and posted a photo with something witty she came up with just then.

We ordered empanadas. And grilled oysters. And I ordered *vacio a la gaucho*. Wilmer brought the hanger steak out a while later, sitting alone atop a simple wooden plate and garnished with a single slice of grilled red pepper.

Emma asked me if I had a date for the gala.

I told her about Tess.

"One day I will get my hands on Ash," she promised me.

"You will do nothing of the sort," I admonished.

She was taken aback.

I stared wistfully out the window. Then I told my friends a story.

"Ava and I were in Santiago de Compostela, in Galicia. In Spain," I began.

I smiled, remembering it all as if it were yesterday.

One night we were sitting at the bar at Petiscos do Cardeal, in the old center city.

Ava wanted another gin tonic. This time with the gin *con fresas*, the stuff made in Sevilla. Our bartender friend laughed, and I explained that this was the last for the night.

"*Es final,*" I insisted. "*Estas las últimas bebidas juntos en Santiago.*"

Por ahora. We both, the bartender and I, had in our minds that this wasn't the end, that Ava and I would return.

He poured me a final glass of the house mencía. God how I loved the stuff. I returned to the bar with Ava's gin.

Later we stepped out into the night. There was something magical about stepping out of your favorite bar in whichever city you were in, out onto the street into the dark night when it was cold enough to see your breath float out in front of you towards the sky, refracted and made delicate by the street lights. There were revelers in the streets, but we knew it was almost time.

"Let's go to Gato Negro," she said. We'd never been to Gato Negro, but she loved the place all the same.

Gato Negro was closed. The bartender was cleaning up, and the door was locked.

We walked the narrow length of Rúa da Raíña, past the Praza de Fonseca and its fountain, gently giving life to the dark with the never-

ceasing marbles of water flowing down into its pool. We stopped at
the Praza das Praterías.

The tower built into the southern end of the cathedral's transept
rose into the night, high above the Christmas lights that had been
strung in a canopy above the plaza. The night was at last completely
quiet. I had never experienced a city so quiet. We were utterly alone
in one another's company.

"Shall we go to the plaza, see the cathedral one last time?" I
asked.

"Yes." She smiled.

We turned back down the Calle de Fonseca, and after a moment,
right into the Praza de Obradoiro. The city hall on our left was lit
with a blue streak down its façade as if it were the Galician flag.
The great Cathedral of Santiago de Compostela towered into the
darkness to our right, lit brilliantly in white light, yet dark down to
the large, seemingly ancient paving stones on which we stood. We
admired it together in silence for several minutes.

I placed my hand on the wall where the steps rose to meet
the door of the narthex. The stone was coarse, weathered by the
years, smooth as if tempered by the gentle hands of time, cold to
the touch, radiantly warm with the memories of nearly a thousand
years of pilgrims and sinners who had stood in this square, laid hands
upon these stones, sought salvation in the shadows of its sturdy
countenance.

I began speaking.

"I don" know if there is a God."

I was surprised when Ava said nothing, just looked at me as if
she were interested in what I had to say next.

"What an incredible sight. Humankind was either inspired by
the divine to build such a thing."

"Or?" she asked softly.

"They were so inspired by faith in the unknown that they built
their own divine . . . in front of which we now stand." I thought for

a moment. "I wonder if God inspired us to build such a thing, or if in building such things we made our own god from the stone itself."

We took one another's hands and disappeared back into the night, back past the Praza das Preterías, up the Rúa da Conga, and quietly into our separate rooms.

‧‿‿‿‿‿‧

I was lost in my thoughts, resigned to another time and place, sitting there glassy eyed looking out on Ninth Avenue when Erik jarred me back to the table.

"I remember this." He smiled. "You had just gotten out of the Coast Guard. And went off to Spain for a month. I visited you in Madrid."

"I spent most of my time in Santiago."

"Peter visited you there."

"Ava visited me there, too."

"You weren't together at that point, though?" he asked.

"We were not." I smiled. "Ava had started school. We thought we might get together in Santiago before the world took us under. We weren't sure if we'd be able to hang on to one another."

Emma interrupted. "Did you hope to get her back?"

"No? I'm not sure what we hoped."

"Chris had gone off to find himself," Erik giggled.

"That's a little trite."

"Alright. He was there to be creative for a few weeks."

Emma asked if I had found any inspiration. I laughed out loud and stared out at Ninth Avenue again.

I thought of a garden hemmed in by stone walls, mossy and green. In the center there was a pool. Dozens of apples had fallen in and floated quietly there, coloring the painting in my mind a brilliant yellow and red. A statue of a man crouched pensively at the side of the pool, unsure if he would pluck out an apple or jump in himself. A simple tin watering can sat beside him.

This was all far up the hill from the cathedral where there had been a small street, the Rúa da Porta da Pena, and a hotel called Costa Vella.

The next morning Ava and I sat together in that garden. The hotel's whitewashed windowpanes looked out at us. Café con leche steamed up at us from the stone table. Vines crawled across the arbors forming a cloister to encircle the bit of tranquil green paradise we had found. A gaggle of excited birds darted in unison between two rows of bushes. One moment aflutter on the left, the next moment racing across the grass to the bush on the right before repeating the whole exercise like energetic children enthralled by the fun they had gotten into.

A girl sat alone, reading and sipping her coffee at the next table. She was younger than us. I guessed perhaps twenty. But I found her strikingly beautiful.

I don't know what Ava and I talked about. She was leaving Santiago that day, so I imagine we talked in circles about what she'd get up to in New York. Peter was to come the next day, and I think I suggested to her then that they get together when both were back in the city. She smiled faintly and told me that she'd consider it.

Then she went inside for a few moments. I argued with myself for several seconds, and at some length looked at the girl sitting at the next table.

"*Hola, buena,*" I chanced.

The girl giggled with surprise, but her smile told me it was all right.

"*¿De dónde eres?*" I asked her where she came from.

"*Depende.*" She shrugged and grinned.

I stammered, wondering where to take it from there with my poor Spanish. She was sympathetic and answered the question properly.

"Chicago," she said.

"*¿Tú eres un Americano?*" I asked surprised.

"Maybe."

"Oh thank God," I exclaimed with relief.

"Why? You don't like Spaniards?"

"Oh, no." Now I was a bit embarrassed. "I just speak terrible Spanish."

"I'll teach you."

"Oh?"

"If you're nice."

"He's nice enough, don't worry." Ava sat down again.

The girl took a hurried sip of coffee and shifted uncomfortably in her chair. I asked her if she lived there in Santiago.

"Oh no. I'm studying here. Actually, I'm returning home next week."

"To Chicago?"

"Well, Chicago for Christmas. Then back to school to finish up."

"Where'd you go to school?" Ava asked.

"Georgetown. In DC." The girl nodded.

Ava threw me a side-eyed glance.

"Chris lives in DC," she said.

"*In* DC, or *near* DC?"

"That sounded uppity, and I don't even know you." I grinned. She laughed.

"Sorry."

"It's alright, I guess you can be uppity. You go to Georgetown."

We talked about how Galicia had been. The girl told us that we should go up to A Coruña. Ava told her that she was leaving in an hour. When I said I might go up to A Coruña, the girl suggested we go together.

I remembered feeling sad at that moment, eight years ago, when Ava reminded me that she was leaving Santiago. We had broken up not long before, and soon after had decided that she would come visit me there. Though our parting of ways had been mutual, the anticipation of our last hurrah in Galicia had softened the blow. Then, watching her befriend this strange girl from Chicago, I was reminded of how warm and genuine my friend Ava Murray really was. It was a really beautiful garden.

I sat smiling and yet on the verge of tears in the restaurant in New York.

Emma asked, "Did you ever see that girl again?"

"Oh," I chuckled and finished my story:

At length Ava had stood up to leave.

"You two should see one another back in Washington," she said.

"I'd like that," the girl said.

"I'm sorry," Ava admitted. "I don't think we properly introduced ourselves. I'm Ava."

"Oh, sorry," the girl apologized. "I'm Ash. Ash Luciano."

I looked at Emma. "Love can't be thrown away," I said carefully. "As I see it, to not love someone today who you loved in the past is to have never really loved them at all. If they were worthy of your love in one time, they are worthy of your love in all times."

Emma contemplated this.

I went on. "These things, these stories. They give us life. And, if you need proof, that insistence on never falling out of love is why we have Ava. Or"—I fell quiet—"at least why I still have Ava."

Tess came in. I got up to hug her. Erik and I introduced her to Emma.

"Finally, another proper sailor in our midst," Erik joked with her. "Did you bring your uniform? Proper Navy thing?"

"Oh, I swore those things off. Haven't got it in London any longer." We sat.

It was a jarring moment, being in that garden back in Santiago and then lurched back to New York—and reality—by Erik's exuberance at seeing our old friend.

"Where have you been?" he asked.

"My flight from London was terribly delayed."

"Fun sounding."

Wilmer brought her a drink. "You're here for dessert?" he asked.

I suggested she try the *panqueque de manzana*. We ordered one and ate it together.

Erik told her how happy he was that she had come. He was very sincere. The last traces of daylight finally slipped away down the street.

"How have you been holding up?" Tess finally asked me. "Ava told me you had been quite the hero in all of this, barely ever leaving them and being good with the kids."

"I'm not a hero." I still felt like having a good cry.

"What drives you?" Erik asked me as if he were clueless in the matter.

Tess laughed. "Isn't that a question you ask when you already know the answer? You know, to prove a point?"

"What do you think of me?" I retorted, a bit cockeyed over my glass.

"Actually, I find you somewhat boring," Erik deadpanned, then giggled a bit into his wine.

A homeless fellow stumbled past on the street.

"I'd have thought you'd have fixed that," Tess poked.

"Oh?"

"You know, with all the Christians running things here in America now? Thought you'd have fixed everything up. No homeless. Doing unto them as Jesus would do. That sort of thing."

Emma squirmed.

Erik jumped in. "Yesterday I saw the Gideons giving out Bibles."

We looked at him, waiting for something more.

"I mean, how about you give out a sandwich? You know, give out something that Jesus would actually care about."

"Funny you should say that." I cast a sidelong glance at Emma as her eyes pled with me to change the subject. "Once I was quite ill, walking not too far from here. Homeless guy saw me and told me that I didn't look too good."

"And?"

"He took me to the pharmacy and got me some medicine. When I had come to my senses I bought him a sandwich."

"That's the America I love." Tess grinned.

"I'm quite attracted to you saying that in Australian." I grinned back. Suddenly those deep brown eyes seemed sultry.

"See, I don't think of you as a highly sexualized person," she laughed and just breezed past my inane comment about her speaking Australian.

I laughed uneasily at where this had gone.

"I'm sorry, where were we?" Emma rescued me, and gave me a look as if to convey that she knew I was dying inside. "The story?"

"I don't know."

"What's the plot?"

"There is no plot."

"Excuse me?"

"That's the point of the story, literally—that there is no plot."

"The plot are all the screwball people you encounter. Billy Grant, Geoff Gamal, and all the rest."

"*Y los demás.*" Emma knew.

Then my head swam with the lyrics of an old Spanish pop song from our younger years.

"You're drunk." Erik looked at her.

"We're all drunk!" she shot back.

"Tess," I proclaimed, "welcome to America!"

Later, at Geoff's place back on the Upper West Side, Tess told me how happy she was to be there. She told me how heartbroken she was by it all, how angry she was with Ash. Then she kissed me on the cheek. I told her that she could sleep in my room. Then I fell into restless sleep on the couch.

There were many nights when I could not sleep. It was as if I had been dissatisfied with the day, and was waiting for the next thing to happen.

Chapter Twenty-Eight

Wine and memories and sadness and anticipation and all the rest sloshed about in my mind when at some point the night before I had sent Ash a message.

It was what it was. It was beautiful, and I'll never regret it. It, and you, will be special to me forever.

No response.

And so we each endure our own heartbreak, some in the sunshine or the spotlight, but more often in the agony of our own mind. It was agony wondering what was happening in her mind just then. Tortured place as it was.

That's how the morning began.

Tess and I drank coffee with Geoff.

"Do you think you might shave today? Or get a haircut?" I looked at him skeptically.

"For what?"

"The gala, where we're going tonight? Ava's return to society?"

"Well, when you put it that way."

There was that place down the street with a big sign: *We buy gold! We sell diamonds! We give haircuts!* I had always assumed they didn't actually cut any hair.

Geoff spent three hours there, and was nearly late for the gala.

I caught a cab over to the Upper East Side whilst Tess waited for Geoff to finish. Then there were frantic comings and goings of settling off the kids with the nanny, Caroline returning from the hospital, and Geoff was still cutting his hair.

Ava had rallied, and didn't want to be late for her big night. She and I left together whilst Peter finished with the children. She looked as on top of the world in that white dinner jacket as ever I had seen her. Erik and Emma arrived before we did.

"You're looking a bit old for a lieutenant," Erik joked with her.

"I have the most beautiful date of them all." I glared back at him, surely treating her as more delicate than she was willing to let on to anyone else.

"At least it fit again. Hooray for cancer treatment!" She was jovial, and it put us at ease.

Caroline had arranged to get ready at Peter's and Ava's because it was closer to the hospital. She arrived with Peter.

The six of us drank gin at the bar. There was a newly minted admiral there for whom Ava and I had both worked when she—the admiral—was a commander. We had not seen her in years, and she was confused when Peter introduced himself as Ava's husband after having seen the two of us arrive together. Nobody mentioned how sick Ava had been.

Around that time Geoff and Tess blew through the door. Caroline, who had been having a drink with me, switched dates with Tess. The admiral shook her head and moved on.

"You look nice." I eyed my cousin.

"Took him hours. We were almost late, right?"

"You *were* late," I laughed.

"He's all yours if you want him." Caroline shot an exasperated grin at Tess.

Ava quietly rearranged the little knot of us so that she stood as

far from Geoff as possible. She laughed and bantered with Erik and
Emma and her husband, and I was amazed at how she had put herself
together for this.

Some other friends and acquaintances passed by. We said hello.
It was all very fun and stuffy wrapped up in our bow ties. Peter wore
a tuxedo.

"I'm surprised you even own a tuxedo," he heckled Geoff.

"I do!" Geoff replied with a high note and a twinkle in his eye,
always self-satisfied with his knack for surprising people.

Erik asked him if he kept it on the boat.

"I keep it in the apartment, where I keep all my things."

"I'll remember that the next time you want me to let you back
in," Caroline suggested.

He smiled sheepishly.

At some point he maneuvered into position such that he might
talk with Ava. I meant to go save her, but an old shipmate sidetracked
me. First he confused Tess for Ash—he had met neither of them—
but became quickly enamored of her accent.

"I have an Australian friend." He mentioned a name. "Do you
know him?"

"Why is it that all Americans think that all Australians know
one another?"

"I never thought of that. Do we?"

"It's a big country. Whole continent in fact!" She turned
dismissive.

He tried to recover, but Tess had finished with him. I slapped him
on the back and told him how good it was to see him again. He told
me how things were on his ship. *His ship?* I marveled at this. My old
shipmate now had a ship of his own.

"And what the hell have you done!" He laughed hard, completely
unaware that I had been wondering the same for some time now.

I thought of the fellow at the garage and of that string of
formative moments when I had looked out on my own departure

from childhood. I remembered how hopeful I had been for what I thought was to come.

The air inside smelled of booze and self-satisfaction. Warm air wafted in from the big open windows. I was wrapped up in layers. Sweat formed at my collar. It was hot.

I grew dour and decided that I'd try not to think of that old fellow again. His kindness had tormented me long enough.

"I shouldn't have said that, about Americans and Australians." Tess rejoined and handed me a fresh glass of Champagne. "I'm sorry."

"He deserved it."

"Oh?"

I told her about what he had said.

"You know, I told you that I think you're the hero of your own story."

"A story without a plot?" I smirked back at her.

She went off to talk with Erik.

Ava had broken free of Geoff and came over to me. We looked out over the city, much as we had done in June at that winery in Virginia, when late-afternoon's warm summer breeze floated over us. Two months ago, when we had still been young.

"I remember you telling me then how much you loved Gee Gee. How you wanted to sail with him from Bermuda."

"I suppose that was a long time ago."

"Try to have a good night. Erik and I will keep him busy."

"It makes me sad." She paused. "I don't know why he had to be like this."

"Religion and remorse do strange things to a man."

"That's for damned sure." Ava thought for a moment. "Are you doing alright?"

"Me?"

"Yeah, you." She smiled a smile that I pretended she only shared with me.

I told her that I had thought about Santiago at dinner the night before.

"Oh God," she asked, "you didn't share that with Tess, did you?"

"Well, no?" I was puzzled. "I think she arrived just after. Why?"

She looked at me as if I were the stupidest man on earth.

"Oh!" I put all the pieces together. "Wait? Oh no. You are a *sneaky little girl.*"

"You were never going to do it on your own."

"I still probably won't do it."

"She adores you."

"And?"

"Consider it my parting gift . . . to you."

"Oh God, don't say that." My eyes glassed over again.

"Fine. My gift to you. And now I should be free of all the guilt I've felt all these years getting you into that mess with Ash."

I had not ever considered this.

"All this time?"

"Yeah." Now it seemed she might cry. She spoke quietly, dryly, almost scratchy trying to choke it out. "I know how much you loved her. I knew you'd keep giving until you had nothing left, until whatever it is that leaves her empty had emptied you completely. And it was my fault. I was the one who suggested you two get together back in Washington. I just wanted you to be happy. That's all I've ever wanted."

She fell silent. We were awash in the golden hour.

"I love you, Chris Jacobson. You know I will always love you."

A tear, and I squeezed her hand. We parted after a moment so that we could pull ourselves together again.

Later, we all sat at the round table Peter had bought. It is a thing that well-meaning wealthy people do. Buying tables at galas so that high-society folks might support the troops, the scholars, the firefighters and teachers. Tess sat beside me, with Peter on the other side. Then Ava, and Emma and Erik, then Caroline, and Geoff back next to Tess. Erik and I, nearly on opposite ends of the table, nodded at each other with satisfaction that we had herded the crowd such that Ava and Geoff also sat opposite of one another.

We waited for everyone to be served. Tess, Erik, and Ava all looked at me. Caroline had a bite. Emma looked uncomfortable. Peter finished with some story he was telling. Several seconds later Ava whispered something to Peter, who then turned to me.

"Ava says that everyone with manners is waiting for you to eat."

"Good Lord," I retorted to him under my breath.

Knife and fork in hand, I cut the beef on my plate.

Tess, Erik, and Ava followed. Emma and Caroline ate. Peter laughed out loud.

"What the hell, man?" he asked.

"It's an old tradition," Erik admonished. "Everyone waits for the senior person at the table to begin eating."

"You're both lieutenant commanders!" Peter added.

"I'm surprised you know what a lieutenant commander is." Geoff smirked, getting even with Peter for the earlier crack about the tuxedo. He had spent enough time aboard ships to know as much.

"Actually, neither of us are lieutenant commanders—not anymore," I suggested.

"Yes, but in either case this is the Coast Guard, not the Navy," Erik clarified. "So, Chris opens the festivities."

Peter raised his glass. "To the smartest, warmest, most devoted and most courageous lieutenant in or out of the Coast Guard." He looked at his wife. "I could not love you more if you were an admiral."

"And what an admiral she would have become!" Erik added.

We toasted to Ava. It felt nice, but also hollow.

"Do you regret leaving?" Peter asked me. He seemed sincere.

The truth was that I didn't know. Erik had once asked me if I felt I could do more good out of the Coast Guard than in. A short time later we both turned it in so that we could chase our unicorns. Now.

Oh God, I had sworn just an hour earlier that I'd never again think about that fellow at the garage.

"I don't think you ever know," I answered half-heartedly. It was a truthful thing, though.

"What would you be now?"

"I'd hope a commander." I gestured to my friend at the next table. "Like my friend, who has his own boat."

"He would have grown up to be an admiral," Ava chimed in from the other side.

I laughed. "There's a funny thing about promotion and winning and random chance," I began.

"You get into the game?" Erik nearly shouted from across the table.

"It's true!" I agreed. "You get into the game. You play hard. You create the chance that you might win."

Erik continued. "It's all about getting into that group of people who might be an admiral. It's not about becoming an admiral. You've no control over that. You can only be good enough to be in the running."

"In the end," I said.

"In the end," Ava picked it up, "the rest turns on a wild pitch."

There was some quieting amongst the hundreds of people. At least it seemed to be so. We carried on bantering with one another, laughing and drinking our wine as if no one else were in the room.

A moment passed and the admiral who had said hello to us much earlier in the night ambled up onto the stage. She was sullen and off-script, seemingly without the words to convey what she was thinking. She stood there for a moment at the podium. The crowd quieted.

"I'm sorry to interrupt, but. . . " she trailed off forlornly. "I am sad to say. . . "

Ava and I exchanged nervous looks. Tess reached for my hand.

"Senator John McCain . . . has crossed the bar."

The room fell ghostly silent.

The admiral stepped away.

I excused myself. Excusing oneself seemed the proper thing to do.

On my way back from the washroom I ran into the admiral. I couldn't help myself, and I hugged her. She seemed surprised.

"I'm sorry."

She put her hand on me. I'd known her for years, and she knew what I thought.

"My father once told me that our mothers had been friends. Never believed it."

"Whose mothers?" the admiral asked.

"Mine and Meghan McCain's. It's stupid, I know, right? He said her mother lent my mother her maternity coat once on a cool night. Honestly I don't know if it's true."

The admiral didn't know what to say.

I sat down at the table. My friends spoke quietly with one another.

There is a rule in uniformed company that politics should not be spoken of at the table. Even Peter was restrained, contemplative, even. It seemed bigger than us, as if—before just then—we might have disagreed, but we still had heroes. These were no politics. This felt the point of no return. The bridge had been crossed, and we were standing, watching it burn. We had lost the last of the great American heroes.

After dinner we moved back out and had drinks at the bar. We mused at what a throwback it had been, that we could have been oblivious to such news until the admiral had spoken.

"I suppose that means we didn't break the convention on putting phones away at the table," Erik joked.

"And what an ancient convention it is!"

"Well now, there is some truth there," he giggled. "I'd say that for the first, oh, two hundred thirty-some years of this country's history there probably wasn't a single man or woman in uniform to take out a smartphone at the table."

Nearby, a group of older gentlemen spoke of millennials and

how difficult it was to get any work out of them, how they couldn't be bothered to wear the uniform as those men had. How few of them probably even knew or cared anything about the death of the senator.

Tess said something unkind.

"Do you think they realize that the oldest millennials are up for captain now?"

Erik cocked his eyebrow at me and asked if I might like to let them know.

"In their minds *millennial* has just become a stand-in for someone in their early twenties," Ava said. "I don't think they realize that millennials age, too."

One of the old men whipped out his phone and passed about some meme he had seen. The irony amused us all.

Erik walked over to them.

"There's something really sick about a country that places the burden of its longest war nearly exclusively on one generation, defers all its bills to them, and then pillories them with memes like that."

They stared at him blankly.

"You've got a lot of damned gall."

He walked away in a huff.

And there we sat. An entire generation on the Group W bench.

"At least nobody punched him." I cocked a smile at Peter.

"He's just more likable than you are."

Desperate to not have the evening end there, I suggested that we go find some drinks.

⁓⁓⁓⁓⁓

Ava surprised us all in wanting to go to Chimichurri Grill. So, we piled into cabs and crossed town to drink wine with Carlos and Wilmer. Peter bought a round of Pappy Van Winkle and kissed Ava on the cheek. He was very generous, and very sweet to her. I loved him for that.

I will never forget how Ava looked then. How she smiled, and laughed, and said witty things and pulled it all together as if it were old times and nothing at all had happened. Looking as she used to, before there were children, or marriage, or Ash. Then she smiled that smile that I pretended she reserved only for me. She said that it was all right.

Geoff and Caroline went straight to bed when we returned to the apartment.

Tess went off to get ready for bed. I had a moment alone, and considered then how stunning she had looked. Hugged in that black dress. Her dark-brown hair framing those beautiful eyes. Delicate white skin. A smile to invite you in, wit to destroy anyone who wasn't careful.

I looked at myself in the mirror. Mostly it had been a good night. But it did not feel like a good moment. There was a bit of grey under my eyes. At least I had shaved. And that blond hair was as golden blond as ever. I had not yet felt what it was like to grow old. I looked at my hands. Hands, they are curious things. For generations a person's hands had been what he or she was worth. That which turned the wrench, molded the clay, chiseled the marble. The bits of fragile humanity from which sprang the great paintings, inventions, literature. These were mine. They worked a keyboard in an office.

"And what the hell have you done?" my old shipmate had laughed.

Others, others had seen more.

My blond hair was disheveled now, unsuited for the world. One day I would grow old. Now I just felt altogether terrified.

I thought about Sweden.

The medals on my uniform stared back from my own reflection.

I was an American. The blood of sinners and saints coursed through my veins.

I heard Tess in the other room, so I went in, and didn't come out until late the next morning.

Chapter Twenty-Nine

Erik and I spent Sunday evening alone in Geoff's apartment after Tess had flown back to London and Emma had returned to Washington. I was suddenly conscious of how long it had been since I was properly home.

A candle burned on the table. It was late August, but the darkness and softly fluttering candlelight reminded me of wintertime, of how all those little lights would shine through each of winter's nights. Then I would hang an ornament from one of the most prominent branches on the Christmas tree. Seven wine corks glued together and splashed in silver glitter. Ava had made it for me, years ago. She thought I hated it. But it was my favorite ornament. I was always sad to put it away after another year.

"Perhaps I've told you about this before," I apologized to Erik.

"No, actually, you haven't."

"Traditions are funny things."

We wondered together if we'd all forever go out to Chimichurri Grill on the twenty-fifth of August each year, as we had done the night before. We agreed that we should, and that we should drink wine, and laugh, and tell stories.

He caught me humming that Spanish song in our moment of silence.

"What's that?" he asked.

"Oh." I was surprised. "Just a song that I used to think was about Ash."

"But you were wrong?"

"Yeah."

We sipped our wine.

"Wine is made great by its ability to share with us things that we didn't know existed," I told Erik as I swirled a well-heeled Chardonnay in my glass. We hated it, but it was one of Ava's favorites. I continued absently. "Takes us to other lands and climates. Teaches us history."

"Anything else?"

I told him a meandering story that began years earlier.

Fist-sized stones clicked together and rattled gently below my feet as I walked through a vineyard in Toro, Spain. To my left, trellised vines crept towards autumn as orange began to color their lowest leaves, whilst to my right I found bush vines of Tinto de Toro, tempranillo's local name. Beautiful mostly flat countryside stretched out far as the eye could see, warmed by the sun beating down from above, wispy clouds sweeping across the sapphire sky as a cooling breeze blew through the vineyard.

I drove west from Austin, Texas, several months later. The wine country of the Texas hills cast a curious mix of green and grey whilst the urban terrain of one of twenty-first-century America's most vibrant cities melted into rolling hills. Rain poured sadly down, but the pastoral serenity of this place was as lovely as it was surprising to be found in a state thought of by most who were not from there as an endless prairie of scorched earth and heat. Ava and I had gone looking for Becker Vineyards, the next chapter in our enduring fascination with wine from places you'd not expect.

There we found tempranillo. Unsurprising, as I suspected that area produces a few similar climatic patterns to some of the world's great tempranillo regions. Hot days, cool nights—Toro, Spain, anyone? We were told that it had been a bit of a dry year. The wine was fruit-forward, yet also smoky, with a bit of spice reminiscent of a good cabernet franc. It was our favorite bottle in the lineup.

Ava possessed a unique ability to articulate very specific details about soil and terrain through just a sniff of the glass. She was matter of fact about it—and everything—though I wasn't sure she would ever have described it in these terms. But to watch her in those moments was to watch someone close their eyes and for an instant be transported through the looking glass unto lands, climates, histories, and people otherwise far away from the moment itself.

Erik and I had recently sat in that wine bar in Prague. Where filament lights hung haphazardly from the ceiling, like the bowed branches of the weeping willow under which I remembered playing as a child. They cast their yellowing glow upon an immense map that spanned the bar's entire wall. Few today would recognize the country it depicts, for it had been a full century since Austria-Hungary ceased to exist. But inside those forgotten borders have grown the curious zweigelt—a hybrid of the red blaufränkisch and sankt laurent grapes—of Austria proper, the intoxicatingly floral whites of Hungary's Tokaj, the dark-red teran of seaside Istria, this earthen pinot noir from South Tyrol, and that enchantingly beautiful natural sparkling wine from Moravia.

Anchoring oneself is terrifically difficult when the currents of technology, politics, and world events seem so determined to unmoor us. The long arc of history is difficult to discern when the days and weeks move so quickly. Yet there in my past I had memories of stones clicking along the ground of a vineyard in Spain, in which was grown the same grapes we found in those grey and green Texas hills. Erik, my childhood best friend, and I had sat there that night in Prague drinking wines celebrated on a map of a country that had not existed in four generations. Grape vines are old creatures that produce new and beautiful things each year.

Portugal has a tradition of field blends. That is, different grape varietals planted in and amongst one another such that they are harvested and blended together straightaway. There was that one particular winery whose terraced vineyards stretch 550 meters up the mountain from the Douro River, older vines near the bottom, younger further up the bank. Their field blends contain about twenty different grape varietals. This old practice in the Douro produces stunningly unique wines.

We need more field blends. We need more maps on walls that remind us of the lands, climates, histories, and people that remain when the fog of fear is lifted and lines in the earth are swept away by time. And, importantly, we need more moments of quiet clarity such that we might step through the stemmed and fluted looking glass long enough to appreciate the majesty of that by which we are surrounded.

Chapter Thirty

That weekend was the last time most of our friends ever saw Ava Murray.

I wondered if she had known. If she had poured it all out in such grand style so that we would all have it to remember.

But the time came quickly when it came at last.

One morning I went up to the apartment and found her sitting with Catherine at the piano. They played together, best Catherine could. Ava told her that she'd have to remember how to play so that she could play for her father and teach her sister and brother. They played on together for some time until Catherine grew tired and wandered off.

I sat there quietly with Ava. She took my hand. I think we talked about baseball.

It's hard to tell when the moment has arrived.

One Tuesday I went down to Washington. Just for the day, with plans to return on the last shuttle. It was all fine.

I had a message from Peter at quarter to five.

Better get up here. Better hurry.

I begged a kind fellow off the 6:30 shuttle.

Peter and the kids had gone when I arrived. A nurse told me that he had wanted to put them to bed.

I went in. Put my hands on her.

She was dreadfully cold, but in my mind I felt only the warmth of a thousand memories of laughter and long nights spent drinking wine with a candle on.

I spoke to her then about those nights. I made all sorts of promises that I cannot now recall. I quietly sang her the lyrics from one of her favorite musicals. I held her hand until I just couldn't stomach it anymore. I knew then why Peter had really left. When it was all over, surely, after a time, there was nothing more to do sitting there.

Eventually some people came to take her away. I kissed her forehead, and realized then that I would be the last person she knew to ever see her.

One Saturday in October we all got together. I think even Peter was surprised by how many turned up. There was the usual crowd. Emma tried to be strong for me, but ended up weeping into my arms. Erik led her away, promising to save me a seat. There was a fellow from the Coast Guard whom I had hated, but he showed up just the same. There might have been 500 people, and separate rooms had to be opened and closed-circuit televisions set up just to find space.

Peter asked if I'd stand next to him, and together we said hello to them all.

Javier came by. Pascual, Carlos, and Wilmer, too. Billy came in with Andrew Jefferson. They walked away, arms round each other. Peter and I looked at one another, astonished that it had never occurred to us what had really been happening there. It didn't matter now. Better for everyone to be with the ones they loved.

Simon came in from Sweden.

"I wasn't sure why, barely knew her, but I like you people," he explained.

Geoff and Peter embraced.

Tess had come back. She sat waiting for me with Erik and Emma, leaving me to wonder what she thought of it all. I wasn't sure what would happen with her, but I marveled at how supportive she had been of me in this moment.

Peter and I shook more hands. I wondered, *Is this what it feels like when your wife dies?* I put my arm around him when they had all gone inside.

We stood there alone, wondering if we were strong enough to take the next steps. I was so grateful for his friendship, for how he had made me a part of this. I was about to say so when he spoke first.

"There is no way," he said quietly, "for me to tell you how much I need you. How grateful I am for your friendship. That you are here with me. I feel so alone, and I cannot imagine what could save me right now but you."

I squeezed his hand in mine, briefly, letting go as we opened the big lonely doors together.

I paused and put my hand on Tess's shoulder as we walked in.

"Thank you," I whispered, hoping she could hear me.

Peter sat with her and Erik and Emma and the children.

I walked quietly to the stage, looking out at hundreds of bright and glassy eyes, for how long I cannot say.

"Last month, I lost my best friend," I choked.

The rest came easier.

"We don't get many of those in life, especially when we grow up and into an ever more complicated world. But Ava was one of them, and ours was a friendship hard fought for. Many of you probably know that we dated and lived together for years.

"The Roman philosopher Seneca wrote, in his play *Thyestes*, 'Truly there is no greater power on earth than natural affection. Strife between strangers may go on forever, but where it has bound once the chain of love will always bind again.'

"Such was true of us. We know that a friendship, no matter how cherished, might fall aside before the forces of life—geographic distance, divergent interests, different paths chosen—and we know that most romances ultimately run their course. But when you've been through all that, when you know one another as we did, and yet you still choose to love one another, it's then when you know you have a friendship soluble not even by death, a friendship for the ages.

"As children, many of us come to think of heaven as this mythical place in the clouds filled with winged, harp-playing babies. Several weeks ago whilst at an orchestral concert—I know it seems untimely, but I wondered if I might find a bit of Ava there—I found myself thinking of that child's vision and wondering how they're getting on with a grown-up, beautiful and brilliant woman who plays a mean clarinet. And piano. And who writes her own enchanting music.

"Well, I don't know what heaven looks like, but I am quite sure that since the evening of October second, its residents have enjoyed one thing in great abundance—cake. Ava was as talented a chef as she was a musician. And for her, cake was the first among equals. Once, years ago, she and I had perhaps a two-week falling-out over something silly wherein for whatever reason she did not come to the Halloween Party I was hosting. She sent us a cake just the same, actually two complete cakes in a Bundt pan. She put them together at the wide flat ends, frosted the thing orange, and dressed it up like a jack-o'-lantern. I also seem to recall a cake in the shape of a pirate ship, and one that she decorated to say *Happy Birthday, Martin van Buren!* She just wanted cake, and Wikipedia told her that it was our eighth president's birthday.

"By the way, for those of you who made that bet with me that Martin van Buren wouldn't come up today, well, you each now owe the Ava Murray Memorial Scholarship fund one Ulysses S. Grant.

"If in music we heard Ava the artist, it was through her cakes that we knew her humor. Do you remember that smile? It was the smile when she'd play this maddening game with the cat, the 'Fun Kitty Game' she called it, bundling him up in a blanket or putting him in a brown paper bag and hanging it on the doorknob.

"'I love smiling; smiling's my favorite!' she'd say, quoting one of her favorite silly movies that was itself a ridiculous tribute to the importance of choosing to live a happy life.

"Yet for all her artistic talent and wonderful sense of humor, it happened that Ava was quite industrious. She was the only philosophy major—those of you who knew her in school might recall—to take summer internships at an investment bank. Later she joined the Coast Guard, where we met. She went to law school. And she always had her hand in a business scheme somewhere. At one job, while every one of her coworkers complained that they didn't have time in the day to get the job done, Ava finished her tasks ahead of schedule and invested her newfound free time in training her beloved Socrates, who was then just a puppy. She loved that guy, and he seemed to share her sense of humor. She once came home from the vet and indignantly said to Peter, 'I am never taking Socrates back there. Can you believe that when I told the girl at the front desk that his name was Socrates, she asked if that made me a soccer fan?'

"That's *Socrates*, not *Soccertees*.

"Yes, Ava was possessed of many talents. Music, cooking, humor, business, a keen intellect and a skeptical approach to the world that made her thoughtful in conversation and resilient in spirit, all talents that make the hole left by our beloved friend so much a greater deficit.

"She loved the Muppets, and each year in December we would share a bottle of wine and watch *The Muppet Christmas Carol*. She was the type of person whose warmth and self-confidence could make a grown man feel good about singing songs with puppets. About a month ago she asked if I'd watch it with her—out of cycle, she called it—one afternoon while Peter took the kids to the park. We came to a scene with the Ghost of Christmas Future. The words of Kermit the Frog as Bob Cratchit were poignant. He said, 'Life is made up of meetings and partings. That is the way of it. I am sure that we shall never forget Tiny Tim, or this first parting that there was among us.'

"When I think of Ava, and the tragedy of her loss at thirty-four years old, I find that what makes me so sad is the amount of life most of us will now live on without her, the road of years stretched out before us upon which we must now 'never forget.' That is when I cry. Because I know that in ten short years many of those assembled today will have been without her for as long as they were with her; and that in thirty-five years, we will have lived more days from this day to that than she lived in her entire lifetime. I don't point this out for grieving, but rather to sober ourselves for the great task we now face.

"If there is indeed life from death, then we must return to this place of remembrance again. In the coming weeks we'll see the pictures of folks with Ava disappear from Facebook profiles as life inevitably marches on, and we move on with it, and we drift further and further away from the sadness we feel at this moment. Though that's when the real work begins, that's also our chance to leave our sadness behind and remember her in better ways, not just every year on her birthday, but day in and day out every time we choose—as she did—happiness from sadness, hope from despair, intellectual curiosity from backwardness, the thrill of the run from the sameness of the sedentary.

"I spoke earlier of heaven. As I am—like Ava—skeptical of dogma, I find myself poorly equipped to make any absolute statements. But what I do believe, something that she and I discussed many times, is that immortality is achieved not at the pearly gates, but rather in the minds and the hearts of those whose lives we changed for good, and who remember us long after we're gone. And if we pass these things, these choices, on to our friends and children . . . well then, Ava really will live forever.

"She loved musicals, and among musicals she particularly loved *Wicked*. There is a wonderful quote from a song in that show, actually the last thing I said to Ava the moment I said goodbye."

I read the words to the crowd.

It well may be, that we will never meet again in this lifetime.
So let me say before we part,
So much of me is made of what I learned from you,

That you'll be with me like a hand print on my heart.
And now whatever way our stories end,
I know you have re-written mine, by being my friend.

Like a ship blown from its mooring by a wind off the sea.
Like a seed dropped by a sky bird in a distant wood.
Who can say if I've been changed for the better?
I do believe I have been changed for the better.
But because I knew you,
I have been changed for good.

I breathed in hard and returned to my seat.

I felt quite alone amongst those hundreds of eyes. The person I loved had died. The person I had wanted to love, well, she had died so many times that I wasn't quite sure that she was anymore capable of living. Santiago was gone. We could never go back to Santiago.

Afterwards there was a celebration of sorts. Best as we could gather. I suspect I will remember very little of it. But there was one moment that I suspect I will never forget.

I scooped Catherine up. She tiredly laid her head on my shoulder. It occurred to me how lucky we were to have her, to have all three of them. There were hundreds of people all about, but in my mind, it was just the little girl and me. And I felt as if I were holding little Ava in my arms, that at least we had her to watch grow up and grow beautiful and wise. Like we would always have Santiago.

"I love you very much," is all I said, in a whisper.

"I know. Mommy told me that you always would," she whispered back.